DIAMOND QUEST

AN ELLIE SPARK MYSTERY

HANNA IRELAND

DIAMOND QUEST

An Ellie Spark Mystery

Copyright © 2023 by Yoko Minor

Paperback ISBN: 979-8-35094-632-1
eBook ISBN: 979-8-35094-633-8

Cover Designed by Yoko Minor

This book is dedicated to YOU.

May you express your heart's desires joyfully into the world.

CONTENTS

CHAPTER 1

Vix Tower and
The Dark Shadow

December 6, San Francisco, California, USA.

Vix Tower felt his blood coursing through his veins as he heard words "*a diamond with magical powers*" from the TV. Daniel Blue, a head curator of San Francisco Museum of Art History, was announcing an upcoming exhibit called "The Great Diamonds" on the local morning news channel. The exhibit would be featuring his discovery—*a purple diamond*—one of the three long-lost diamonds with magical powers.

"One down!" said Vix Tower, his fists shaking. "*We* must have the three diamonds by the magical night. This time, no tricks and no mistakes are allowed." He said with conviction, but nobody else was around.

Vix's shadow was darkening and expanding behind him in the morning sunlight.

"Daniel Blue must find the two missing diamonds in two weeks. And then the infinite total power will finally be our own!" Vix's *shadow* spoke as it filled the entire room.

As soon as Nicholas Blue opened the door to his house, the aroma of spicy Mexican sauces hit him. Sure signs that his Aunt Joyce was working her magic in the kitchen. Tonight Nicholas and his father Daniel were celebrating Daniel's TV announcement.

Daniel invited Jerry Goldman over for dinner. Jerry was an art historian on Daniel's museum staff. Daniel had been supportive of him since he hired Jerry five years earlier. Somewhat Daniel saw himself in Jerry.

"Long time no see." Jerry gave Nicholas a big hug. "Sorry I couldn't make it to your 13th birthday party." His usual cheery face saddened for a moment.

"That's OK."

"So what's new with you, pal?" Jerry asked Nicholas.

"Not much, I guess."

"Jerry, he got straight-A's on all his report cards this year," Aunt Joyce said, "All right you three. Enjoy your dinner. I've got to get home. My husband and I are leaving for a trip to Europe tomorrow morning."

It didn't take long for them to polish off the last of Joyce's enchiladas.

"Your Aunt Joyce still knows how to cook." Jerry leaned back in his chair and patted his stomach. Jerry's eyes twinkled. "Do you still want to become a curator like your father?"

Nicholas shrugged and looked down at his plate.

"Every object of historic art has its own story behind it," Daniel said. "And when you discover the story, you really appreciate what you have in your life."

Oh, no, Nicholas thought, *here he goes again.*

Daniel gave lectures on archeology at California colleges and universities a few times a year. And Nicholas was the first person to listen to his father's lecture about his new subject.

"The story of our magical purple diamond is a good example." Daniel said, "Following an earthquake about two-and-a-half-years ago I discovered the diamond by accident.

The size of it is the size of a large cherry. There is a legend behind these powerful gems and it was passed on from generations to generations for 500 years in the village of Chiesa, Italy. The legend is 'the magical diamonds bring great fortunes and social powers to the owner.' In fact, the owner significantly thrived but one day the gems were stolen from the owner. And shortly after, the owner's family and the land were devastated by a mysterious curse—black clouds shrouded the land and nothing could grow and thrive there. Today in the result of the curse the dark gray sky is as good as Chiesta gets. Their population has decreased."

"Supernatural stuff," said Jerry, "in those days folks were pretty gullible, Nicholas. Although I guess there are still people today who believe supernatural diamonds can work miracles."

Daniel nodded. "Lots of them, Jerry. And many of them are deadly serious."

Later that night, Nicholas shivered in his room as he changed into his pajamas. He turned on the old radiators in his room, but it took an hour for the heat to warm up the room. Nicholas wished that his father would have decided to move into a modern house rather than living in this old and cold Victorian house. Somehow Daniel had been procrastinating it for years.

Nicholas went to the living room to say good night to his father. "I'm going to—"

Nicholas stopped at the sound of the doorbell.

"Who could that be, Dad?"

It was almost ten-thirty.

"I don't know." Daniel went to the front door and looked through the peephole. A well-dressed man was standing on the porch, someone Daniel had never seen before. He looked back at Nicholas and shrugged. The security chain on the door was fastened, and he cracked the door open as far as it would go. "Can I help you?"

In the glow from the porch light, the stranger's pale gray eyes gleamed hypnotically. "Pardon me, Mr. Blue," the man said. "I hope you'll forgive me. I realize that dropping in on you unannounced at this hour may be inappropriate. I'm Vix Tower, president and CEO of the Oxford Company in downtown San Francisco."

He passed his business card through the crack. "You see, I heard about the magical purple diamond on today's news. I was busy all day and didn't get to it until this evening. But I'm very excited to know more about it. It's really important to me, and I couldn't wait until tomorrow to see you."

Magical purple diamond!

The words sounded like a beautiful melody to Daniel's ears. He looked at the business card. "I recognize your company, Mr. Tower."

"What I want to tell you, Mr. Blue," Tower said, "is that the legend is true. The purple diamond is one of the three magical diamonds—and it belongs to me."

"Are you sure, Mr. Tower? We actually discovered the purple diamond in an ancient cemetery in Italy."

"The cemetery of the Adamo Balducci family. Am I right?"

"Well, yes, it was, but—"

"I'm the last descendant of the Balducci family," Tower said. He smiled. "The other two diamonds also belong to me."

"This is amazing!" Daniel said. "For two-and-a-half years we haven't been able to find any information on the other diamonds." He unfastened the security chain. "Please come in, Mr. Tower."

Nicholas felt a little embarrassed about being in his pajamas in front of a stranger. He ducked behind the kitchen door. It was partially open, the light was off, and he peeked at the man through the space between the hinges.

Tower was a little taller than Daniel. He appeared to be in his mid or late forties. Like Daniel, he looked fit. His jet-black hair was combed back sleekly, and in the light from the living-room floor lamp it looked almost blue.

Daniel sat down on the couch, and set the business card Tower had given him on the coffee table. "Please sit down," he said.

"No thank you," Tower said. He stood near the lamp, his hands clasped in front of him. He looked toward the kitchen, and for a moment Nicholas wondered if he could see him through the space between the partially open kitchen door and its frame.

He turned back to Daniel, and Nicholas noticed that his shadow on the rug—like his hair—seemed oddly dark.

"To start with," Daniel said, "could you tell me where the other two diamonds are?"

Tower shook his head. "That's the problem. I've had my people searching for the three diamonds for years. Thanks to your efforts, I know where one of them is. Now I need to know where the others are, and you seem the most likely person to find them. When you do find them, of course, I'll loan all three to the museum for your exhibit."

"I can't tell you how excited I am about this," Daniel said. "But at the same time it's a too serious matter for me to go into right now. Why don't we discuss it further at the museum tomorrow?"

Tower frowned. "There's nothing more to discuss," he said. "I want you to find the green and the pink diamonds and then bring all three diamonds to me before midnight December twentieth. That will be a night of miracles.

You've got two weeks to complete the job. Needless to say, I'll provide you with a generous incentive for that."

Daniel stood up. "This is ridiculous," he said. "Maybe you think there's nothing more to discuss, but that's not my opinion. First of all, you haven't shown me any proof of ownership for the purple diamond. And second, you say you don't know where the other two are now. Even if I *could* find them, it would surely take more than two weeks—maybe a lifetime. I do my job at the museum because it means a lot to me and it is important work. But I don't do my job just for money. You're asking the wrong person."

"Mr. Blue," Tower said, "I'm a wealthier and more powerful man that you can imagine. I'm offering you a golden opportunity to work for me. And believe me, the rewards will be enormous. You can visit my empire, tomorrow. I think that will change your mind."

"I tried to make it clear that I've pledged my life to my work," Daniel said. "And frankly, to me, it's richer than all your assets." He looked up at the clock. "It's getting late, Mr. Tower. I'm sure you need your sleep as much as I do." He crossed the room and put his hand on the doorknob.

"Not so fast," Tower said. Although he stood still, his shadow grew larger, spreading up the walls and across the ceiling until it enveloped the entire room.

Nicholas couldn't believe what he was seeing. He looked away for a second. His back accidentally pushed the serving cart behind him. A wine opener fell off from the cart and clacked the kitchen floor.

Tower turned his head, trying to locate the sound. He looked toward the kitchen, then turned toward the front door as a municipal bus rumbled by. He muttered something under his breath and looked up toward the center of the shadow.

"Now!" he said.

The Dark Shadow disintegrated into black particles that floated in the air and then gradually formed into the giant face of an angry man. The giant face and Tower spoke in overlapping, threatening tones that echoed throughout the house: "You will bring the three diamonds to me by midnight December twentieth or you will die."

The shadowy face moved toward Daniel, opened its mouth wide, and swallowed him.

Daniel tried to break free, but the face wouldn't let him. Nicholas watched his father struggling within the shadowy figure and tried to cry out to him, but no sound came out. Paralyzed with fright, Nicholas turned his face away from the scene.

Tower scooped up his business card from the coffee table, took a few steps toward the front door, and stopped. He turned toward the kitchen and sniffed the air.

Nicholas held his breath, tried to be silent, though his body was trembling.

Tower walked across the room and stepped into the kitchen. He flicked on the light.

Crouched behind the door, Nicholas closed his eyes, wishing that if he couldn't see Tower, Tower wouldn't be able to see him—knowing it was childish and useless.

He opened his eyes just as the kitchen light went out. He held his breath and heard Tower's footsteps cross the living room. He peeked through the space between the kitchen door's hinges. The shadow, now its normal size, followed Tower to the front door. Tower opened it, took a last look at Daniel's figure—now stretched out on the floor—and stepped into the night, slamming the door behind him.

Nicholas resumed breathing, but cautiously. He waited awhile, fearful that Tower might be playing a trick—might come storming back into the house. The silence was broken by the shriek of an ambulance's siren. When the sound finally faded out, Nicholas rushed into the living room.

Daniel lay there, gasping for breath. His eyes were open, but only the whites showed.

"Dad! Dad!" Nicholas cried out.

His father didn't respond.

CHAPTER 2

The Cup of Mirrors

December 7, San Francisco, California.

Nicholas woke and sat up in his bed. Then the horrific event that happened last night came to his mind. He looked around. The lights in his room were on. He threw off his covers and realized he was already dressed and wearing his shoes. Then he remembered he'd changed from his pajamas to his regular clothes last night in case he had to leave the house to get help. The alarm clock said five. He probably slept only forty five minutes or so last night. Tossed and turned, the horror of the night kept him awake all night.

"Hah!" He turned to the door. An unusual sound of drawers and cabinets being yanked open and slammed shut came from his father's bedroom across the hall. He got out of bed and went out to the hallway. The door to his father's bedroom was cracked open. It was actually partly a bedroom and partly an office where his father often brought work home from the museum.

Nicholas stepped into the room and saw his father standing by his desk, his back to the door. His books, magazines, and maps were scattered on the floor. He was busy talking on his cell phone.

First he called Jerry.

"Hey, Jerry," he said, "it's Daniel. As soon as you get this message, give me a call. This is an emergency. I got a visit last night from the owner of our purple diamond and we've got to get to work pronto. Something amazing is going to happen on December twentieth. It's really fascinating. I'm rushed now, but I'll give you a brief summary of what happened last night."

He mentioned that the man was named Tower and that he owned all three magical diamonds, but he entirely left out the part about the Dark Shadow.

As soon as Daniel hung up, he called Allison Kenwood, another one of his team members. Then he called his manager, Philip Rose, to leave a similar message. He then made two long distance calls to Italy, the first to the Tuscany Museum of Treasures. He asked their researchers to find any historical exhibits of green and pink diamonds anywhere in Europe.

The second call was to his trusted priest friend and archaeologist, Father Luciano Ugolini of Chiesta. Daniel had worked with him back in Italy and highly had talked about him.

"Father Luciano," he said, "I've got amazing news. That legend about the three diamonds is actually true. I met the owner of the magical diamonds last night. He's a descendant of the Balducci family, and he said the other two diamonds actually exist." He paused for a moment and then said, "No, he doesn't know where they are. But he says it's vital we find them by December twentieth. If you can get any information on them, please let me know as soon as possible."

He listened again. "Of course, I understand, Father," he said, his disappointment obvious in his tone of voice. "But when you *do* get back from your trip, please let me know. And I'll let you know what's happening at our end."

He said goodbye, took a deep breath, and dropped his phone on the desk.

Nicholas felt a knot in his throat. His father hadn't mentioned the Dark Shadow to Father Luciano either.

"Dad . . ."

Daniel spun around, his eyes flashing. He didn't seem to recognize his son. "What are you doing here?" he said, his voice angry.

"I just wanted to—"

Daniel turned away from him and picked up his phone from the desk. "Who cares what you want?" he said. "It should be obvious that I'm busy and don't have time to talk to every Tom, Dick, and Harry who wants to pester me."

"Are you okay, Dad?" Nicholas said, his voice trembling.

Daniel turned back to him. "Oh, good morning, Nicholas," he said. "I must find the other two diamonds and return all three to Vix Tower by midnight December twentieth. They belong to him. Our time is limited. I have to work much harder and faster on this. Help me, would you?"

"Dad, Vix Tower isn't human!"

Daniel smiled. "Yes, he owns the three magical diamonds."

"You're not making sense, Dad. Don't you remember what the Dark Shadow did to you? Vix Tower is dangerous. You can't trust him."

"What I want to know," Daniel said, "is where the other two diamonds are."

"Please, Dad, listen to me," Nicholas said. He clutched at his father's arm. "You're talking crazy."

Daniel's face grew red. He pushed Nicholas away from him and sent his son sprawling on the floor. Daniel stepped forward and crouched down, his face inches from Nicholas's, their noses almost touching. "Listen to me—whoever you are—don't ever interrupt me again!"

Daniel rose from his crouch and walked out of the room, slamming the door behind him. Nicholas got to his feet, started toward the door, and stopped. Could his father be waiting in the hallway for him, ready to launch another attack? There was something terribly wrong with him. He might be capable of anything.

A moment later, Nicholas heard the sound of the garage door opening and then closing. He hurried to a front window and saw his father's car heading off down the street. He stood at the window for several minutes, confused, angry, and frightened—and without any idea in the world about what to do.

It was time for his ride to arrive. Every day his friend Hunter and his mother Kayla took him to school and back. Nicholas stuck a Cup of Mirrors in his pocket with no reason and hurried out of the house.

The Cup of Mirrors was the shallow, red-lacquered cup just about filled his hand. Inside the cup was an octagonal mirror covered the bottom and eight smaller mirrors lined the sides. A little wooden knob was attached to the outside of it. It was given to Nicholas a few months ago by Allison Kenwood for his 13th birthday. She was a curator and worked under Daniel. Nicholas met her for the first time at his birthday dinner. He felt awkward getting a gift from somebody he didn't really know. At first, he thought the Cup of Mirrors was just a strange object. He tilted the mirrors toward the overhead light and studied the flashing reflections from its various facets. It was interesting. He put it on his desk instead of storing in his closet.

On the ride to school, Nicholas kept his thoughts to himself. Hunter, as he often did, took up the slack.

Throughout the school day, Nicholas had trouble concentrating. When the dismissal bell finally rang, he still felt distracted. As he and Hunter headed out to the sidewalk, he felt a chill surge up his spine. Would his father be there when he got home? Would he still be acting and talking crazy?

When the boys got to Kayla's car, Nicholas was surprised to see that she wasn't behind the wheel as usual. She stood on the sidewalk, a worried look on her face.

"Hi, Mom," Hunter said. He got into the back seat and buckled up.

Nicholas started to follow him, but Kayla put a hand on his shoulder. She pulled him close and gave him a hug. "I'm sorry, Nicholas," she said, "but a serious situation has come up."

The chill he felt earlier struck again, only stronger. He knew instinctively: *It's about Dad.*

"Allison Kenwood called me a little while ago," Kayla said, "She told me your father fainted at work today. They couldn't wake him and they called 911. The emergency-response team took him to the hospital in an ambulance. Allison's there now, and she says he's resting comfortably. She asked if I'd bring you there."

Images of the Dark Shadow and Vix Tower leaped to Nicholas's mind.

When Nicholas, Hunter, and Kayla got to the hospital, Allison Kenwood greeted them in the lobby. Nicholas could tell she was making an effort to smile. Daniel couldn't have visitors except for family members.

Aunt Joyce was on her way to Paris so Allison called Daniel's neighbor Renee. She was Nicholas' friend Ellie Spark's mother. Nicholas could stay with her family until Daniel was released. That way Nicholas could stay close to this hospital.

The Spark family moved from Seattle a month ago and lived across from Nicholas' house. Ellie would be thirteen in a couple of months and went to a school close to his. Something about Ellie was mysterious to him. It was not logic. It was an instinct.

Her house had been previously vacant for a few months. Nicholas and Hunter called it "The Dream House" because it was like a castle with Spanish architecture and at least four times bigger than any other house on the block. The boys had imagined it would take a lot of moving truck for the new residents' furnishings, but only one U-Haul trailer was parked in front of The Dream House on the day Ellie moved in. He recalled an embarrassing bike accident he had in front of her house on that day:

One of the trailer's doors was open and Nicholas decided to take a closer look. He got his bike from the garage and pedaled up the sidewalk. The trailer's door was still open, but there was nobody there. Disappointed, he tried once more, this time pedaling hard. As he passed the trailer again, he glanced up at the Dream House and—*WHAM!* He crashed into a big cardboard carton Ellie had just taken from the trailer.

She staggered back a step, and the carton flew from her hands. It landed upside down, its contents spilling out onto the sidewalk. One of the items was a jewelry box of large glass beads. Its cover opened in midair and the beads scattered everywhere, some smashing on the sidewalk, others rolling into the gutter.

The impact sent Nicholas reeling. He slammed down on the sidewalk, banging his head and gashing his knee. He laid there for a moment, eyes closed. When he opened them, he was dazzled by several of the colorful beads sparkling in the sunlight.

"Are you okay?" Ellie asked.

She was leaning over him.

Dizzy from the fall, he couldn't see her face clearly, but he noticed a shiny gold pendant hanging from her neck. Ellie and her mother Renee helped Nicholas up and took him inside the Dream House to patch him up.

There was a spacious foyer inside and two staircases led to the right and left wings on the second floor. They led Nicholas to the living room on the first floor and had him stretch out on a long leather couch. As Renee applied some ointment and bandaged his knee, Nicholas looked up and examined Ellie's face. Her eyes were unusual: amber colored with a slightly blue tint to the whites. Her straight mahogany colored hair seemed to float in the air when she moved her head. *There is something mysterious about her*, he thought.

He said with embarrassment, "I'm sorry I ruined your things."

She smiled. "That's okay. Beads break. There's nothing we can do about it. It's just part of life."

Ellie sounded more mature than the girls in his class.

"Why don't you rest for a while," Ellie said. Then she headed for the front door to go clean up the sidewalk.

Renee went to the kitchen. While she was there, Nichols looked around the room and appreciated the beautiful décor of the Dream House he'd long wanted to visit. It had a high ceiling and two tall French doors that led out to a patio and garden. There were a few unpacked boxes by the entrance, but most of the furniture was already tastefully arranged in the room. Two framed paintings of Asian landscapes hung on one wall. Nicholas thought they might have come from overseas. A black lacquered coffee table, some oversized ceramic pots, and a three-fold black screen decorated with inlaid gold and colorful gems made the room seem like an elegant parlor in an Asian emperor's palace.

Renee came back to the room carrying a tray with three cups of cocoa and set it on the coffee table. Nicholas sat up and she handed him one of the cups of cocoa. It was much tastier than the cocoa he made at home. He felt comforted and welcomed. For the first time he hoped that—just this once—his aunt would be late for dinner today.

Ellie came back and joined them on the couch. Nicholas looked at her and said, "I'm really sorry about the accident. It was totally my fault, and—"

"Shh!" said Ellie, giving him a fake frown. "No more apologies." She opened her hand and showed him four of the large beads. "These were my very favorites, so there's no need to apologize, *again.*"

Nicholas couldn't resist giggling, as Ellie's fake frown turned to a smile. She gently touched Nicholas's bandaged knee. He was about to wince, but her touch was like a butterfly landing on a flower. There was a tiny soothing tingle but no hint of pain.

Later that night, Nicholas checked the wound on his knee. He gently peeled back the bandage to see if the bleeding had stopped. He was shocked to see the cut had already healed. He put his hand over the spot where the cut had been and pressed. It wasn't even sore. That was a miracle…

As Hunter headed out of the hospital, he turned and waved goodbye to Nicholas.

Nicholas could see that Hunter's face was pale, and he knew his friend was holding back tears.

Nicholas and Allison took the elevator to the second floor and got to Daniel's room just as a nurse was leaving. She held the door open for them. "Mr. Blue hasn't regained consciousness yet," she said. "But all his signs are fairly stable now. He does have a slight fever, but we don't think it's anything to worry about." She pointed to a call button next to Daniel's bed. "If you need anything, just press that button. I'll be back in a minute."

"Thank you," Allison said.

She took Nicholas's hand and they went to Daniel's bedside.

Nicholas' eyes watered as he looked at his father. Just then Daniel made a moaning sound. He began panting as if he were having a bad dream. Nicholas reached out and touched his arm. "He feels hot," he said to Allison.

She put a hand to Daniel's forehead. "He does." She reached for the call button. As she did, the door opened and a nurse with a small injection in her hand stepped into the room. The nurse noticed the look on Nicholas's face and smiled at him.

"This kind of fever is normal in these cases," she said, "and we'll soon have it under control. For now though, we'll have to ask you to step out of the room while we tend to him."

"I understand," Allison said. They left the room and went down the hallway to the waiting area next to the elevator. There were several comfortable chairs, a couch, and a small table with magazines and newspapers on it there. She and Nicholas sat down on the couch.

"You *see*, Nicholas," she said. "These people are really good at what they do."

"I guess so," Nicholas said. From his expression, he didn't look all that confident.

Nicholas' mother died from a heart attack brought on by a rare disease two weeks after giving birth to him. Since then Aunt Joyce had come by to cook for dinner every day during the week.

They sat in silence for a while until a thought came to Nicholas. He reached into one of the inside pockets of his jacket and pulled out the Cup of Mirrors Allison had given him.

She noticed it.

"I just stuck it in my jacket this morning before I left for school." He paused. "Is there a story behind it?"

Allison's face grew excited. "There is indeed a story behind it. I wasn't sure if you liked my gift or not. That's why I didn't tell the story on your birthday. I'm not a good story teller like your father, but would you like to hear it now?"

"Please," Nicholas said.

Allison smiled. "Good…"

"Just inside the mouth of an alley in a poor section of a city, a blind man sat on the sidewalk. His back rested against the wall of a building. A white cane leaned against the wall, and a small open briefcase sat beside him.

An old woman slowly approached the alley, her body bent, and her steps unsteady. She paused a moment and looked into the alley. She noticed the white cane and realized the man was blind.

She stepped into the alley. 'Do you need help?' she said.

'No, thank you,' the man said, 'I'm just resting.'

The woman peered into the briefcase. Among the jumble of the man's possessions, she spotted a wallet. 'This is a very bad neighborhood,' she said. She knelt down slowly, reached into the briefcase, and removed the wallet. 'You should be careful about your belongings.'

'Good advice,' the man said. 'Now please put the wallet back in the briefcase. You'll see that there's a Cup of Mirrors in the briefcase. Take it out.'

'But I wasn't—'

'No need for excuses. Just take the Cup of Mirrors and look into it.'

She got frightened because the blind man had caught her in the act of stealing, she did what he said. The Cup of Mirrors was shallow and multi-faceted. It just fit in her hand. A large octagonal mirror covered the bottom of the cup and was surrounded by eight smaller mirrors that lined the sides.

'What do you see?' the blind man said.

The woman looked confused. 'The mirror in the center is blank and . . . wait! In the side mirrors I see the faces.'

She looked at the blind man. 'Are they all me?'

'They are. Now tell me what is happening at each stage of your life.'

She looked into the cup again.

'I'm a baby in my mother's arms and I'm smiling. I'm a little girl and my family is poor. And their love for me is fading under the heavy burdens in their lives. I feel unhappy, unwanted. I'm a teenager now and feeling worse about everything in my life. I'm screaming inside. I'm an adult, selfish, never satisfied. I'm a middle-aged woman and I've lost my love. I'm miserable and alone. I see myself as I am today—old and miserable, with a sorrow that has penetrated my soul with a permanent stain. My heart is empty.'

She lowered the cup once again and her body shook with her sobs.

'Now,' the blind man said, 'look at the mirror in the center and tell me what you see.'

The woman hesitated, let out a sigh, and raised the mirror. She gasped. 'It's me as a baby,' she said. 'And I'm smiling. I seem happy, without any cares. I feel worthy of being loved.'

'That is you,' the blind man said. 'That is the truth of you that you are always lovable and worthy of love. Somewhere in your life that was chipped away, but the truth about you still remains. You don't live in the past anymore. Let the truth in and express your true self. Remember that feeling of worthiness. You are not alone. The Universe is always with you because you came to this world from the Universe. We all did.'

The woman burst into tears and he let her cry until she got calm.

'What are these mirrors?' the woman said sobbing again but now with tears of joy.

'Those mirrors are my eyes,' the blind man said. 'They show you hidden truths that you never knew before.'

The old woman put the Cup of Mirrors back into the briefcase and closed it. She wiped away her tears. 'Thank you,' she said. 'And God bless you.'

She turned back toward the main street and began to walk away; her body straightened now, her steps steady."

"That's an awesome story," Nicholas said.

"The Cup of Mirrors could help you discover hidden truth around you. The eight small mirrors might show what has happened to you from the past to the present. The large mirror could show you the truth deep inside your mind that even you don't realize." Allison said.

"You mean that with it I can see something that is invisible to me?" he said. "Or maybe learn something I don't know?"

"That could happen."

"That's a lot to think about." Nicholas said.

They sat together quietly for a while, until Nicholas broke the silence. "I heard the messages that Dad left for you, Jerry, and Mr. Rose this morning.

They were all pretty much the same, but there's more about the diamonds you should know."

"Oh?"

Before Nicholas could tell her about the visit from Vix Tower, Jerry stepped out of the elevator.

CHAPTER 3

An Invitation from Vix Tower

"Hi." Jerry sat down in a chair across from Allison and Nicholas. His normally cheery face looked serious.

"I'm so glad you could make it. We just came from his room," Allison said.

"How's he doing?"

"He's fairly stable, but he's still in a coma and his temperature went up. They're taking care of that now, but he can't have visitors for a while."

"I was at my parents' house in Los Angeles when I got his message," Jerry said. "He sounded really strange, so I cut my vacation short and caught the first flight back to San Francisco. I went straight to the museum, and Philip told me you were all here."

"Nicholas heard Daniel make the calls to Philip, you, and me. But he says there's more to the story than he told in the messages."

Jerry turned to Nicholas. "Hey, Pal," he said, "I didn't mean to ignore you. I was just so worried about your Dad."

"That's okay, Jerry."

"So what else should we know about the mysterious Mr. Tower?" Jerry asked.

Nicholas had to think for a moment whether he should tell them the whole story. Should he leave out the part about the Dark Shadow and what it did to his father? And would they believe that Tower said his father would die if he didn't bring him the diamonds? He wasn't sure whether that part really happened or whether he and his father had been hypnotized. Either way, Jerry was skeptical about supernatural and might think he was making it up. Maybe he'd tell Allison later. For now, he decided, he'd just tell them what they needed to know.

"Mr. Tower—Vix is his first name—came to our house pretty late. Like Dad said in his messages, he claimed he was the owner of the three magical diamonds. They talked for a while and Tower thanked him for finding the purple diamond and said the museum could use all of them in the Great Diamonds exhibit, but he'd have to find the other two first. Then he got really bossy about it, and he and Dad started to argue."

Nicholas paused to gather his thoughts. "He told Dad he had to bring him all three diamonds by midnight December twentieth."

"What's so special about December twentieth?" Jerry said.

"Well," Allison said, "there's going to be a total lunar eclipse that night."

"Yeah," Jerry said, "but what's that got to do with Daniel?"

"I don't know," Nicholas said. "But Vix said if Dad doesn't bring him the diamonds by then he'll be in big trouble."

"That's outrageous!" Allison said. "Did he have any proof that he owned the diamonds?"

Nicholas shook his head. "That's a part of what they were arguing about."

"Where was this guy from?" Jerry said. "Did he say?"

"He gave Dad a business card, but I don't know what happened to it."

"Do you remember anything else about what he said to your father?" Allison said.

"He said he was very rich and powerful. Dad said he didn't care, and told him to leave."

"I wish we had the business card," Allison said. "It would make it easier to do some research on Tower and maybe untangle Daniel's story."

"I agree," Jerry said. "I've got to get back to the museum now, but I'll go online and see if I can get any information on Tower." He paused. "His first name's Vic?"

"*Vix*," Nicholas said.

"Hmm," Jerry said. "Odd name."

"I'm staying here tonight," Allison said, "but Daniel's neighbors Renee and Ellie Spark are coming by for Nicholas. He'll be staying with them until Daniel can come home. And I've already informed the Italian team and Father Luciano that now you and I are the contact persons on this project under the circumstances. Unfortunately Father Luciano will be soon out of town for his religious business trip."

"Okay, Thanks." Jerry said, "Stay in touch." He gave Nicholas another hug and headed for the elevator.

Just as Jerry's elevator closed, Ellie Spark and her mother stepped out of the elevator the one next to it. They soon joined Allison and Nicholas on the second floor, where she was talking with the nurse. The nurse told them all that they could see Daniel, but they could only stay for a few minutes. The four of them followed her down the hallway to Daniel's room.

Daniel didn't seem to be as feverish as he was earlier. His eyes were closed and his breathing was steady. After several minutes, the nurse looked at her watch. "He's a little better," she said, "but he needs plenty of peace and quiet now."

She walked to the door and held it open. Nicholas, Allison, and Renee followed her, but Ellie lingered at Daniel's bedside. She put her hand on his arm and whispered, "Nicholas will be safe with us."

Daniel's eyes remained shut, but his eyelids twitched. The hint of a smile flickered across his face.

Ellie turned and joined the others in the hallway.

It was growing dark when Renee, Ellie, and Nicholas got to the parking lot. Renee noticed how quiet Nicholas was. "I tell you what," she said. "I'm not in the mood to cook dinner tonight. How about we hit a pizza restaurant and then catch an early movie?"

"What movie?" Ellie said.

"Let's Nicholas decide," Renee said. "It'll be a late birthday present for him."

"Okay," Ellie said. "But I get to pick the pizza restaurant."

Jerry got back to the museum from Daniel's hospital. There wasn't much to do in his office. He hadn't left a backlog when he went on vacation, and Daniel and Allison had made sure that his workload would be covered. It was actually good to be back to work. He'd spent his vacation helping his parents move from their house in southern California to an apartment in a gated retirement community in the same small town. His two sisters lived on the East Coast, and were too busy with their children to come across the country to help in the move.

Now that his parents were settled, he'd have more time to focus on himself. He was ready for a change. He'd worked hard all his life, and most of his debts were paid off, except for his student loans. Sometimes he regretted not following his father into the business world. His job at the museum was rewarding in terms of personal satisfaction—but a nice fat bank account would be more than welcome.

A large envelope on his desk caught his eye. It was from a courier service. It must have come in while he was at the hospital.

He checked the return address and almost fell out of his chair.

It was from Vix Tower!

Inside the large envelope was a small envelope containing a formal invitation to dinner at seven that evening. There was no phone number, but an address was printed at the bottom of the invitation. A handwritten note said: "Mr. Goldman—Please join me at my residence for dinner and a discussion that should prove highly interesting to you."

It was signed simply, "Vix."

Jerry read the invitation again. Was this the change he'd been waiting for? He tucked the invitation in his pocket and got up from his chair.

When Jerry exited the downtown MUNI subway station, he had to push through the flow of commuters who were leaving work. He'd considered taking a taxi, but he figured public transportation might be faster. Certainly cheaper.

He checked his watch. Quarter to seven. The sidewalks were crowded with holiday shoppers and tourists, but he got to the address with ten minutes to spare. It was a high-rise building with a marble entranceway. Its tall glass doors were set in from the street. He pulled on one of them, but it was locked.

Inside, two uniformed security guards stood talking near a desk, their backs to Jerry. He found an intercom on the entranceway wall and pressed the button.

One of the guards moved around behind the desk. A moment later a voice came over the entranceway speaker. "Can we help you?"

Jerry leaned toward the intercom. "I'm Jerry Goldman. I've got an appointment with Mr. Tower."

The man checked a clipboard on his desk and then walked to the doors and opened one.

"Mr. Tower is expecting you, sir," he said. "This way please."

Jerry followed him through the lobby to a bank of elevators.

Like the rest of the lobby's décor, the holiday decorations were tasteful and luxurious.

The guard ushered Jerry into an elevator and slid a card into a slot just inside the door.

"This will take you directly to Mr. Tower's penthouse, sir. Just leave the card in the slot. No one else will be using the elevator this evening." He pressed the "Up" arrow and stepped back into the lobby. Seconds later the door closed, and the elevator began to move upward swiftly and silently.

When the elevator glided to a stop, the door opened and Jerry stepped into a softly lit foyer that was richly paneled in some kind of dark wood. A large painting of boats on San Francisco Bay hung on one wall illuminated by a pin spotlight mounted on the ceiling. Jerry stepped close to it to see if he recognized the artist's name.

"It's a late Gideon Jacques Denny work from the 1860s, one of my favorites."

Jerry turned and saw a man in a stylishly tailored black suit coming through the doorway to an interior room.

"Welcome, Jerry," the man said. "I'm Vix Tower. I'm so glad you could make it on such short notice."

Jerry shook his hand. "That's a beautiful painting."

"I love beautiful things. That's why I invited you here tonight." He moved closer to Jerry. "Please," he said, "let me take your coat."

"Thank you." Jerry slipped out of his coat and handed it to Tower.

Tower hung it on a brass coat rack that stood near the inner door and gestured for Jerry to follow him into the other room.

Jerry could see that Vix's taste was exquisite—from the furniture, to the art objects on the mantel above the white-marble fireplace, to the paintings on the walls.

Tower guided Jerry to a matched set of easy chairs on the other side of the spacious room. On the glass-topped coffee table in front of the chairs two champagne glasses sat next to a towel-wrapped bottle of champagne in a silver ice bucket. When Jerry was seated, Tower opened the bottle and filled both glasses. He sat down in the other chair and pressed a button on the arm of his chair. With a soft hum, the dark red drapes that covered a wide picture window separated and revealed a spectacular view of San Francisco by night.

Tower lifted his glass. "A toast," he said.

Jerry raised his glass.

"Here's to what I'm sure will be a successful business arrangement," Tower said.

They clinked glasses and each took a swallow of champagne.

"That's excellent," Jerry said.

"I'm accustomed to excellence," Tower said. "I hope you soon will be too." He set his glass down. "This is primarily a business meeting, but I think we should relax and get to know each other first. To start with, do you have any special dining requirements? Vegetarian? Allergies to seafood, and so on?"

Jerry laughed. "No, Mr. Tower, I suppose you could call me an omnivore."

Tower smiled. "Please call me Vix."

Jerry nodded. "Certainly . . . Vix."

"I think you'll enjoy tonight's offering. We'll start with lobster bisque with cognac and a seasonal salad with raspberry vinaigrette. The entrée is filet mignon and jumbo shrimp. My cooks are working on some side dishes of vegetables, which I'm sure will be delicious. Dessert is white-chocolate cheese cake topped with strawberry and peach purées."

"Sounds wonderful," Jerry said.

Tower handed him an engraved formal business card. "I've written my private phone number on it," he said. "I don't usually give out my number, so please keep it to yourself."

"Thank you," Jerry said. He glanced at it and tucked it into his wallet.

"Jerry," Tower said, "I had a courier take my invitation to you because I heard about Mr. Blue's sudden illness this morning, and we were scheduled to meet tonight. I hope he recovers soon. According to what he told me, you're more than well qualified to handle a matter he and I discussed last night."

Jerry had been prepared for unpleasant dealings with Tower, but he was now having second thoughts. His preconceptions were based on the report Nicholas had given him and Allison at the hospital.

Nicholas had seemed sincere then, but he was also under a lot of stress because of Daniel's situation. The boy had said Tower wasn't a nice man, that he was bossy, and that he'd argued with Daniel. Yet in Daniel's brief voicemail there hadn't been even a hint of all that. And so far this evening, Tower had been nothing but gracious.

"Vix," Jerry said, "I'm really looking forward to that fabulous dinner, but perhaps we could get some business out of the way first."

"Of course, Jerry."

"First of all," Jerry said, "we at the museum feel we should see some proof of your claim to ownership of the three, uh, *magical* diamonds."

"I spoke to Mr. Blue about that," Tower said. "And they are indeed *magical*. I inherited those diamonds from my younger brother when he passed away many years ago. They are family keepsakes—tangible memories of my brother."

"I understand," Jerry said. "But the purple diamond was found in the grave of Adamo Balducci, who was buried 500 years ago. How does that—"

"I'm the last blood of the Giovanni Balducci family," Tower said, his voice rising. "Mr. Blue started this whole business when he discovered the

28

purple diamond, and I want him to finish it—once and for all. I want him or someone else from your museum to find the other two diamonds and bring all three of them to me. How complicated is that?"

"Please don't be offended," Jerry said, "but we really need official paper-work to prove your claim to the purple diamond. As for the other two, I understand you mentioned a deadline that would be virtually impossible to meet—if it could be met at all."

"I need those three diamonds before midnight of December twenti-eth," Tower said. "And let me assure you, for a man like myself, *nothing* is impossible." He smiled. "Listen, Jerry," his voice calmer, "I overcame a great many obstacles on my way to becoming who I am today. And why was that? Because I had a brilliant vision that I would possess whatever I desired. What I most desire now is to have my rightful inheritance. It is my destiny to have the magical diamonds in my hands at last."

Jerry gave him a blank look.

Tower shook his head, seemingly frustrated that he wasn't getting through to Jerry.

"Jerry, I have a fantastic proposal to present to you. This is your once-in-a-lifetime opportunity. Either you can quit working soon and enjoy a life of unbelievable affluence, or you can remain stuck in your current position under Mr. Blue with no chance to rise in your organization. Your talent and passion will be doomed for the rest of your life. This isn't guesswork. My people have conducted thorough investigations of your background and Mr. Blue's. What I've said is beyond question the truth. I'm proposing to give you a guaranteed annual income of two million dollars for life—which will be adjusted upward to account for inflation. You will never need to work again. All you have to do is bring those three diamonds to me by midnight of December twentieth. Any expenses you foresee will be paid in advance." He gave Jerry a sly smile. "And there's actually no need to involve Mr. Blue or the museum itself. How you manage the task is entirely your own business."

Jerry got up from his chair, his face reddening. "Mr. Tower," he said, "please bring your ownership paperwork for all three diamonds to the museum and we'll try to work out an agreement. We'll decide if your deadline is possible. If not, there will be no agreement. The business will be conducted through the museum. And, by the way, I'll require no compensation for my part in the matter other than my regular museum salary. I don't like to have my integrity questioned, Mr. Tower. I find it insulting. This meeting is over. Please excuse me, but I'll have to skip dinner. There's no need to see me out. I know the way."

Jerry headed out to the foyer and grabbed his coat from the rack. The elevator was still open, and he stepped into it and hit the down button.

As the elevator door closed, he heard Tower call from the other room: "You'll be back, Jerry!"

Tower finished his champagne in one long swallow and watched the Dark Shadow expand until it enveloped the room.

An angry, inhuman voice said, "I can feel her force coming back. She's trying to attack us again. We must get the diamonds before she destroys us."

Tower gripped the stem of the glass with one hand and with the other covered its rim. "We won't let it happen!" he said.

His fingers clenched the rim tighter and tighter until the glass shattered into pieces and the bloody shards clattered onto the hardwood floor.

CHAPTER 4

Time Travel

The movie theater Nicholas, Ellie, and Renee went was packed. Nicholas wanted to enjoy the movie he had long waited for, but he was distracted. The image of his father in the hospital bed was in his mind for the whole time.

Renee pulled up the car in front of her house and left the engine running.

"Ellie, I've got to pick up a few things at the drugstore. You can show Nicholas his room and give him a tour of the house."

"Okay, Mom." Ellie and Nicholas got out of the car.

"Ellie, could you put this leftover pizza into the refrigerator for me? You both didn't eat much this evening. You might be hungry later." Renee handed it to Ellie.

"Okay."

Ellie and Nicholas started heading for the house.

"Oh, wait, Ellie. Do you have the key?" Renee said.

Ellie turned and gave her mother a look. "Of course, Mom."

"Just checking," Renee said. She watched them until they entered the house, and then pulled away from the curb.

"Moms can get a little over protective," Ellie said. "Sometimes they can drive you crazy."

"I suppose so," Nicholas said.

Ellie felt herself blushing. She remembered that Nicholas didn't have a mother. She wished she could take her words back. To compensate, she took his arm and said in a cheery voice, "If you're ready for the grand tour, let's start with the basement."

He'd really never seen much of the house except for the entrance and living room.

"Sure," Nicholas said, secretly pleased. He and Hunter had often speculated about what lay within the house, particularly in the basement. They'd often entertained the idea—half seriously—that it might contain a secret treasure cave.

When Ellie and Nicholas reached the bottom of the stairs, he realized the prospects of finding a treasure cave were dim. He had little interest in the washing machine or the dryer. But the door across from them suggested possibilities.

"Do you have a key to that door, Ellie?" He smiled and pointed to her pendant. It was a gold key with a heart-shaped head—the shiny object he'd noticed when he was dazed from his bike accident. "I think that's an ancient key to a secret room full of treasures."

"Uh-uh," she said. "It's never locked." She pulled it open and flipped a light switch on.

"It's our hot-air furnace. And, boy, it does a great job. On a cold morning where we lived before, you wondered if the place was ever going to warm up." She smiled, "my mother gave this pendant to me on my last birthday. And I certainly don't think there's a secret room full of treasure in our house."

The rest of the house was as empty of secrets as the basement, but it still impressed Nicholas. In addition to the first-floor rooms he'd seen on the earlier visit, there were Ellie's father's office; a play room with a billiard;

a guest room; and a recreation room with a couch, easy chairs, and a huge flat-screen TV.

Ellie's parent's room was the master bedroom on the second floor. It had two walk-in closets and a bathroom with a shower, tub, and sauna. A small balcony off the bedroom looked out on the front yard. Nicholas opened the door to the balcony and stepped out on it. There were eight torches in the yard below. Stone steps led down to the detached street-level garage. A cold gust of wind made him shiver, and he stepped back into the room.

There were three other bedrooms on the second floor. All were nearly as spacious and elegant as the master bedroom. Ellie's room was next to the master room.

Nicholas was given the guest room on the first floor next to the recreation room.

The guest room including its own rest room and bathroom was at least four-times bigger than his room at home. Besides a king-size bed, it held a desk and office chair, a comfortable leather easy chair, a table and two chairs, a chest, and a bedside table with a reading lamp and a radio alarm clock on it. Unlike his room at home, it was warm in there.

"The heater in this house does a great job." Nicholas opened one of the windows a crack.

"I told you." Ellie said.

She opened the door to the walk-in closet. "Plenty of room for your stuff," she said. "Are you ready to go and get some of it?"

Nicholas hesitated. Images of last night's events in the living room of his house flashed through his mind, accompanied by a memory of the words Vix Tower had said to his father: "You will bring the three diamonds to me by midnight December twentieth or you will die."

If only he could tell someone about everything that happened to his father that night—someone who would take his story seriously.

Jerry?

He'd probably say it was all in his imagination. Supernatural stuff.

Hunter?

He might think it was another of the fantasy games he and Nicholas liked to play.

Allison?

He liked her a lot, but he just didn't know her that well.

If only . . .

"Nicholas . . . Are you okay?"

"What?"

"You had a look on your face that—"

"No, no . . . everything's fine. I was just thinking about a quiz we're going to have at school next week."

Ellie nodded. "Oh, good," she said, but she looked worried.

"Well," Nicholas said, "I'd better head over there now."

"I'll go with you," Ellie said. "Who knows how much stuff you'll want to bring back?"

Nicholas looked relieved. "Get your coat," he said.

When Nicholas stepped into his living room he felt a chill. It wasn't just that the heat was off. He couldn't completely block memories of the previous night. He was glad Ellie was with him. She was more than just a friend; sort of like a sister.

They packed his stuff into one of Daniel's large wheeled suitcases.

"I think that covers it for now," Nicholas said. "I can always come back later if I remember something else."

As soon as he said it, he remembered he had to find the business card Vix Tower had shown to his father for Allison. They left the suitcase in the bedroom and went back to the living room.

Nicholas checked out the magazines on the coffee table where Daniel had set the business card. It wasn't on or under any of them. He got down on his hands and knees and searched under the table and couch. *Come on, where is it?*

No luck.

"What are you looking for?" Ellie said.

"It's just a business card," Nicholas said. "There's some information on it that Allison wanted. Maybe it's in Dad's office."

It wasn't on Daniel's desk or his worktable, and a search of the books, magazines, and maps strewn around the floor came up empty.

"Never mind," Nicholas said. "I'll try to find it later."

"Wait," Ellie said. She stood absolutely still, and stared at Daniel's bedside table.

"What's the matter?" Nicholas said.

Ellie pointed to the table. "Maybe he put it in the drawer."

Nicholas shrugged. "I'll check it out."

"I'll get the suitcase," Ellie said, and left the room.

He opened the drawer. The only thing in the small table's drawer was a wallet-size color photograph of a young woman. She had long curly brown hair, piercing hazel eyes, and a heartbreakingly beautiful smile. He took the photo from the drawer and stared at it for several moments. He felt a gnawing sense that he knew her, yet he couldn't place her.

Who could she be?

He turned the photo over and gasped.

A short handwritten message on the back read: "To Daniel—With all my love—Olivia."

"Mother," he said softly, and tucked the photo into his shirt pocket.

He closed the drawer and headed out to the living room, where Ellie was waiting with the suitcase. His mind was racing. His heart was filled with an incredible joy that alternated with deepest sorrow.

If only she were here to help me now!

By the time Ellie and Nicholas got back to the house from Nicholas's house, Renee was back from the drugstore and in the kitchen cooking.

"Your Dad's working late again," Renee said to Ellie. "I'm making him something he can zap in the microwave when he gets home."

"Okay," Ellie said. "Nicholas and I'll be unpacking his things and getting his room settled."

When Nicholas's clothes were hung up in the closet and stashed in the chest, and his books arranged on the desk, Ellie sat down at the table by the window. Nicholas pulled the other chair and sat down opposite her.

"I've got something to ask you, Ellie," he said, his voice betraying his nervousness.

"Okay," she said.

"There's something I have to tell *someone*, and I finally figured you might be the best one."

Ellie nodded, her expression showing curiosity.

"It's going to sound really weird, so can I trust you to hear me out?"

"Of course," she said. "What is it?"

He took a deep breath. "Well," he said, "it's about the magical purple diamond my Dad found in Italy."

"The one that will be shown at the diamonds exhibit next year."

"Right. In the legend surrounding it, there are two more magical diamonds in existence besides the purple diamond. Last night, a stranger named Vix Tower visited us. He said he saw the purple diamond on the TV and that he's the owner of it and the two other magical diamonds. He wanted my Dad to bring all three to him by midnight of December twentieth. He said if Dad doesn't bring them, he'll die."

"Oh, no!"

"It's true. I haven't told this to anyone. I thought of Jerry and Hunter, but I didn't think they'd take me seriously. I like them and trust them, but they seem too ... I don't know *what*. But you seem to have some special qualities."

She nodded, her face serious.

"Nicholas," she said, "some people have certain gifts that others don't have. They can see in a different way, hear in a different way, and experience the world in a different way. I'm one of them. When I was little, I thought everybody could sense things the way I could. As I grew older, I came to realize most people couldn't. I decided it would be best to pretty much keep those gifts to myself."

"My knee?" Nicholas said.

"What about it?"

"After your Mom put ointment on the cut the day of the accident, you put your hand on the bandage and I felt a little buzzing sensation. Was that what made it heal so fast?"

"Let's just say it helped," Ellie said.

Nicholas shook his head in wonder. "That is really something."

"And now," Ellie said, "I think you have something very serious and very mysterious to tell me. Believe me, Nicholas, I won't laugh at you, and I won't doubt you. We have to trust each other."

A wave of relief swept over Nicholas, and he began to share with Ellie the nightmarish events that had been haunting him. As he talked, Ellie listened intently, making no comments, allowing him to unburden his soul.

When Nicholas finished, he let out a great sigh and slumped down in his chair. "That's it, Ellie," he said. "If I can't get those diamonds, Vix Tower and the Dark Shadow will kill my father. I don't know what to do."

"I'll help you, Nicholas," Ellie said, "but first we must know what happened to the two lost diamonds. And we need to know the relationship between them, Vix Tower, and the Dark Shadow."

"But where do we even start?" Nicholas said.

"We start in the past," Ellie said. "Tonight I'm going to take you on a journey that few people have ever been on. We'll have to travel back in time. Whatever happens, you must trust me. It's the only way we can help your father."

Nicholas looked confused. "How in the world could we ever do that, Ellie? It doesn't seem possible."

"Many things don't seem possible—until they happen," Ellie said. "I'll tell you about my another gift.

When I was five years old, my grandmother—who I loved very much—was diagnosed with stomach cancer.

One day my mother came to my room while I was playing with my dolls. 'Put your best dress on, Ellie,' she said, 'and be sure to brush your hair. We're going to the hospital to see Grandma.'

When we got to the hospital, I didn't recognize Grandma first. She had lost her hair and was as skinny as a skeleton. Her eyes looked sad and blank. My mother pulled aside her covers and began stroking her boney legs. Grandma sighed with pleasure and gave me a weak smile.

'Ellie,' my father said, 'why don't you stroke Grandma's legs for her?'

Grandma looked so awful, I was too scared to touch her—or even talk to her. I ran from her room.

My parents didn't scold me. But when we got home, I went to my room and cried because I felt so bad about not comforting Grandma. I don't remember how long I sobbed, but I stopped when my mother came to my room.

'Put your best dress on, Ellie,' she said, 'and be sure to brush your hair. We're going to the hospital to see Grandma.'

I felt an incredible thrill come over me.

Everything happened as it had happened before, until we got to the hospital. This time I rushed to Grandma's room and pulled back her covers. I said, 'Grandma, let me stroke your legs for you.' She looked at me and smiled.

I stroked her legs until she drifted into sleep. I was so glad to see her happy. At the same time, I couldn't believe that I got to make it up on the same day.

I said to myself, 'is this real?'

Just as I doubted that moment, my body was literally dragged back to home from the hospital by force, like time was rewound. When I opened my eyes, I was back in my room where I was before.

Somehow I'd traveled back in time and had a chance to change a sad part of my life."

Ellie smiled. "I don't know how I learned to go back in time, Nicholas. But ever since then I've secretly practiced that ability. And now I'm taking you back in time with me."

"Is that really true?" Nicholas said.

"I'll let you be the judge of that," Ellie said.

She headed for the door. "I'll be back in a minute."

Ellie came back with a white candle about 5 inches tall and a candleholder from the dining room and set it on Nicholas's table. She turned the overhead light off but left the bedside lamp on.

She came back to the table and handed him a lighter. "Not yet." She held up her hand, palm toward him.

Nicholas waited for her direction. She glanced at the radio alarm clock on the bedside stand. It was a few seconds before nine o'clock.

"Light it!"

As the wick caught fire, she said, "Close your eyes, take a deep breath, and clear your mind. Focus on our wish: We want to go back to the root of the diamonds. You must trust your power and be strong willed. That's the only way we can return safely to the present time."

She took both his hands in hers and closed her eyes. "Focus your mind," she said.

Nicholas closed his eyes and tried to concentrate. The harder he tried, the more tightly he squeezed her hands.

Images of his father's suffering, of the Dark Shadow, and of Vix Tower flashed through his mind.

He fought against them.

I must go back to the past to find the missing diamonds . . .

I must go back . . .

I must . . .

"I *will* go back!"

Nicholas was swept up in a whirlwind, losing all perceptions of time and place. His hands grew damp and he no longer could feel Ellie's hands—

"Nicholas," a familiar voice said.

Nicholas opened his eyes. "Ellie! I thought I lost you." He sighed with relief. "Are we in the past?"

She looked around at the surroundings; there were a long beach and a jungle behind it. That was all she could see. "I don't think so." She furrowed her eyebrows. *What am I doing here? I must focus on going back to the time and place where I was supposed to be.*

From behind them came the trilling of a bird's song. They turned and saw a large green, yellow, and black bird—some kind of parrot. It was sitting on a tree limb in a jungle that bordered the beach. The limb extended over the beach. Beneath it an eight-foot wooden picnic table was set up on the sand.

They exchanged glances, and then hurried over to it.

"Wow!" Nicholas said.

The table was loaded with an unusual feast: a large platter of various sorts of biscuits and pastries, two baskets of fresh fruits—some were kinds they'd never seen before—and a crystal bowl of swirled white and pink whipped cream.

"Is this for us?" Nicholas said.

Ellie looked up and down the beach. In both directions, as far as the eye could see, it was deserted. "Who else?" she said, and reached for one of the pastries.

Nicholas took one, too, and they each dipped them into the whipped cream bowl and took a bite.

"Wow!" Nicholas said again.

Ellie said nothing. She closed her eyes, and the smile on her face spoke for her.

When Nicholas finished the pastry, he took a fruit from the basket. It was shaped like a peach, but it was multi-colored. He broke it in half, and it gave off an enticing fragrance. Instead of a pit, it had a soft aqua seed at the center. He popped it into his mouth. Incredible! It was like a candy drop that tasted of peach and condensed milk.

"I've been hungry because I couldn't eat enough pizza tonight after I saw my dad like that in the hospital." Nicholas said.

"Me, too. We've been hungry. That's why we were drawn to this place." Ellie said and bit into a yellow pear that turned out to be a sponge cake layered with creamy vanilla frosting and white chocolate syrup.

The two looked at each and shook their heads.

"I wish they served stuff like this in the school cafeteria," Nicholas said.

Ellie smiled, "That would be great." She reached for a silver-and-gold-striped banana and peeled it open, wondering what in the unknown period of time it would taste like.

When they'd had enough of the curious and delicious taste sensations, Ellie said, "We should get going."

Nicholas looked up and down the beach. "Which way?"

Ellie pointed toward the jungle.

"Why that way?" Nicholas said.

"I don't know, exactly," Ellie said. "I just have a feeling—and it's strong enough so that I think we should follow it."

The jungle seemed too thick to get through, and they walked along the edge of it until Ellie came to a halt. "Wait," she said.

A moment later the jungle leaves rustled softly and a narrow opening appeared in it. It was a clear trail, about 75 feet long. On the other side of it, a huge stone wall stood. A tall iron gate in it was open wide. They looked at each other and nodded, and then proceeded into the opening.

As they were moving toward the gate, it began to close.

Ellie grabbed Nicholas's arm. "Run!" she said. "We've got to get through it!"

They dashed toward it. But the faster they ran, the faster it closed, finally slamming shut when they were just a few feet from it.

Frustrated, they pounded on it with their fists.

"What should we do now, Ellie?" Nicholas said.

Ellie thought for a second, and made up her mind. "We back up and then we run right at it," she said calmly.

"What?" Nicholas looked at her in confusion.

"Come on," she had already started backing up. "We don't know when it will open again."

He followed her back about twenty feet, and they both turned to face the gate.

"Trust me; we'll be okay," she said confidently. "Are you ready?"

"As ready as I'll ever be," he said.

"Then let's go!"

They charged straight toward the gate.

CHAPTER 5

The Balducci Brothers

Italy in the year 1536.

Giovanni Balducci, a ruler of a vast area in Tuscany, came to a decision regarding his two sons: Savino, who was twenty-nine, and Adamo, who was four years younger. According to tradition, the oldest son in a family inherited a deceased parent's holdings.

Giovanni Balducci had other ideas.

Because he loved both his sons equally, he believed Adamo deserved to share equally in the Balducci inheritance. He had his secretary draw up a last will and testament to that effect.

Seven years ago, to prepare his sons for their responsibilities, Giovanni put each in charge of one of the villages under his control. Savino was to rule Torre, a walled village that was dominated by a great stone tower at its center. Adamo was given charge of Chiesta, another walled village that was several miles from Torre. Its distinguishing feature was a large church that served as the hub of the village's activities.

He recognized that each son would use a different style in ruling his designated village. However, he didn't intend that they would be in competition with one another; he wished only that each would develop his personal potential for governing.

Giovanni realized that, like most brothers, his sons indulged in friendly rivalry, although he was a bit concerned that Savino's rivalry seemed to get stronger with age. At one point they even courted the same woman, Foresta Bollai, the daughter of his old friend Romano Bollai.

When it became obvious that Foresta's preference was for Adamo, Savino graciously yielded, and went on to Magarita Capello, the daughter of another of Giovanni's old friends, Cosmo Capello.

Savino and Margarita were married. And six months after that, Adamo took Foresta for his wife. Giovanni felt a deep sense of relief.

Giovanni Balducci had never considered that his sons were frivolous. Still, he was filled with both pride and relief that they both were now started on the serious and mature pursuits of a man's life.

Within a year of the wedding, Margarita gave birth to a son, Mariotto. Savino and Margarita occupied a large estate that overlooked Torre. It was an impressive property with spacious grounds and an elegant house that featured furniture and artwork selected by Margarita. Her father was a wealthy lord and had tutored his daughter well in the finer things of life. Savino's contribution to the artwork was a bas-relief of his profile carved by a Torre artisan in a block of granite at the entrance to the grounds.

Adamo and Foresta took up residence at their own estate, which overlooked Chiesta. Although less elegant than his brother's estate, its grounds proved suitable for Adamo's agricultural studies. In the more than six years that he and Foresta dwelt there, Adamo developed numerous techniques that greatly improved the way Chiesta's farmers grew and harvested their crops. Although Foresta was unable to conceive a child, she and Adamo were content with their lives. Foresta was well read and an accomplished writer. She maintained a journal that chronicled Adamo's agricultural experiments, the affairs of the village, and the day-to-day life that she and her husband shared.

Just before dawn of a damp spring morning, Adamo Balducci mounted his horse and headed out to do some business in Chiesta. A short distance from his house, he was startled by strange cries from an area near the edge of the cliff his estate was situated on. He hurried toward the source of the sounds.

He peered over the cliff and saw a young child perched on an outcropping some twenty feet below. She clutched a cloth bag in one hand. A yellow kitten poked its head out of the bag's opening.

"Please stay still!" Adamo said, his heart pounding. He returned to his house for some rope, and then rushed back to the cliff's edge.

The mingled cries of the kitten and the child filled him with hope. *If only they could hold on!*

He tied one end of the rope to a tree nearby on the ground, dropped the other over the edge of the cliff, and began to lower himself hand over hand. When he reached the outcropping, he tied the rope around his waist and picked up the little girl, who was now clutching her kitten with both hands.

"You're safe now," he said.

He could see how terrified she was, and smiled at her. "Your kitten is very sweet," he said. "You must love her very much."

"I do," the girl said.

"And what is your little friend's name?"

Her expression brightened. "Piero," she said. "I named him myself."

"A wonderful name."

He looked to the right and could see in the early morning light how the girl might have ended up where she did. A long ridge of rocky material slanted down from the cliff's edge. To a child it might appear to be a path. There was now a gap of several dozen feet between the ridge and the section he was standing on. It had probably broken off in the previous night's rain.

Before he could begin to pull himself up, he heard a cracking sound. The outcropping gave way and vanished into the abyss. He swung away from the cliff and twisted in the air. On the return swing, his back slammed into the cliff, jarring him so severely he nearly lost his grip on the child.

The situation was more dangerous than he'd first thought. How could he pull himself up hand over hand and also hold onto his precious load.

"Put your arms around my neck, dear," he told the girl, and he started to make his way up the cliff.

"I can't hold on," the little girl said, her voice weak.

"That's all right," he said, freeing one hand from the rope and wrapping his arm around her. "We'll be up there soon." He hoped his voice conveyed more confidence than he felt.

Would it be possible to jerk himself upward with one hand and catch onto the rope at a higher point?

He gave it a try. At best he gained a few inches. He tried again, with the same result. It took all his strength, and he didn't know how much longer he could keep it up. He began to feel the task was hopeless, until the rope gave a jerk and he found himself raised half a foot or so.

Someone was pulling him up!

"Thank you!" he shouted.

There was no answer, but little by little he was hauled up the cliff face.

After a few minutes, he was close enough to the cliff's edge to hoist the child and her kitten over it. Moments later he pulled himself up and onto solid ground.

"Papa!" the little girl said. She set her kitten down and hugged the shoulders of the man who lay face down near the edge of the cliff.

Covered by a blanket, the man lay on a couch in the Adamo Balducci family's living room. He'd been gasping for breath when he was brought into the house, but his breathing was more normal now, although still labored.

Foresta cradled the little girl in her arms; the little girl cradled Piero in hers.

Adamo sat next to the man, supporting his head with one hand. He held a cup of herbal tea that Foresta had prepared in the other hand and moved it to the man's lips.

The man took a small sip, swallowed, and took another. When he finally finished the tea, he was able to sit up. He looked at his daughter, who was now sleeping in Foresta's arms. "God bless you both," he said. "And . . ."

He began to cough.

Adamo patted him gently on the back until the man's coughing finally subsided.

"Just relax now," Adamo said. "You don't need to talk."

The man shook his head. "I do," he said. "I don't have much time." He looked at his sleeping daughter again and smiled. Then he opened his shirt and revealed a makeshift bandage that was secured to his chest by a belt. It was soaked with blood.

Foresta gasped. "We must send for a doctor!"

The man shook his head again. "It won't help. I was a soldier once. I know what such wounds do."

Foresta stood up, the girl still in her arms. "I'm going to put your little one to bed. You must try to relax." She left the room, but before putting the girl to bed in her room, she told a servant to take Adamo's horse and to ride like the wind to get a doctor.

As soon as Foresta had left, the man reached for Adamo's arm. "Please listen to what I have to say; it's very important."

Adamo nodded, and the man began to tell his story:

47

His name was Lorenzo de Canal and his daughter's name was Caterina. He was a gem cutter from Venice and was heading to Florence to study detailed gem engraving with a master. His wife had died a few years earlier, and he had no relatives who could care for Caterina while he was away.

"Two days ago," he said, "as our coach was traveling through the mountains, three bandits came out of nowhere and attacked us. They first killed the horses. The coachman fought bravely, killing two of them. But the third villain stabbed him in the back and then came for Caterina and me."

Lorenzo brought his hand to his mouth and stifled a cough. He held up the other hand to Adamo. "I'm all right," he said, and continued his story.

"As I said, I was a soldier once. There was no way I would let this animal harm my child. Like many people in my trade, I carry a weapon with me when I travel. When he yanked open the door to our coach, I drove my dagger into his heart."

Lorenzo paused. "Unfortunately, he drove his sword into my chest."

He coughed again, and this time a clot of blood slipped from his lips and fell to the blanket.

"Look," Adamo said, "you mustn't—"

"I must!" Lorenzo said, his eyes wild. "Hear me out! We left the coach and began to walk. We walked that night, all the next day, and most of last night. Finally, not far from where you found my daughter, we collapsed on the ground, exhausted. I covered her with my coat and we fell asleep. Sometime after that she must have awakened and wandered to the cliff's edge and . . . well, you know the rest."

Lorenzo glanced around the room, a worried look on his face. "My coat! Where is it?"

"Please be calm," Adamo said. "It's in the foyer."

"I must have it. Bring it to me, please!"

Foresta came back into the room, and Adamo stood up.

"Sit with him for a moment, dear," Adamo said. He left the room and was back moments later with Lorenzo's muddy coat in hand.

"Thank you," Lorenzo said, taking the coat from Adamo. He reached into it and pulled on a thread that dangled near the armpit. A concealed pocket fell open. He reached into it and pulled out a small velvet sack.

A weak smile appeared on Lorenzo's face. "Please listen carefully," he said. "This may be the last time I ever tell this story."

He opened the sack and tipped its contents into his hand: three cherry-size octahedral gemstones. One was green, one purple, and one pink.

"What are they?" Foresta said.

"Rare diamonds," Lorenzo said. "I come from a family of jewelers, and they have been passed down from generation to generation. According to legend, one night a nobleman brought them to my great-great-grandfather—Carlo de Canal—and hired him to set them in a necklace as a surprise gift for his lover. He swore Carlo to secrecy and said that no one else knew about the diamonds.

The next morning when Carlo opened the box, the three diamonds were gone, replaced by a red one much larger than the others. He was terrified. How did it happen? No matter the cause, he was sure that the nobleman would never believe his story. He'd have him arrested, tried as a thief, and hanged.

As fate would have it, when the nobleman was on his way to pick up the necklace, his carriage lost a wheel while it was crossing a bridge. It plunged into a canal, and the nobleman was drowned.

My great-great-grandfather realized that there was no one to return the red diamond to. The three diamonds might belong to the nobleman's family, but not the red diamond. Out of fear of arrest—rather than greed—he kept it.

After that incident, he worshiped the red diamond as a gift from God, believing it had kept him from being hanged.

Over the years he prospered in his business and became very wealthy. He thanked the red diamond for saving him from the gallows and for all the good fortune he believed it had brought him. His life indeed seemed blessed. On his deathbed, he passed the box on to his son and told him what it contained. He also told him how he had come by the diamond. He said to pass it on to succeeding generations—along with its story—and surely success would come to them.

After his death, his son opened the box and discovered that instead of a red diamond it contained the three diamonds that Carlo had claimed the nobleman left with him years earlier.

No one ever saw the red diamond again, and these three diamonds were finally passed down to me. My faith in their magical power is uncertain, but I am proud that I didn't sell them for my own profit. If what I fear will soon happen to me *does* happen, I pray you would pass two of them on to Caterina."

"Two of them?" Adamo said.

"Yes. And I would ask you to keep one for yourselves. Any one of the three would more than pay for her upkeep and education until she is of age—if you would be willing to care for her until then."

Adamo and Foresta looked shocked. "Of course we would care for the child," Foresta said. "But not for any payment."

Lorenzo smiled at Adamo and Foresta. "God bless you."

His eyes grew misty. "Only the true owner of these diamonds will ever know their secrets," he said. And he drifted off into sleep.

Adamo greeted the doctor at the door and thanked him for coming so promptly. "Unfortunately," he said, "you're too late."

After arrangements were made to take Lorenzo de Canal's body to the church in Chiesta, Adamo and Foresta sat in the living room, both of them feeling drained. He held the three diamonds in his hand and stared at them blankly.

Piero came into the room and began to purr. He rubbed against Adamo's legs and then jumped into his lap. Adamo stroked the cat gently, as if moving in rhythm with his purring.

Foresta watched Adamo for a while and sighed. "Adamo, what shall become of that poor little girl?"

"I think good things will come to her, my dear, if we raise her as if she were our own. What do *you* think?"

"Oh, Adamo, for us to have a child . . ." Tears streamed down her cheeks. "I am so happy to have a daughter. I am so ready to be a mother."

"And I to be a father."

He eased Piero to the floor, stood up, and put the diamonds back in the velvet sack. "I think we should store the diamonds someplace where they'll be safe," he said. "For now I'll put them in the chest upstairs. Whether they're magical or not is not clear. But they are certainly precious: They are little Caterina's inheritance."

He and Foresta headed for the stairs.

CHAPTER 6

We Are Not Orphans or Beggars

Nicholas found himself lying face down on a wooden floor.

"Ellie?"

"I'm right next to you," she said.

"Thank God," he said. It was dark, but his eye began to adjust to the dim light that shone through a small dusty window.

"Where are we?" he said.

"I think we're in an attic."

He looked up and saw wooden beams that formed a triangle above the two of them.

"Look!" Ellie said. She was peering through a crack in the floor. She gestured for Nicholas to join her.

An empty room lay below them.

"Where do you—"

"Shh," Ellie said. "I can hear footsteps."

The door to the room opened and a man and a woman entered. He was wearing a dark purple slashed doublet and matching hose. She was dressed in a teal colored long silk dress with long balloon sleeves and gold trim. Her long hair was tucked into a bonnet.

They crossed the room to where a chest stood, and the man pulled the top drawer open. He turned to the woman. "The magical diamonds will be safe, Foresta."

"Adamo, do you think they would turn into one red diamond like they did when Lorenzo's great-great-grandfather had them?"

"Perhaps," Adamo said. He put the sack in the chest drawer and pushed it closed.

"Wherever we keep them," she said, "we'll preserve them for dear Caterina—our little gift from Heaven."

They kissed for a moment, and then left the room.

"Everything is so weird here," Nicholas said. "I knew they were speaking Italian, but it sounded like English to me. I understood what they were saying. How can that be?"

Ellie shook her head, "I don't know exactly, Nicholas. There are many things I can't explain to you—or to myself. But somebody is helping us translate Italian into English in our minds."

"Who?"

"They are our angels, who help us during this time-travel and everyday in our time."

"I don't understand." Nicholas said.

"I don't understand all of what's happening either. I'm relying on the feelings I've been getting from somewhere. Let's stay here for a while and see if we can find out what happened to the diamonds."

"So can we take the diamonds now and bring them back to San Francisco?" Nicholas said.

Ellie shook her head. "We can't take *anything* back to San Francisco. But we do need to find out where the diamonds ended up."

"How long will that take?" Nicholas said, his voice desperate. "Remember I've only got two weeks left before—"

"Don't worry about that," Ellie said. "The time in this realm doesn't affect the time back in San Francisco. We'll find out what we need to know here, and when we get back to our own world, it will be the same time it was when we left it. Trust me."

"Okay. What do we do now?"

"Find a way to get out of this attic and find a place to get some sleep. From then on, we just play it by ear."

Early next morning, Ellie and Nicholas woke up in the hayloft of Adamo's barn, where they'd spent the night.

A short while later, Adamo came into the barn with one of his servants. "Make sure the horses are fed," he told the servant. "Then hitch them to my carriage. I'm leaving in half an hour to visit my father and my brother."

"Will you be staying long?" the servant said.

"Not really," Adamo said. "I just want to tell them in person that Foresta and I are adopting a little girl."

When Adamo's driver stopped to open the Adamo's gate, two figures hurried from behind a clump of bushes and climbed onto the back of the carriage.

The carriage drove through the walled village of Chiesta. On the way, Nicholas saw a big church made of stones. It was the church in the picture Daniel had shown him. He appreciated the beautiful round stain glass window set into the stone wall above the front door. An hour later they hopped to the ground just outside the gate to Giovanni Balducci's estate.

Giovanni was delighted to hear Adamo's news about Caterina. He'd now have two grandchildren, a boy and a girl. Adamo didn't mention the diamonds to him. He would someday, but for now he wanted to show him that he could develop his village and land through his own ingenuity and efforts, not through any kind of magical powers.

As Adamo left his father's estate and headed for Savino's, Nicholas and Ellie sneaked back on the carriage again.

On the way there, the carriage passed through the village of Torre. The bells in the great tower rang out and Nicholas noticed that the tower—except for not having a clock—looked very much like the tower on his father's pictures.

The village was bustling with life. In the open square in front of the tower, merchants with booths or wooden tables displayed their goods. Potential customers eyed tools, clothing, jewelry, produce, and a variety of other goods.

At one end of the square, a line of people with bottles, bowls, pots, and buckets waited their turn to draw water from a community well. An old man in the line nudged the woman in front of him, and they both turned toward the wagon and laughed. They waved to the little thieves who were stealing a ride.

Nicholas and Ellie waved them back.

Another woman stared at them with a bewildered look on her face.

"What's wrong with her?" Nicholas said.

"It's probably our outfits."

The carriage exited Torre through its rear gate, and the horses picked up speed. They finally slowed when they drew near to Savino's estate.

The carriage stopped in front of the gate to Savino's estate, and Adamo hopped out. He approached the gate and shouted something. A moment later it swung open. As Adamo stepped forward, the driver snapped his reins and followed him in.

Once inside the walls, the driver turned his horses toward a stable that was located fifty feet or so from the entrance.

"Now!" Ellie said.

She and Nicholas jumped to the ground. A cluster of bushes bordered the wall. They scooted behind them and dusted themselves off.

"We made it," Nicholas said. "So what do we do now?"

Ellie chuckled. "What I told you last night. We play it by—"

"Hey!" a deep voice said.

The bushes parted, and a huge baldheaded man stepped in front of Nicholas and Ellie. He crossed his brawny arms over his massive chest and frowned down at them.

"Where did you two come from?" he said. "And why are you wearing such strange clothes. It's a little early in the day for a masquerade ball, isn't it?"

"We've been traveling for days," said Ellie.

"That's not what I asked," he said. "And it's not likely either. You're both too clean for that." He grabbed them by the scruffs of their necks. "Let's go!"

Adamo's purpose in visiting his brother was to tell him he was going to adopt a daughter. He'd also considered discussing the magical diamonds with him. Savino's wife, Margarita, was from the north, where the jewelry business thrived, and her father, Cosmo Capello, was acquainted with many of the fabled jewelry dealers in Venice. Could she have heard about those diamonds from him? On the other hand, since he hadn't mentioned the diamonds to his father, would it be wise not to bring up the subject with his brother?

He'd think about it. First, though, he'd tell him about Lorenzo and Caterina. But he'd leave out the business with the diamonds.

"Amazing," Savino said when Adamo had finished. "A brave man, that Lorenzo. A pity he couldn't get help sooner."

A knock sounded on the office door.

"Come in," Savino said.

The door swung open and the man who'd caught Nicholas and Ellie pushed them into the room.

"Excuse me, my lord," the man said, "I found these two lurking about on your property."

Savino eyed the two. "Are you brother and sister?" he said.

Ellie and Nicholas shook their heads.

"Do your families live near here?"

"No, sir," Ellie said, "they live far from here."

Savino nodded. "And where exactly is that?"

Ellie and Nicholas exchanged glances, but neither spoke.

"Well," Savino said, "you don't look like villagers, and you don't seem to know where your families are. That suggests to me that you are orphans and probably beggars."

"We're not!" Nicholas said. "We have families but we're separated from them."

"And you don't know where they live?" Savino gave them a crafty smile. "I see. You're not orphans, you're not beggars, you have no homes hereabouts, and you have no means of support. Is that right?"

The two looked at each other again and nodded.

"All right," Savino said. "I think we can find something to keep you busy until your . . . *families* . . . decide to find you."

He looked at Nicholas. "What's your name, boy?"

"Nicholas."

"Well, Nicholas," he said, "Mariotto, my young son, needs a play-mate—a big brother, so to speak. You will have a good life with us here. My son will be glad to have you around."

"And you," Savino said to Ellie, "what's your name?"

"Ellie."

"A lovely name." He turned to Adamo. "Brother, would you take care of the girl? She needs a home and somebody to look after her. She can be a big sister to your new daughter."

"A wonderful idea," Adamo said. He turned to Ellie. "My wife and I would welcome you to our family. And don't worry; we live nearby, and you and Nicholas can see each other often."

"Ristro," Savino said to the big man, "take these children to the kitchen and tell Agnola to feed them."

Savino made a dismissive gesture with his hand, and Ristro led Nicholas and Ellie out of the room and closed the door behind him.

The unexpected arrival of the two children gave a boost to Adamo's spirits. In almost no time at all, he and Foresta had acquired two lovely daughters. Maybe there was something to the story of those diamonds having magical powers. His luck was indeed changing for the better.

He made up his mind. He would share the secret of the diamonds.

"Brother," he said to Savino, "I received a wonderful gift from Lorenzo, a reward for looking after Caterina."

Savino raised an eyebrow. "What is it?"

"He gave me three unusual diamonds: one green, one purple, and one pink. According to him they have magical qualities. He says they might make my wishes come true." He chuckled. "I don't believe that story entirely, yet I'm still curious about it. Foresta and I thought we'd always be childless, but you yourself have seen how we've come to be doubly blessed."

Savino shrugged and said nothing, stroked his beard. Adamo recounted the story that Lorenzo told him; however, he held back the part about the transformation of the red diamond—just in case.

When Adamo finished, he said, "Have you or Margarita ever heard of such a legend?"

"I never have," Savino said. "Margarita may have heard something about it from her father. I'll ask her and let you know. If the story's true, I'd like to get my hands on some diamonds like that." He smiled. "In fact I'd like to get my hands on *any* kind of diamonds. So, Brother, be content with them—even though the claims of their magical powers are doubtful."

"I'm skeptical too," Adamo said.

"What size are they?"

"They're big. Like cherries."

"Hmm," Savino said, "that is big. You're a lucky man, Adamo."

"I am," Adamo said. He felt a wave of joy sweep over him. It was brought on by both his good fortune and by the pleasure of sharing the news of it with his brother.

In the kitchen, Agnola, a young servant, bluntly put two bowls of stew and some dry bread on the table for Ellie and Nicholas. She was incredibly skinny. Her eye bowls were so big, almost sticking out from her skull, that Nicholas and Ellie could see their own reflections on her eyes. Nicholas thought she must eat like a sparrow.

Agnola handed spoons to Ellie and Nicholas and hurried from the room.

"Ellie, what should we do now?" Nicholas said. "I'm trapped here, and you're trapped with Adamo's family."

"Don't worry," Ellis said. "We'll be okay if you trust what I told you: Try to keep track of where the diamonds are located, but don't do anything to them. And find out what is the relationship between Vix Tower, the Dark Shadow, and the diamonds. These will help us find the missing diamonds when we get back to our own time."

Nicholas nodded. He stared at the food, but didn't really feel like eating.

Oh, well, he thought, *who knows when I'll see another meal?*

He reached for a piece of bread.

Agnola climbed the stairs to her lady's room. Margarita had gone to Florence for the day to shop for jewelry, clothing, and maybe some delightful sweets. Agnola hoped she'd share some treats with her. Her mouth watered at the thought of the only kind of food she really craved.

Savino's six-year-old son, Mariotto, was out in the garden playing hide and seek with another servant. Savino was in his office talking with his brother. The coast was clear.

She opened the door to Margarita's room, stepped in, closed the door behind her, and went to a bookcase across the room. She knelt on the floor and pulled out a thick leather-bound book from the bottom shelf. She took an envelope from her apron. It was folded into a small rectangle and closed with a string. It was a letter for Savino from a lord in another region that had been delivered that morning. She opened the book, tucked the envelope into it, and returned it to the shelf.

Ristro, who was fiercely loyal to Savino, handled his outgoing messages. Still, Margarita was able to garner a great deal of information about her husband's doing from the messages that came in.

She stood up and went over to a portrait of Margarita and Mariotto that hung next to a couch. She tilted it slightly to one side—a sign to her lady that a letter was waiting for her inside the leather-bound book.

"Are you done eating?" Agnola said sharply when she got back to the kitchen.

"Yes," Ellie said. "And we've cleaned the dishes and put them in the cupboard."

Agnola looked surprised. She stood there for a moment, her bony hands resting on her hips. "Hmm!" she said. She frowned at the two children, and then turned and walked out of the kitchen and off down the hallway.

Ellie and Nicholas waited in silence. When the sound of the servant's footsteps finally faded away, they turned to each other and burst into laughter.

CHAPTER 7

A Smart Mischief

As soon as Margarita returned from her shopping trip, she went to her room and sank into the couch. She took a deep breath and let it out with a sigh. She was exhausted but pleased with the onyx pendant and long gold chain that she'd purchased in Florence that morning. She held it in her hand and turned it this way and that, admiring the delicate craftsmanship. As she let it fall back on her chest, she noticed that her portrait was slightly out of kilter. She smiled.

"Mariotto, are you here?" she said.

There was no answer. That didn't mean he wasn't nearby. Her son was a little prankster. He sometimes hid in her room and surprised her. She checked the room thoroughly, including the closet and under the bed.

Satisfied he was gone. She went over to the bookcase and removed the leather-bound book. She took out the folded envelope, untied the string, and removed the letter. She read it quickly, and made a little sound of disappointment. The letter concerned a regular meeting of lords. Nothing important.

She put the letter back in the envelope, retied it, and put it back in the book. She straightened her portrait, a sign to Agnola that she could now take the letter to Savino.

She dropped back on the couch and examined her pendant again. She'd wear it to dinner tonight and see if Savino would notice it. She gave a short, weary laugh. She doubted it. Although she didn't doubt he'd notice it if Foresta were wearing it.

"Mother!"

Margarita looked up. Mariotto dashed into the room and hopped the chubby body into her lap.

"Mother, I want the magical diamonds that uncle Adamo has. I want them before Father gets them!"

"What are you talking about, Mariotto?"

"Today I was hiding in Father's office and heard Uncle Adamo tell him about them. They're green, pink, and purple diamonds—and they're magical. They make his wishes come true." He paused for a moment. "And they're big."

Margarita smiled at the boy. He was given to exaggeration. "How big, dear?"

He made a circle with his thumb and forefinger. "They're as big as cherries."

"Did you see them?"

He noticed the sly smile on her face. "No, Mother—but they *are* real! I don't care if you don't believe me!" His eyes started to water.

Margarita stared at him for a moment. He was serious. She pulled him onto her lap and kissed away his tears. "I do believe you," she said. She hugged him tight. "Dear Mariotto, if they're real we must own them—you and me."

"Do you think you could get them for me?"

She nodded. "I will try," she said. "You are such a good boy. But you mustn't tell anyone. Do you understand, my beautiful angel?"

Mariotto blushed with pleasure. "Yes, Mother."

She set him back on the floor. "You run along now, and I'll think of a way to get them."

62

Alone in her room, Margarita entertained visions of what awesome power the three magical diamonds could bring if they were real—and in the hands of the right person. That person certainly wouldn't be Adamo, Foresta, or Savino.

I *must* have them, she thought.

I *will* have them!

She could feel her blood coursing through her veins. She felt at that moment that she was radiating like the magical diamonds themselves.

After Adamo left for home with Ellie, Ristro escorted Nicholas to Margarita's room. The door was open, and Ristro stopped at the threshold. Nicholas saw a large painting on the wall opposite the doorway. It depicted a seated young woman with a small book in her hand. A little boy stood beside her, his hands resting in her lap. It reminded Nicholas of the paintings in the Renaissance Art Annex at his father's museum.

In one corner of the room a little boy—who Nicholas figured must be Mariotto—was jumping up and down on the couch. He was obviously the boy in the painting. In the other corner, the woman in the painting—clearly the boy's mother—sat in an upholstered chair and read a book.

Agnola and a much older woman watched the boy's alarmingly dangerous activities.

"Please, Mariotto," the older woman said, "you must be more careful."

Mariotto ignored her, and jumped about even more vigorously.

The woman turned to Agnola. "It's your responsibility, not mine, to make sure my lady's son is safe. Don't you understand that, Agnola?"

Agnola nodded. "I do, Serafina. I try my hardest."

Serafina shook her head. "That may not be enough," she said.

Agnola's hands trembled. "I just don't know . . ."

Before she could finish, Ristro stepped into the room. "My lady," he said.

Margarita lowered her book and turned toward the door. "Yes, Ristro." Her eyebrows shot up. She narrowed her eyes and stared at Nicholas. "Who is that boy?"

Ristro poked Nicholas in the back, pushing him forward.

"His name is Nicholas, my lady. He's an orphan. My lord wants to keep him here as a companion for your son."

Margarita sized him up for a few more seconds, and then turned to Mariotto. "Do you want this boy to be your companion, my love?"

"Yes!" Mariotto said. "I want him to play with me!" He ran to Nicholas and took his hand, his face showing his delight at the prospect of a new playmate.

"Then it's settled," Margarita said. "Nicholas can stay here."

"As you wish, my lady," Ristro said. He bowed to Margarita and left the room.

Margarita gestured toward Agnola and Serafina. "I won't need you two. You can take Mariotto out to the yard. Nicholas will join him in a minute."

Mariotto made a face, and she pulled him toward her.

"Mariotto, dear," she said, "go out to the yard now and Nicholas will be right with you. Then you two can play until supper time."

She kissed him on the forehead, patted his bottom, and sent him on his way.

When she and Nicholas were alone, Margarita said, "If you are going to be my son's companion, you must never hurt him or put him in danger in any way. You are allowed to play with him and entertain him, but you must *always* keep him from harm. Understood?"

Nicholas nodded. Margarita's love for her son was obvious. He touched his shirt pocket, which held the photograph of his own mother. He was surprised at the tinge of envy he was feeling toward little Mariotto.

"Come closer," Margarita said.

As he walked toward her, he caught a scent of her perfume.

She patted the couch with her elegant hand. "There you are, sit here next to me." She put her arm around his shoulder.

"I think you'll be a good companion for my son. And you must tell me all about your adventures together. Will you do that?"

"Certainly," he said.

Just then, Mariotto burst into the room. "Mother," he said, "I can't wait!"

Mariotto dashed across the room and tugged at Nicholas's arm. "Come on, Nicholas. Let's go outside and play!"

Nicholas stood up and turned to Margarita. "I guess I better protect my little brother."

"Keep him safe," she said.

The yard was filled with statues, marble benches, trees, bushes and several rows of flowers. It was easily fifty-feet wide and stretched for a hundred feet or more to a low wooden fence. A forested area lay just beyond the fence.

Nicholas and Mariotto stepped out of the house and into the yard. Serafina was sitting on one of the benches, her back to the house.

Mariotto put his finger to his lips. "Shh," he whispered to Nicholas. "Watch how I trick the fat old lady."

He ran to the other side of the yard and hid behind a bush next to a row of trees. "Serafina!" he yelled. "Help me! My foot is caught!"

The face of the old servant grew pale. She got to her feet and stumbled her way across the yard. By the time she reached the bush, Mariotto had run to the other end of the row of trees. He peeped out and watched her go behind the bush. As soon as she was out of sight, he dashed back across the yard and crouched behind a marble base that supported the bronze statue of a lion.

"Mariotto, where are you?" Serafina called out in a shaky voice.

"I'm over here, you silly old woman," he called back to her. "Why did you go over there? You must hurry; I'm bleeding!"

Her face now red, she rushed to the other side of the yard. Before she reached the statue, she stumbled and fell face first on a dirt path.

Mariotto jumped out from behind the statue. "I fooled you!" he said. "Just like I always do!" He ran back to the steps where Nicholas was standing. Tears of laughter rolled down the little boy's cheeks.

Serafina struggled to her feet. Frustration and anger showing on her face, she stared at Mariotto but said nothing.

Agnola came out to the yard as Serafina was dusting herself off.

"All right now," Mariotto said to Agnola, "it's time for hide and seek. You and Serafina must cover your eyes and count to a hundred."

He grabbed Nicholas's hand and pulled on it. "Come on," he said, and headed for the wooden fence at the far end of the yard.

"Let's hide from them. Bone is tough to get away from."

"Bone?"

"That's what I call that skinny Agnola. It's a better name for her. Follow me!"

As the two women covered their eyes and began to count, Mariotto headed toward the wooden fence, with Nicholas right behind him.

A crude hut stood just off a pathway on the other side of the fence. "We'll hide in here," Mariotto said.

The hut was about four-feet high. It was made of tree limbs and open on one side. Mariotto darted into it. Nicholas crouched and followed him in.

"Do you like it?" Mariotto said. "I made Big build it for me."

"Who is Big?"

"Ristro," Mariotto said. "I call him that because he's so big. I have names for lots of people."

"Hmm," Nicholas said. The little boy could be bratty, but he was certainly clever. He wondered what nickname Mariotto would choose for him. Another thought struck him.

"Mariotto, you know a lot of people. Have you ever heard of Vix Tower?"

"No," Mariotto said, without much interest. He brought a finger to his lips. "We must be quiet now, so that Serafina and Bone can't find us."

Agnola and Serafina came wandering along the path. Nicholas and Mariotto watched through a gap in the limbs as the two passed the hut. The women seemed not to notice the hut, but it was obvious to Nicholas that they were purposely avoiding looking at it.

"Where could they be hiding?" Agnola said in a loud stilted voice.

"I don't know," Serafina said. "Mariotto is always so smart."

The two servants continued down the path. When they were out of sight, Mariotto nudged Nicholas. "We can go back to the house now while they wander around the woods. Isn't that a good trick?"

"Quite a trick," Nicholas said.

Mariotto smiled. "I always hide there, and those dumb servants never can find me."

Nicholas and Mariotto left the hut and headed back to the house. Just before they reached it, Nicholas glanced over his shoulder. Serafina and Agnola stood by the gate to the wooden fence. He couldn't make out the expressions on their faces, but he could imagine what they would be like.

Back in the house, Mariotto led Nicholas to a room next to his father's office. "I have something good to show you. Come on." Savino wasn't there, but the door was open. "He calls this his armory."

Nicholas was impressed by Savino's collection of weaponry. Daggers, a mace, and a variety of swords, of different lengths and styles hung on one wall. A metal helmet and other sections of armor rested on a rack. A full set of armor was displayed on a stand. It looked as if a real warrior were standing there.

There was a fireplace on the other side of the room, along with a small table, armchairs, a bookshelf, a desk, and a straight-back chair.

Mariotto pointed to a long steel sword. "That's Father's," he said. "And that's mine." He pointed to one of a pair of short wooden swords. "Get them down, Nicholas, and we can practice sword fighting."

Nicholas took the two wooden swords from the wall and handed Mariotto his.

Nicholas wagged the other one this way and that, testing its weight. He'd once written a report on swords for his history class, but he'd never actually held a sword, not even a wooden one.

Mariotto waved his sword in the air. "Come on," he said. "Let's fight!" He lunged toward Nicholas.

Nicholas blocked Mariotto's sword from hitting him, but his own sword was knocked from his hand.

"Wait, Mariotto," he said, and knelt to pick it up.

Mariotto wasn't listening. He thrust his sword at Nicholas's chest, and Nicholas deflected it just in time.

Mariotto frowned and jabbed at Nicholas's belly. This time his aim was true.

"Ow!" Nicholas said.

Mariotto laughed. "I won!" he said. "Let's do it again."

Nicholas raised his sword and gripped it tightly. Mariotto swiped at his legs, and he blocked the blow. Before he could raise his sword again, Mariotto jabbed straight at his throat.

Nicholas twisted away, but he lost his balance and tumbled to the floor.

"Be careful, Mariotto!" he said. "That was dangerous. Remember, we're just practicing."

"I won, again!" Mariotto said. "Get ready!"

He rushed forward.

This time Nicholas was prepared. He quick-stepped to the side and stroked upwards.

Mariotto's sword went flying across the room.

"This time, *I* won," Nicholas said.

Mariotto stood still for a moment, his face twisted into an ugly frown. Without a word, he ran to the wall, climbed up on the desk, and grabbed Savino's sword. He jumped down to the floor and ran toward Nicholas, the long sword raised high above his head.

"Stop!" Nicholas shouted.

Mariotto ignored him and swung the sword down.

Acting on instinct, Nicholas fended off the blow with his wooden sword. It shattered, but it deflected the steel sword enough to make it miss Nicholas's head by inches.

The attack sent Nicholas reeling again. He ended up on his back by the fireplace. He stared at Mariotto.

There was a demonic gleam in the little boy's eye as he edged toward Nicholas, his father's sword again raised above his head.

As he drew nearer, Nicholas grabbed a metal poker from the fireplace stand and got to his feet.

"You . . .!" Mariotto screamed. He swung the sword down with all his might.

This time Nicholas stepped forward to meet the attack. He swung the poker upward and shook the sword loose from Mariotto's hand.

The little boy looked terrified.

Nicholas raised the poker to Mariotto's throat and glared at him.

"I surrender," Mariotto said in a piping voice.

Nicholas nodded, but said nothing. He went over and picked up Savino's sword and put it back in its place on the wall. He put the poker back in the fireplace stand and turned to Mariotto. "Sword-fighting practice can be fun," he said, "but it mustn't be dangerous."

Mariotto sniffled and wiped tears from his eyes. "You're my playmate," he said. "You're supposed to entertain me. You shouldn't win. I must win!"

Nicholas went over to him, knelt down, and gave him a hug. "If I let you win all the time, Mariotto, you wouldn't acquire the skill to win in a real fight."

That didn't seem to console the little boy. He continued to whimper.

"Mariotto!" A voice called out.

Nicholas stepped to the door. Margarita was coming down the hallway. He felt relieved. Maybe she could calm her son down.

"He's here," Nicholas said.

As she came into the room, Mariotto rushed to her. She bent down, lifted him up, and held him close.

"Mama . . ." he said, his voice quavering. He pressed his head against her chest.

Margarita noticed the pieces of the shattered wooden sword scattered across the floor. She turned to Nicholas, her eyes blazing. "What did you do to him?"

"Nothing. We were practicing sword fighting."

She narrowed her eyes. "If he's hurt, I will never forgive you!"

"I didn't hurt him. He shattered that wooden sword with your husband's sword. When he saw he was losing, he tried to hurt *me*!"

She stared at Nicholas for a moment, preparing a response. She stood up and looked at him with contempt. "That's ridiculous," she said. "My son doesn't lose. He's a winner!"

She stepped into the hallway. "Agnola!"

Agnola emerged from the kitchen. "Yes, my lady."

"Take the orphan boy to your room and try to get him clean before dinner."

CHAPTER 8

Who Is the Liar?

After putting Mariotto down for his afternoon nap, Margarita headed for her own room. Halfway down the hallway she ran into Savino, who had just returned from a business meeting.

"Margarita," he said, "you look magnificent—as always." He kissed her hand.

Her expression registered no emotion.

"My dear," he said, "I heard an unusual story today about diamonds."

"Oh?"

"I wondered if your father ever mentioned magical diamonds."

Her heart beat faster, and she sucked in her breath. *Mariotto's story was true. Adamo does have them!*

"Magical diamonds?" she said. "No, father's a practical business man. Fairy tales don't interest him."

Savino noticed her hesitation. *She's a clever one*, he thought. *But so am I!*

"I guess it *was* a fairy tale," he said. He brushed his hands together, as though dismissing such a foolish idea, and changed the subject. "So how is our new orphan boy doing? Is Mariotto having fun with him?"

"Fun?" She raised an eyebrow. "I don't think so. They were practicing sword fighting, and I think he tried to hurt our son."

"Oh?" Savino said, looking concerned.

"One of the wooden swords got broken, and he blamed it on Mariotto. He said Mariotto got mad because he'd beaten him in a sword-fighting contest. I don't know if he did or not. Either way, he shouldn't be bullying Mariotto."

Savino's expression hardened. "My son is meant to be a great swordsman. Defeat should not figure in his development."

"I suppose not," Margarita said. She headed for her room, fantasies of magical diamonds dancing in her head.

Agnola's room was next to the kitchen. It held a rickety bed with a straw mattress, a crude wooden shelf on one wall, a table, and a chair. There was barely room on the floor for the washtub she carried in from the kitchen. The tub itself was just big enough for Nicholas to fit in.

"There're some clothes on the bed for you," she said. "Take off the ones you got on. You can put on some others when you're clean. I'll be right back."

She headed back to the kitchen, and Nicholas examined the clothes on the bed. He could see right off that they were too big for him. He figured they belonged to one of the adult servants. The baggy pants could be held up with a belt and their bottoms rolled up a few turns. He could roll up the shirtsleeves too. He shrugged. He really had no choice—and at least the clothes were clean. He transferred the photograph of his mother from his shirt to the shirt on the bed.

When Agnola came back to the room, staggering under the burden of a large bucket of hot water and another of cold, she gave a start.

"Why aren't you undressed? How do you expect I can give you a bath if your clothes are still on?"

"Give me a bath?" Nicholas said, an amused look on his face.

"Of course. You heard what my lady said."

"I prefer to bathe myself."

Agnola looked surprised. "But you heard . . ." Her voice trailed off.

Nicholas felt pity for her. Her life seemed to be one of taking orders from everyone, never getting respect, and always being afraid. On the other hand, there was no way he was going to let her bathe him.

"I tell you what," he said. "Where I come from, people of the opposite sex aren't allowed to bathe one another. If you step out of the room, I'll bathe myself. And if anyone asks, I'll say that you bathed me."

"But . . ."

"I promise it will be all right."

Agnola thought for a moment. To tell the truth, she didn't really want to bathe this strange orphan. Who knew what bugs or diseases he might have?

"All right," she said. "If you really promise not to tell."

"Absolutely," he said.

She handed him a sponge and a bar of hard soap. "Don't use too much of this. It comes all the way from Venice." She turned away. "I'll be out in the hallway," she said, and left the room.

When Nicholas was bathed and dressed, he called Agnola back to the room.

She looked him over and seemed pleased. "You need a belt for the pants," she said. She went over to the shelf and found a length of thick cotton cord. "It isn't fancy, but it'll do." She tied it at his waist and then combed his curry hair from the side to the other. For the first time since Nicholas had seen her, a little smile came to her face.

"Well then," she said. "You're now cleaned up and ready for dinner."

The dining room table could easily seat twenty people. This evening there were only four. Savino sat at the head of the table. Margarita and Mariotto sat on one side of the table next to him. Nicholas sat across from them.

When Agnola brought in a tray with a vegetable and egg dish along with a plate of bread and cheese, Mariotto reached for a piece of cheese.

Savino pulled the plate away from him. "You must wait, Mariotto," he said. "Nicholas is our guest. Let him try it first and tell us how it tastes."

He beckoned to Nicholas. "Please, tell us what you think."

Nicholas reached for the cheese, took a bite, and smacked his lips.

"It's good," he said. "I've never had any cheese quite like it."

"And the other dish?" Savino said.

Nicholas scooped a spoonful from the vegetable and egg dish and brought it to his lips. "Mmm . . . it smells good," he said. He popped it into his mouth, swallowed it, and paused. "It *is* good. Really tasty."

Serafina brought out the main course, a roasted chicken. Again Nicholas was first to try it. And again, he thought the food was delicious.

"I'm hungry," Mariotto said, pouting. "When can I eat?"

"Mind your manners," Savino said. "We'll eat when we know that our food agrees with our guest."

He snapped his fingers in the air, and Agnola disappeared into the kitchen. A moment later she reappeared with a large bowl of pudding. She set it in front of Nicholas and stepped back from the table.

Two cooks came out of the kitchen and stood against the wall next to Agnola and Serafina. The four of them looked tense.

"If you find our dessert is to your liking," Savino said, "we'll congratulate our cooks and our servants."

Nicholas dipped a small spoon into the pudding. "Is this caramel?" he said.

Savino nodded.

Nicholas put the spoonful into his mouth. He waited a moment, and then licked his lips.

"Wonderful!" he said.

Agnola, Serafina, and the two cooks broke into smiles. Savino nodded to them, and sent them off with a wave of his hand.

"Thank you, Nicholas," he said. "We're all delighted that our food suits you. Shall we begin?"

"Of course, Papa!" Mariotto said.

When the last of the pudding was gone, Savino turned to his son. "Mariotto," he said, "someday you are going to be a great swordsman. Starting tomorrow, Ristro will give you sword-fighting lessons every day."

"Oh, thank you, Papa," Mariotto said. "I know I'll be the best!" He picked up his knife and thrust it into the remains of the roasted chicken.

Savino, Margarita, and Nicholas couldn't hold back their laughter.

How things can turn around, Nicholas thought. The unpleasant encounter with Margarita in Savino's armory was fading from his mind. Of course she'd be protective of her son if she thought he was threatened. But that seemed to be resolved now. The family was treating him as a special guest. Mariotto was a little spoiled, true. But that could happen in any family where the parents loved an only child as much as Savino and Margarita loved Mariotto.

He touched the shirt pocket that held his mother's photograph.

After dinner Savino called Nicholas to his office. When they were both seated, he said, "I hope you feel comfortable in my home."

"I do," Nicholas said. "You and Margarita treat me well."

"I'm glad you feel that way," Savino said. "My son is glad to have you as his playmate."

Nicholas was about to speak, but hesitated.

"What is it, Nicholas? If you have any questions, please feel free to ask me."

"There *is* something I'm curious about," Nicholas said. His face grew serious. "Have you ever heard the name Vix Tower?"

"No," Savino said. "An unusual name, but I've never heard of it."

Nicholas sighed.

Another dead end.

"I have a question for *you*," Savino said. "Do you think Margarita takes good care of our son? Speaking to you man-to-man, I think it's something all father's worry about."

Nicholas felt a thrill go through him.

Man-to-man! Savino was treating me like a grown-up.

"I think she spends a lot of time with him."

"Yes. But how does she spend her time when she's not with him, hmm? I'm curious." He thought for a moment. "Perhaps you could keep track of what she does each day and let me know."

"Why?" Nicholas said.

Savino seemed annoyed. "Curiosity," he said. "Just curiosity. Think it over, Nicholas." He stood up. "It's growing late. I'll have Ristro show you to your room."

Two candles in hands, Ristro led Nicholas past the kitchen and Algona's room to the end of the hallway, where some heavy logs were stacked. He pushed the pile aside with one hand, revealing a door. It was about the same height as Nicholas. A curved piece of wood served as a handle. He opened the door and passed the candle to Nicholas.

"This will be your room," Ristro said. "There's a blanket on the shelf. You have to make your own bed."

The light from the candle illuminated a large tapestry on the stone wall across from the door. It bore an image of the tall tower in Savino's village. The room was more poorly furnished than Agnola's. It had only a small bed with a straw mattress, a shelf, and a bed stand. There was no window in the room.

"Get your sleep," Ristro said. "My lord gave you a job. You'll be a stable boy soon."

"What's that?"

"You're going to take care of my lord's horses."

Ristro took a new candle from his shirt, lit it from his other candle, and stuck it in a candleholder on Nicholas's bed stand. Without a word, he turned and left the room.

A four-foot length of wood leaned against the wall in his room. Nicholas dropped it into the iron brackets on either side of the door, barring it for the night.

He took the blanket from the shelf and arranged it on the bed. He slid under it and tried to go to sleep, but with little success. He tossed and turned throughout the night. He'd occasionally sit up in a sweat and see his shadow projected on the wall by the flickering light of the still-burning candle. When it finally burned out, he lay there in the dark; his eyes still open, seeing nothing but blackness as dark as the single thought that occupied his mind.

If I can't trace the missing diamonds, my father will die.

The next morning at breakfast, the tasting ritual was the same as the night before. Nicholas tasted everything before the family did and then commented on it. At lunch it was also the same.

In the early afternoon, Margaret called Nicholas to her room. Savino and Ristro had left the manor on business.

She was sitting on the couch and, as she had the day before, she asked him to join her.

He sat down next to her.

"Nicholas," she said, "I'm sorry I acted cross to you yesterday. I hope you'll forgive me."

"There's nothing to forgive," he said. "You were worried about your son."

"That is kind of you to say that. You are a remarkable young man."

Nicholas blushed.

"I feel I can trust you now and . . . and I hope you feel you can trust me."

"Of course!"

She clasped her hands together at her breast and beamed. "Oh, I prayed you would say that." Her expression became serious. "I'm worried about my husband. He works so hard, I'm afraid his health will suffer. If I knew more about what he did, perhaps I could help ease his load. Do you understand?"

"I think so."

"I'd like you to do me a big favor . . . to do *Savino* and me a big favor. If you'd keep track of his doings and report them to me at the end of every day, it would be so helpful. He's such a busy man that I don't often have a chance to talk with him. As his wife I should know what's going on in this house and in this village. He's so proud, doesn't want people to think he has to get any help from his wife, so you mustn't mention it to anyone. Would you be willing to help us both?"

Nicholas hesitated.

She's asking me to spy on Savino just like he asked me to spy on her last night. But they both seem to have good intentions. I guess there's no harm in it, as long as I don't lose my focus on the diamonds and Vix Tower.

"Is something the matter, Nicholas?" Margarita said.

"Oh, no," he said. "I just had something else on my mind. I'd be glad to help you."

"Thank you," she said. "But you look very concerned. Is something bothering you?"

"In a way. I'm trying to find information on a man named Vix Tower and three magical diamonds, and I'm getting nowhere."

"Oh, I see," Margarita said. She forced a laugh. "I did hear about some diamonds that had magical powers. I thought it was just nonsense. But I've never heard of . . . what was that name?"

"Vix Tower. He wants to get those diamonds."

"Whoever this Vix person is," she said, "I'd say he was chasing rainbows. Perhaps just having a little fun."

"No!" Nicholas said. "He's deadly serious. He told my father to bring him the diamonds or he'd kill him. And because of him, my father is already dying." He lowered his eyes.

Margarita put her arm around him. "Shh . . . don't worry, Nicholas. I'm sure things will work out all right." She kissed him on the forehead and stood up. "I have to get ready to go into town now, but we can talk about your worries later."

Once she was alone, Margarita stared into her mirror, her brow furrowed in thought.

How did the orphan boy find out about the diamonds? Did Mariotto tell him? And what should I do about this Vix Tower? Savino wants the diamonds, and now Tower. Another enemy!

At least the boy's father is dying . . . and he may not be the last one.

Margarita smiled at her image in the mirror. She felt more radiant than ever.

CHAPTER 9

What Would You Wish For?

On the day of Lorenzo de Canal's funeral, Foresta Balducci was busy dressing Ellie in a black dress, part of an outfit suitable for the solemn occasion. Adamo himself was in his office, contemplating the diamonds Lorenzo had given him. As he gazed at them, a voice from outside cried, "Adamo!"

He quickly returned the diamonds to the velvet sack and put it in his top desk drawer.

Moments later his brother breezed into his office without knocking.

Adamo was both surprised and pleased by Savino's visit. It was rare for him to come to Adamo's house unescorted by his bodyguard, Ristro.

"What brings you here today, Brother?" Adamo said.

Savino closed the office door. "I know you're busy today because of the Venetian's funeral," Savino said, "but I have important news for you: Margarita knows about the magical diamonds—and the Venetian's story is true."

"The diamonds really *are* magical?"

"Without a doubt."

"This is fantastic news!" Adamo said. "I'm overwhelmed."

He went to a cupboard and brought back a bottle of wine and two goblets. "We should celebrate. This is wonderful news for our villagers and for the whole Balducci family."

"Yes," Savino said, "good fortune should be shared."

He took the goblet Adamo passed to him and raised it high. "A toast to good fortune for all!"

"A fine toast, Brother!" Adamo said, and clinked his goblet against Savino's.

Savino started to speak, but stopped when the door popped open. Caterina came in, a few tears trickling down her cheeks.

Adamo assumed it was because of her father's funeral. He came from behind his desk and crouched down in front of her. "There, there," he said. "I know you feel sad, but remember what Foresta said: Your father is now in Heaven."

She ignored his comment. "I'm afraid," she said, her lower lip trembling. "It's getting dark outside."

"Don't worry Caterina; it could be just rain clouds coming."

She shook her head. "No. The sun is going away."

"What?"

She didn't answer, but began to cry in earnest.

Adamo went to the windows and parted the curtains. "My God!" he said. "Look at that!"

Savino went to the window. "What's happening?"

"The Black Sun. It's a total eclipse," Adamo said. "I should tell Foresta, Ellie, and the servants not to look right at the sun."

He scooped Caterina into his arms. "I'd better hurry, Savino," he said. "Help yourself to more wine. I'll be back in a few minutes and join you."

He turned and hurried from the room, the little girl clutching his neck and weeping her heart out.

Savino's mind raced.

God has given me a chance!

He closed the office door and scanned the room.

Where would Adamo keep those diamonds?

He wouldn't have much time to search the room, but the desk seemed the best starting point. He rushed to it and slid open the top draw.

He let out a cackling laugh. "Stupid brother!"

He seized the velvet sac and tipped its contents into his open hand: a single diamond. Its radiance and size took his breath away. He shook the sack, but there was nothing else in it.

Adamo had said there were three diamonds: one green, one purple, and one pink. But there was only this one. Why had he lied? He'd said they were as big as cherries, but this one was much bigger—the size of a fig. And not green, purple, or pink, but bright red.

He glanced at the office door. Should he take it? No. That would raise suspicions when Adamo returned. "Hellfire!" he said in frustration. He began a frantic search for the two missing diamonds.

When Adamo got to Ellie's room, she was sitting by the window and staring out at the growing darkness.

"Don't be afraid," he said. "This is a natural phenomenon."

Ellie turned to him and smiled. "I know. It's an eclipse."

Adamo looked surprised. "You know about them?"

"Yes," she said. "But I've never seen a total one before. They're rare."

He seemed impressed by her knowledge. "They are indeed," he said. He set Caterina down. "Ellie, could you look after her for a while?"

"Of course," Ellie said. She opened her arms, and Caterina rushed into them.

Adamo smiled. "Thank you, Ellie. Now I need to look for Foresta."

"I think she's in the yard," Ellie said.

"Good. I'll find her." He headed for the door and paused. "And be sure not to look right at the sun."

"We won't," Ellie said, and drew the curtains closed.

When Adamo got to the yard, he saw Foresta standing before a gathering of servants. She was explaining to them about the eclipse. "A total eclipse is unusual," she said, "but not unnatural. There's nothing to fear. It will soon be over. The Sun will soon appear. You shouldn't stare at it."

The servants seemed to be somewhat calmed by her words, but not completely. A few stood and gripped the hands of their neighbor. Others knelt on the ground—their eyes closed—and said their prayers.

Adamo felt a wave of love for his wife wash over him, as he so often did. She had a natural way with people, a true motherly instinct for everyone. She seemed to have matters under control, and he headed for the stable to see if the eclipse had affected the animals.

After a few minutes, the surroundings became bright and sunny again. The servants exchanged looks and began to smile.

"Well," Foresta said, "I've got chores to do. I suppose we all have." She smiled at the servants and turned toward the house.

Back in Adamo's office, Savino pounded his fist on the desktop in frustration. He'd searched the desk thoroughly, looked behind the bookshelf and paintings for hidey-holes—even looked under the rug for a possible trap door. He knew time was running out. The two missing diamonds just weren't to be found. At the sound of footsteps in the hallway, he dropped the velvet sack back into the drawer and closed it.

The office door opened and Foresta stepped in. "Adamo, I was . . ."

She stopped, a surprised look on her face. "Oh, Savino," she said, "I thought Adamo was here."

Savino stood up and bowed to her. "He should be back shortly," he said. He crossed the room, took her hand and kissed it. "It's always delightful to see you, Foresta. It has been a long time. I think last year at my son's birthday."

"You look well, Savino," she said. "Excuse me, but I didn't know you were visiting us today. You certainly came at an exciting time, what with the eclipse and all."

"I'm always excited to see you, my dear," he said.

Foresta gave a nervous laugh, but said nothing.

"You see," Savino said, "I have always—"

"Ah, Foresta," Adamo said, stepping into the room. "I just checked the stable and our horses are all fine."

"That's good news for you," Savino said. "But if you'll both excuse me, I have to be heading back to Torre. Who knows how my people have reacted to today's cosmic events?"

"They say it's good luck to experience one," Adamo said.

"Indeed," Savino said. He turned to Foresta. "And you're having much good luck lately. I congratulate you on your new daughter. Caterina is such a lovely girl." He nodded to his brother, bowed to Foresta, and left.

After Savino left, Foresta looked puzzled. "I haven't seen your brother for quite a while, and I don't think I've ever seen him without that big, sullen bodyguard of his."

Adamo laughed. "Ristro," he said. "And I have to agree, he's not exactly a ray of sunshine."

"So what was the occasion for Savino's visit?"

Adamo could hardly contain his enthusiasm. "He brought wonderful news! Margarita has heard of the legend of our diamonds. My brother thinks they truly are magical. And by the way, I'll take them with me to Lorenzo's funeral to show our respect for him and his ancestors."

"That's a noble gesture," Foresta said.

Adamo took the sack from the drawer and emptied it into his open palm. He stared at the large red diamond, stunned.

"What's wrong?" Foresta said.

"Nothing, dear, nothing at all. It's true! Lorenzo's story is true! The three diamonds have become one big red diamond, just as the legend says."

"Oh my Lord above!" Foresta said.

She took the diamond from his hand and examined it closely. "Do you really think it will make our wishes come true?"

Adamo shrugged. "Well . . . I guess we'll just have to see."

She shook her head, overcome by the possibilities the diamond might offer. "Oh, Adamo," she said, "What would *you* wish for?"

Adamo thought for a moment. "I suppose I'd want my work for my people in Chiesta to be recognized. And I'd want to have the power to improve people's lives here, in this region, this country . . ." He paused and a giddy smile came to his face. "Even throughout the world!"

She rushed into his arms, and for a moment they stayed together in an embrace.

"And what about you, my love?" Adamo said. "What would *you* wish for?"

"Oh, what a question!" She sighed. "I suppose I'd wish that my journals that document our lives would be passed down from generation to generation so that our descendants could learn from us. And I'd wish that Ellie would find the family she's been separated from."

"Beautiful wishes, Foresta," Adamo said.

Foresta smiled. "I'm not finished, Adamo. I'd also wish that our soulful work stays true to God's intentions, and that our dear Caterina would always cherish our love and carry on our missions. God bless us all."

The funeral ceremony for Lorenzo's was held in the large church at Chiesta's center.

Few people in the village were in attendance, only Adamo, Foresta, Ellie, and Caterina. They were the only ones who realized that a remarkable man was being laid to rest.

When the village priest finished his ritual, Lorenzo's coffin was taken to the cemetery that lay just outside Chiesta's walls and buried.

That night Foresta documented the dramatic events of the day in her journal:

Lorenzo's funeral; the total eclipse; and the transformation of the purple, pink, and green diamonds to a single red one.

Before closing her journal, she wrote: "Caterina is the Sun, Adamo is the Earth, and I am the Moon."

By the glow of a candle, Foresta looked at Caterina, who was sleeping in her own little bed next to Foresta and Adamo's. Piero, Caterina's little cat, was curled up at her feet. Watching the child and her pet brought Foresta the joy of her new motherhood along with a sadness for Caterina, who had been through such turmoil.

"Papa, Papa, . . ." Caterina said in her sleep.

Foresta sighed. "Your father rests in Heaven, little one," she whispered. "But he will always be with you. Adamo is your father now, and I am your mother, and we will love you with the deepest love forever."

She blew out the candle.

The next morning after breakfast, Foresta told Ellie and Caterina she was taking them on a special outing. They were going to a monastery not far from Chiesta. Foresta was a frequent visitor there. She and Adamo donated food, clothing, and household goods to the monks. They also made financial contributions to the monastery. The monks distributed the gifts to the poor and to visiting travelers who stayed overnight at the monastery.

Besides carrying out her charitable work, Foresta spent a great deal of time with two of the older monks. They kept records of the comings and goings in the monastery, in the village of Chiesta, and in the surrounding countryside. Their work was similar to the recording of local activities that filled Foresta's own journals. She delighted in having long conversations and sharing notes with them. Today Foresta was excited to talk about the total eclipse she saw yesterday with the monks. She wrapped her journal with a piece of leather and left her room.

When the two girls were ready, they followed Foresta out to the carriage that was waiting near the stables. The donations had already been loaded aboard it. As they approached the carriage, Foresta noticed that Caterina looked nervous.

Of course, she thought, *the little girl is probably remembering what happened when the bandits attacked the coach.*

She gave Ellie a look. "Why don't you and Caterina sit up front with the driver?" she said. "You'll get a much better view from there."

Ellie had heard the story about the bandits. She nodded to Foresta. "A wonderful idea," she said. "Come on, Caterina, you can sit on my lap and we can talk to the horses."

Caterina's eyes lit up. She took Ellie's hand, and Ellie helped her up to the driver's bench.

Foresta smiled. *What a gem Ellie is!*

When they got to the monastery, several monks helped the driver unload the donations and take them inside.

"I've got some business to do in the monastery," Foresta said to Ellie. "It shouldn't take long. You and Caterina can explore the grounds."

Caterina grabbed Ellie's hand, a big grin on her face.

Foresta watched as the girls headed for the vegetable garden on the side of the monastery. She sighed. Ellie filled the role of big sister so beautifully. Caterina's sorrow would never fade away completely, but time would eventually ease the pain.

When the girls rounded the corner of the monastery, Foresta headed inside, her eyes misty.

Dragonflies of different colors buzzed about the yard. In the vegetable garden, the yellow flowers of the squashes gave a colorful accent to the simplicity of the property. A young monk came out of the monastery, a basket in hand. He went straight to the garden and began picking squashes.

Meanwhile Ellie and Caterina dashed about trying to catch dragonflies. A yellow one landed on Caterina's arm. "Ooh!" she said. Her mouth opened wide in awe, and she took a deep breath. Before she could exhale, the dragonfly flew from her arm, its wings buzzing.

A blue dragonfly hovered enticingly near them. A green one joined it, and the two hovered together. Caterina and Ellie reached out to them. With an extra loud buzzing of wings, they shot into the sky and out of sight.

Laughing and shouting, the girls chased another dragonfly back to the front yard. It zigzagged every which way, with the girls in hot pursuit. Finally it zoomed close to their heads, and the girls crashed into each other. They fell to the ground, laughing harder than ever.

The monk who'd been harvesting zucchinis saw them tumble down. He dropped his basket and rushed over to them.

"Are you all right?" he said, a worried look on his face.

"We're fine," Ellie said.

"What happened?"

"We were trying to catch dragonflies," Ellie said. "But we didn't have much luck."

The monk smiled. "Watch this," he said.

He walked over to a tree where a red dragonfly was sitting on the tip of a branch. He moved his hands slowly toward it and—in the blink of an eye—cupped it in his hands.

He came back to the girls and said to Ellie, "Stick out your finger."

She did, and the monk set the dragonfly on it. Ellie and Caterina held their breaths for a moment, their eyes wide.

A soft puff of breeze made the dragonfly's wings ripple, and it took to the air.

"I want to do it," Caterina said.

The monk pointed to a yellow dragonfly that was resting on the tip of another branch.

"Go slowly," he said, and guided her over to the tree. "Now hold out your hand."

Her little hand reached out—but too fast.

The dragonfly flew off the branch and buzzed out of sight.

Caterina made a face.

"Wait," Ellie said. "I'll try to get you one."

Another yellow dragonfly settled on the same branch the last one had been on.

Ellie eased her way toward it. She held her breath and moved her hand closer and closer to the branch. The dragonfly's big round eyes seemed to stare into Ellie's. She stretched her hand forward, palm up, until it was just under the branch. The dragonfly twitched its wings several times and dropped onto Ellie's hand.

Caterina sucked in her breath, her mouth wide open with amazement.

Ellie moved back to her and nodded.

Caterina stuck out her finger, and Ellie slid her hand under it. The dragonfly fluttered its wings, slid onto Caterina's finger. It stared into her eyes, as it had done with Ellie.

Ellie and the monk looked at each other and smiled.

Their smiles were nothing compared to the smile on Caterina's face.

Foresta came out of the monastery. "It's time to go home, girls," she said.

The dragonfly wasn't disturbed by Foresta's voice, but when the monastery bells began to toll, it fluttered its wings once more and took flight. It soared high into the sky and vanished from view.

Adamo was waiting to greet Foresta and the girls. When Foresta stepped down from the carriage, he rushed forward and threw his arms around her.

Foresta stepped back, a smile on her face. "Well, that's certainly a warm welcome!"

Adamo laughed. "My love," he said. "I have wonderful news. An envoy from the Duke arrived this morning with an amazing message."

He paused, a mischievous smile on his face.

"Well, what was it?" Foresta said.

"He plans to make me a count!"

He hugged her again. "And I owe it all to you. It's because of the work we've done for the villagers and the monastery. Without your efforts, we'd never have achieved our goals. The Duke will give us lands and a castle."

"Have you sent word to your father and brother?" Foresta said.

"Not yet. It becomes official a week from today, and the Duke wants us to keep it a secret until then."

"Does anyone else know about it?"

"Not really," Adamo said. "The envoy, of course. And our doorman, who escorted him to my office."

"It's overwhelming," Foresta said. "I can't wait to tell the monks. I know how pleased they'll be."

"And I can't wait to tell my father and brother. They've always been so supportive of me."

Foresta stepped forward and kissed him. She turned from him and headed for the house. "Excuse me, dear," she said over shoulder. "I've got to start planning the most wonderful celebration party Chiesta has ever seen."

CHAPTER 10

Give A Taste of
The Same Medicine

At Savino's estate in Torre, at six in the morning, Nicholas reported to Savino's stable for his first day as a stable boy. He stepped through the main doorway and saw a skinny old man brushing a horse's coat. His hands and face were wrinkled and dark, an indication of a long life spent laboring in the sun. He glanced at Nicholas and went back to brushing the horse.

There were seven horses in the stable: four large black horses and three smaller brown ones. The old man was brushing one of the black horses; the other six horses were in their stalls.

Nicholas waited in the doorway, not knowing what he should do. He sniffed the air, and made a face.

The old man turned to Nicholas and chuckled. "It's only horse manure, boy," he said. "You'll get used to it." He looked Nicholas up and down. "I don't suppose you've ever taken care of horses before, eh?"

"I've ridden them before . . ." Nicholas said. He paused. No need to say they were rented horses from the Golden Gate Park Stables. "But I've never taken care of them."

The old man chuckled. "Well, don't worry. I'm going to teach you all about it. My name is Lacopo. What's yours?"

"Nicholas."

"Welcome, Nicholas," Lacopo said. "Let's start from the beginning. First off, you check the horses from the head to toe for swellings or cuts. You've also got to check their hooves for pebbles. If you see them, take them out. And you've got to groom the horses—like you saw me doing.

"Okay." Nicholas said and nodded.

"Then you give them fresh water, and take them to the pasture to feed on grass. When they're out there, that's when you clean the stable. You should always make sure that the stable floor is dry and clean, especially in the stalls. That's to protect the horses' hooves from getting white or pasty. Horses get sick easily."

He pointed to a long-handled wheelbarrow with a shovel in it. "Every morning you have to muck out the stalls and throw the manure into the barrow. Then you wheel it down to the open door at the end of the stable and dump it into the pit below. It might not smell so nice now, but when it's composted, it's going to make everything in our gardens grow real good."

He indicated a pitchfork that was leaning against one of the stalls and then gestured toward the hayloft. "The next thing you do, you throw some hay down and spread it on the main floor and on the floors of each stall." He smiled. "The horses will love you for giving them a nice clean home every day. You think you can handle that?"

"I guess so."

"I'm sure you can," Lacopo said. "There's more stuff too, but I'll show you how to do it later. For now, why don't you try brushing this old fellow?"

He handed Nicholas the brush.

The horse was so tall Nicholas had to stand on an upended bucket to brush its back. The horse seemed happy about the way Nicholas groomed it.

Lacopo told Nicholas that the three large black horses still in their stalls were warhorses. The first two belonged to Savino and the other was for Ristro. Two of the brown horses were used to pull carriages. The third was for Margarita to ride.

He patted the horse Nicholas was grooming. "Giotto, here, is also a warhorse, but he's too old to do much charging now." He shook his head. "He was really something in his day. He still earns his keep by carting water, hay, food, and household goods." He rubbed the horse's muzzle.

"So, boy," he said, "When you finish brushing Giotto, we'll get some fresh water for the horses from the well in Torre. I've got to get something from the house, but I'll be back in a minute."

Nicholas speeded up brushing Giotto, switching the brush from one hand to the other. It was harder work than he thought, but when he was done, the horse's coat seemed to glow.

He sat down on the bucket and rested for a moment. He blocked the sunlight that came through the side door with one hand and saw Mariotto and Ristro practicing sword fighting in the yard. He had to smile; Mariotto looked so small in comparison to the giant Ristro.

Savino stood to the side, watching the two practicing. Nicholas remembered that Savino had said he wanted Mariotto to become a great swordsman someday. It looked like that day would be far in the future.

"What's this, Nicholas? Are you already sitting down on the job?"

Nicholas turned to see Lacopo coming through the main door. "Just taking a rest," he said, an embarrassed look on his face.

"Well," Lacopo said, "from the looks of Giotto, I'd say you earned it. But now it's time to head for town. You can help me hook up the cart."

There was only room for one on the driver's seat of the cart. Nicholas got in back and sat down on a large, upside-down wooden bucket between two empty water barrels. Lacopo gave Giotto a gentle flick with the reins and the cart started moving.

Nicholas looked back and saw Mariotto lower his sword.

"Nicholas," Mariotto shouted, "where are you going? I want to go with you!"

"I'm afraid you can't do that," Ristro said. "You're in the middle of practice."

Mariotto frowned. "But, I want to go with him!" He pointed his sword at Ristro's belly.

Ristro lowered his own sword.

Mariotto took a step toward Ristro and thrust the sword forward.

With a clang, the sword flew through the air.

Ristro hadn't moved a muscle.

Savino, his sword in hand, looked down at his son. "The next time you disobey Ristro, I won't just disarm you, I'll wallop you so hard you won't be able to sit down for a week. Do you want to be a swordsman or do you want play with that boy who defeated you? That boy didn't even know how to use a sword, and you let him win. Now pick up your sword!"

Mariotto picked up his sword. Holding it over his head with both hands, he ran toward his father and slashed downward.

Savino took a quick step to the side. He stuck out his foot, tripping his son and sending him sprawling to the ground.

"Get up, you weakling!" Savino said.

With tears in his eyes, Mariotto raised his sword and charged his father again.

This time Savino stepped to the other side. He swatted Mariotto's legs with the flat of his sword and knocked him to the ground once more.

Savino glared at his son and shook his head. "Don't be weak like a loser," he said. "Be strong like a king!"

As the cart passed through the main gate of the estate, Nicholas saw Margarita rush from the house and pick up Mariotto. She held the weeping boy in her arms and said something to Savino. By then the cart was too far away for Nicholas to hear what she said.

He imagined it wasn't very pleasant.

The trip to Torre was uneventful—even restful. Weary from rising so early that morning, Nicholas stretched himself out on the cart floor and dozed as Giotto plodded his way to the village. He woke with a jolt when the cart came to a halt at the village well that he and Ellie had passed on the trip from Giovanni Balducci's estate to Savino's.

It was still early, but merchants were already arranging their goods in their booths and at their tables. The square wasn't as crowded as it had been when he and Ellie had passed through it, but there was already a line at the well. The people in line recognized Lacopo and stepped away from the well. Several of them gave Lacopo a friendly greeting. They obviously didn't hold it against him personally that he represented Lord Savino, whose authority they must yield to.

An empty wooden bucket was attached to an iron hook at the end of a rope that ran through a pulley suspended from an iron bar over the well.

"Here's how we do it," Lacopo said to Nicholas.

He pulled on the rope, lowering the empty bucket into the well. As the empty bucket descended, a bucket full of water hooked to the other end of the rope rose up. "It's about twenty feet to the bottom," Lacopo said.

He unhooked the full bucket and emptied it into one of the barrels on the cart. He re-hooked the bucket and repeated the process.

After he'd poured the second bucket into the barrel, he handed it to Nicholas. "We'll take turns," he said, "until we've filled both barrels."

Nicholas hooked up the empty bucket and began pulling on the rope. It wasn't as easy as it had looked when Lacopo did it. The rope was rough, and pulling the full bucket wasn't the only difficulty. Some water slopped to the ground when he carried the bucket to the cart. More water spilled to the floor of the cart when he emptied the bucket into the barrel.

When he re-hooked the bucket, Lacopo took the rope from him. "I'll do two turns to your one today, because I'm used to it." He smiled. "Later on you'll be doing two or three to my one, because you'll be getting stronger as I get weaker."

When both barrels were filled, they headed back to Savino's estate. Despite his morning nap, Nicholas was exhausted. His hands were almost raw from pulling on the rope.

"You will get use to it soon," Lacopo said. "Your hands will get strong and protected by calluses. In this world we must work in order to eat, and we must eat in order to live, eh?"

"I guess so," Nicholas said.

Lacopo chuckled. "You guess right." He reached back and patted Nicholas's head.

Savino sat at his desk, a scowl on his face. Ever since he'd seen it at Adamo's, he couldn't get the sight of the magical red diamond from his mind. What a spectacular ring it would make! He could picture his subjects kneeling before him, kissing his hand, worshipping him and the red diamond that would signify his power.

He now wished he'd taken it when he had the chance. But why cry over spilt milk? He needed to think of the best way to get it from Adamo. There was another problem too. Had Adamo lied to him about the diamonds? He'd said there were three diamonds: green, purple, and pink. The diamond had certainly looked red, but maybe it had been pink or purple, and the black sun had made it appear red. Adamo had also said the diamonds were the size of cherries, but the red one was the size of a fig.

He slammed his fist on his desk. *There is a way to solve the problem!* He needn't be straightforward about it; after all, Adamo had probably lied to him. Now he'd give his brother a taste of the same medicine.

"You called, sir," Ristro said. "How can I be of service?"

Savino looked up from his desk. "Close the door and take a chair," he said.

When Ristro was seated, Savino said, "Go to Adamo's tomorrow and tell him that Margarita and her father, Lord Cosmo Capello, want to see his three diamonds. Tell him that we will guard the diamonds diligently and return them safely as soon as they have examined them."

"Yes, my lord. Do you know what those diamonds look like?"

"Why do you ask?"

"I want to make sure that they will give you the real ones, my lord."

"Very well, Ristro. There are three of them: green, purple, and possibly red or pink. And they're as big as figs. Take Nicholas with you. He might be useful to soften up Adamo and Foresta."

"Yes, my lord."

When Nicholas and Lacopo finished distributing the water to the troughs and putting the barrels away, Mariotto rushed into the stable.

"Nicholas," he said, "Take me for a horseback ride!"

"I don't know if I can," Nicholas said. "I've still got work to do."

Mariotto looked petulant. "That's not fair," he said.

Lacopo laughed. "He may be right, Nicholas. You did good work this morning. I think you've earned some time off. We'll saddle Giotto up. Carrying a small boy around the estate is easier than hauling a cartload of water. I don't think he'll mind."

Nicholas lifted Mariotto into the saddle and made sure he was seated comfortably. Lacopo handed Nicholas the reins. "You can lead him up to the pasture and circle it a few times. He knows the way and there won't be any problems."

Mariotto gave the horse a tap with his heels, but it didn't move.

"Come on, Giotto, let's go," Nicholas said.

Giotto started walking.

As they left the stable, Mariotto straightened his back and put his chin up. "I am riding my warhorse," he said, "and everybody must obey me."

Giotto wasn't having any of that. Although Mariotto frequently kicked his sides, the horse continued at a steady pace.

As they were finishing their second circle of the pasture, Mariotto said, "Nicholas, everybody must obey me. You must do whatever I say because I'm more powerful than anybody."

Nicholas chuckled. "I think your father is the most powerful one," he said.

"No, my uncle Adamo is."

"Why is that?" Nicholas said.

Mariotto didn't answer.

Nicholas looked up at Mariotto. He had a serious expression on his face.

"Tell me," Nicholas said. "Why is Adamo the most powerful?"

Mariotto shook his head. "I can't say. I promised not to tell. When I'm king, I can tell anybody anything I want to."

Nicholas smiled. "You can ride a warhorse and swordfight now, so you might become a king some day."

"I will!" Mariotto said. "And I will employ you in my castle. Would you want to be my closest knight who always stays beside me to protect me, Nicholas?"

"Maybe," Nicholas said.

A fly landed on Giotto's nose and he tossed his head.

"Ouch!" Nicholas said as the reins were yanked from his grip.

"What happened?" Mariotto said.

Nicholas retrieved the reins with his other hand. He showed the sore hand to Mariotto.

"My hands got chafed from pulling up water buckets at the well today."

"Be my knight," Mariotto said. "Then you wouldn't need to pull buckets anymore."

"Maybe someday," Nicholas said.

They headed out of the pasture and down to the stable.

That night as Nicholas lay in bed he pondered over the purpose of this trip into the past. Was the journey really the key to saving his father's life or was it just a waste of time?

A pounding on the door interrupted his thoughts.

Ristro's voice rang out. "Open up!"

Nicholas got up and crossed the room. He lifted the wooden bar from the brackets and opened the door.

Ristro stepped into the room. "You're not working at the stable tomorrow. I'm going to Lord Adamo's, and Lord Savino wants you to go with me."

"Why?"

Ristro frowned. "You don't question what Lord Savino asks. You just do it."

"All right," Nicholas said. "When should I be ready?"

"Be outside the stable by eight o'clock. And I warn you, don't be late."

"I'll be there," Nicholas said.

"You'd better be," Ristro said, and left the room.

Despite Ristro's rude behavior, his message was good news to Nicholas. A visit to Adamo's might give him a chance to connect with Ellie. They could share whatever information they'd come up with.

He started to bar the door but turned at a sound from behind him. "What. . .!"

Mariotto giggled. He was sitting on Nicholas's bed, his legs crossed, a mischievous smile on his face.

Nicholas was dumfounded.

"How did you get in here, Mariotto?"

"I am a magician," Mariotto said. "I am an invisible man. No one can catch me! I know everything. You are going to my uncle's place tomorrow to get the magical diamonds for me."

"But—"

"I'm magic!" Mariotto said. He hopped off the bed and dashed from the room. His laughter echoed in the hallway before fading away.

Nicholas closed and barred the door and went back to his bed. A jumble of thoughts whirled through his mind. Were he and Ellie really accomplishing anything? Why did Savino want him to go to Adamo's with Ristro? And how had Mariotto sneaked into his room?

Another thought struck him. The secret that Mariotto had mentioned must mean Savino knows about Adamo's diamonds. Would Margarita also know about them? And who made Mariotto promise he wouldn't tell the secret?

Before he could come up with an answer to any of the questions, exhaustion overcame him and he drifted into sleep.

CHAPTER 11

The Secret of The Dark Shadow

T he next morning, Nicholas was having a dream. A voice said; "*I must let you get through this phase, Nicholas. You must not neglect my remedy. I've given you a gift. What you do with it is up to you....*"

Nicholas woke up to pains. The dream resonated in him awhile thinking what was all about, but gradually faded away. He tried to get up, "Ouch!" His body was sore from yesterday's labors. His muscles ached and blisters had formed on both hands.

At the stable, Lacopo had already readied the carriage for Ristro and Nicholas's visit to Adamo's, and one of the servants was seated on the driver's bench. As soon as Ristro and Nicholas were inside the carriage, the driver gave a shake to the reins, and the horses began to move.

Around eight o'clock, the carriage passed through Torre. The giant bells in the tower resonated as they tolled the hour.

The carriage continued on through the village of Chiesta and climbed the roadway to Adamo's cliff-side estate. As they neared it, they passed through colorful patches of lilies that bordered the cliff.

The gate to the estate was open, and the driver brought the horses to a halt in front of Adamo's house.

Nicholas sensed that Ristro's mood had improved from the night before. He dared to venture a question. "Excuse me, Ristro," he said, "but what is it we'll do here?"

Ristro laughed. "Today Lord Adamo is going to be kind enough to loan his brother three diamonds."

They got out of the carriage and approached the house. Ristro pounded on the front door. A moment later the doorman opened it. "Can I help you?" he said.

"We've been sent by Lord Savino Balducci to see Lord Adamo Balducci," Ristro said in a commanding voice.

The servant seemed intimidated by Ristro. "I'm sorry, sir, but my lord and his family have gone shopping in preparation for the ceremony."

"What ceremony?"

"The Duke will appoint my lord a count in this region, and a grand ceremony will be held five days from today."

Ristro scowled. "When will they return?"

"Not until this evening. If there's anything I can do—"

"There's nothing you can do!" Ristro said. His jaw clenched and his face flushed, he grabbed Nicholas's arm and headed back to the carriage.

Back in Savino's office, Ristro reported what Adamo's doorman had said.

Savino hammered his fists on his desk and stood up. "A count! Why him? What did he do to deserve this honor? Adamo kept this from me. He made me a fool!"

A knock sounded on the door.

"What is it?" Savino shouted.

Serafina stepped in. "My lord," she said, her voice trembling, "One of your father's messengers is here. He says he has a vital message for you."

"Hellfire!" he said. "All right, send him in."

Serafina stepped back from the doorway and a gray-haired man entered. His expression was somber. "Lord Savino," he said, "I bring ill tidings." His voice choked, and he paused for a moment. "I deeply regret telling you that your father passed away this morning. He wasn't feeling well last night, and when we checked on him this morning . . . he was . . . he was no longer with us."

Savino sank into his chair and his rage seemed to fade away. He reached for a bottle of wine on his desk and poured some into his goblet. He drank it down and stared at the ceiling. The messenger watched him and a tear came to his eye. He brushed it away. "I'm so sorry," he said. "God be with you, sir." He turned and left the room.

Savino's eyes were still focused on the ceiling.

"My lord," Ristro said, "are you all right?"

Savino dismissed the question with a wave of his hand.

Ristro nodded, but said nothing. What could he say? He had never seen Savino so pensive. He felt that his employer's sorrow must be unbearable.

That wasn't the case.

Savino stared at the ceiling as if in a trance. All his thoughts were focused on a single reality:

At long last, my father is dead. His fortune is now mine!

Savino got his feet. "Ristro, ready my horse. I have urgent business to attend to."

The serving staff at Giovanni Balducci's house was assembled in the main hall, their expressions somber. Many held back tears; a few wept openly.

Savino Balducci thanked them for their years of good service to his family. "A few years ago," he went on, "our mother passed away. Now my father is gone. I know some of you are concerned about your positions here. Please don't worry. As the first son of the Balducci family, I'll maintain the operation of this household as it has been in the past. You will all keep your jobs."

Despite their grieving, there was a sigh of relief from some of the staff. Many of them were advanced in years, and finding new employment would be difficult.

Savino excused most of the staff, but asked his father's longtime secretary to stay. "There are a few matters I need to discuss with you," he said.

"Certainly, Signor Savino," the secretary said. "I think you'll find your father planned his estate with an eye to the future for you and Signor Adamo."

"I'm sure he did," Savino said.

The secretary took a parchment from his leather case. "His will is not complicated," he said. "He put great trust in you and your brother to carry on after him. Basically the will states that you and your brother will share equally in his lands, personal wealth, and social power."

He handed it to Savino.

Savino looked confused. "Traditionally the inheritance goes to the oldest son, isn't that so?"

"It is," the secretary said. "But because your father loved you and your brother equally, he wanted you each to have an equal share of the inheritance."

"Hmm," Savino said. He scanned the document. "I see it's signed by my father and witnessed by you."

"Yes," the secretary said.

"Is there a copy of this?" Savino said.

"No, just this original."

"I see," Savino said. "That simplifies matters. That will be all."

"Is there anything else?"

105

"Yes there is," Savino said. "You have one hour to collect your belongings and leave this property."

"But—"

"There *are* no buts!" Savino said. "Once you leave this house, you have one day to leave this territory. You are banished."

Savino smiled at the secretary and ripped the will into shreds.

The secretary's face drained of color.

"Best get moving," Savino said. "Time and tide wait for no man."

That night, Serafina knocked on Nicholas's door.

"Come in," he said, "it's not locked."

She opened the door and poked her head into the room. "My lady wants to talk to you," she said.

"Now?"

"Of course, now." She flicked her fingers against her chin. "Don't dawdle. Go!"

Margarita was alone in her room, seated on the couch. "You look exhausted, Nicholas," she said. "Come sit by me."

He sat down next to her, and she looked at his blistered hands. "Poor boy, you've been working so hard."

Nicholas took a deep breath. "You smell so nice."

She brought her silk handkerchief to her face and inhaled. "Roses, lilies, patchouli, and musk. My favorite scent." She stroked his head.

The tension he'd been feeling seemed to melt away. He closed his eyes, lost in thought:

This is what a mother's loving touch must feel like.

"I understand you and Ristro visited Adamo's house this morning," she said.

"Yes," Nicholas said.

"I imagine Foresta was wearing beautiful new diamonds. Is that so?"

"I don't know," Nicholas said.

"What do you mean?" Margarita said. "You'd certainly notice if she had new diamonds."

"What I mean is, I didn't see her. She and Adamo were out making preparations for the grand ceremony."

"What ceremony?"

"The Duke is going to make Adamo a count five days from now. There's going to be a big celebration."

"Does my husband know about this?"

"I guess Ristro must have told him."

She stood up abruptly and glared at Nicholas.

"You *guess*?" she said. "What's wrong with you? You promised you'd let me know what my husband was up to."

"I didn't think—"

"You certainly didn't!" Margarita said. She shook her fist at him. "Get out! Go to your room—I don't want to see any more of you!"

Back in his room, Nicholas stretched out on his bed. His mood was dark. His feelings were hurt, and what made it worse was the fact that Margarita had seemed so warm until she turned on him. Why had she spoken to him so harshly? He hadn't tried to hide anything from her.

The incident with Margarita gnawed at him as he stared at the walls of his room. Would she treat Mariotto that way? Would she go from a loving mood to one of rage so easily with her son?

The thought of Mariotto brought another question to his mind. How had the little scamp managed to sneak into his room undetected?

He flashed back to the days when he and Hunter would fantasize about the Dream House. They were sure it was filled with trap doors and secret passages.

Could that be Mariotto's secret?

He scanned the room, from the two wood-paneled sidewalls and the wall the door was in to the stone wall where the tapestry depicting the village tower hung.

He got off the bed and moved it away from the corner where the sidewall met the back wall. By the light of the candle, he examined the panels. They were snugly joined, not a crack between any of them. He moved the table away from the other sidewall and repeated the process. The results were the same. The wall the door was in was equally solid.

The back wall, where the tapestry of the village tower hung, seemed unlikely. The stonework above and below the tapestry was smoothly covered by stucco. But could there be a crack behind the tapestry?

He slid the table in front of the tapestry and climbed up on it. An iron rod ran through the hem at the top of the tapestry and was suspended from two iron hooks. Nicholas lifted the rod from the hooks and jumped to the floor.

The area that the tapestry had covered was slightly lighter than the rest of the wall. But the stucco there was as smooth as glass.

He climbed back on the table and put the tapestry back on its hooks, slid the table to its previous position, and pushed his bed back toward the corner. One leg of the bed snagged on a rough spot on the floor, and he gave it an extra hard push. The bed slammed into the wood-paneled sidewall, and one of the panels in it opened like a door.

There *was* a secret passage!

He took the candle from the table and peered into the opening. The passage was large enough for an adult to stand up in. He stepped through the opening. There was a handle on the other side of the panel. He pushed it closed and followed the passage for a dozen feet or so to where an unlit torch was stuck in a socket on the wall. It was a single stick with one end wrapped with a waxed burlap rag. He lit the torch with his candle, and the passage became alive with light.

The passage continued for another thirty feet and dead-ended at a short flight of stairs. At the top of the stairs was a door handle similar to the one on the inside of the secret door to his own room. He extinguished the torch and set the candle on the floor about ten feet back from the stairs.

He climbed the half-dozen steps to the door and gripped the handle. He opened it a crack and peered into Savino's armory. Savino and Margarita seemed to be engaged in a heated argument.

Savino took his sword from the armory wall and glared at Margarita. "Hellfire!" he said. "You just don't understand!"

"I understand completely!" Margarita said, her tone as hostile as her husband's. "When Adamo becomes a count, he'll be able to take over our lands. I'll be stuck in this country house, but Foresta will live in a castle!"

Savino shook his sword at her, the veins at his temples swelling. He cast it aside and it skidded across the floor, ending up in the fireplace. He clenched and unclenched his fists, trying to regain his composure. "Listen, Margarita," he said, his voice icy cold, "I've had enough of your whining. You think I am just the lord of a little village—but you're wrong."

"What do you mean?" Margarita said, her voice less harsh.

"My father passed away today." Savino said. "I now own all of his lands. I am the sole heir of Giovanni Balducci! Adamo's land is mine now. I can do whatever I want with his properties. I now have a greater fortune and more power than he does."

"But if Adamo becomes a count, he would have power over you."

"*If!*" Savino said. "But it's not official yet. The ceremony is five days away."

"You must do something about it."

"I intend to."

"You'd better," she said. She spun about and hurried from the room. Ristro was standing in the hallway. She brushed by him without even a glance his way.

Ristro stepped into the armory. "My lord, you wanted to see me?"

"Oh, my faithful Ristro," he said, Savino shook his head. "I am surrounded by enemies. You are the only one I can trust."

"But Lady Margarita is—"

"Treacherous!" Savino said. "She is capable of killing me so that she can gain all my worldly goods. Why do you think I have a new poison taster in my house?"

A shock went through Nicholas. *So that's why he has me tasting the food before anyone else eats!*

"My lord," Ristro said, "I didn't realize—"

"She hides it well from most people," Savino said. "I should have known from the start. But nothing stays hidden from me long. And no one can keep me from what is rightfully mine."

He paused in thought. "Ristro, there is no way in this world that Adamo could be made a count before I was one—unless magic was involved."

"No, my lord."

He turned to Ristro. "Are you with me?"

"I am, sir!"

"Good man," Savino said.

Savino walked across the room and took his sword from the fireplace. The blade was hot and smeared with ashes.

He turned back to Ristro and said, "I curse Adamo!"

A log in the fireplace flared up behind Savino and it projected his shadow on the wall.

"I must take my life back. I want those diamonds!"

The log flared up again and made his shadow monstrously big.

"This curse is for my brother! I would give my soul to possess them!"

Savino flung his sword at the shadow.

His sword stuck in the wooden panel, inches from the crack Nicholas was peering through.

Still facing the wall, Savino said, "Tomorrow is my father's funeral, and I must present a good front to everyone. But on the following day I will see you at the stable just before dawn. Bring three or four of your friends with you. People who are ready for any occasion—if you get my meaning."

"I understand my lord," Ristro said. He bowed to Savino and left the armory.

Alone in the armory, Savino headed across the room to retrieve his sword from the wooden panel.

Nicholas began to tremble. If he pulled the panel shut, Savino would know he was there. If he didn't, Savino would see that the secret panel was partially open and discover him.

A knock sounded on the door.

Savino turned toward it. "Ristro?"

The door opened and a figure in a black robe glided into the armory.

Savino grabbed the hilt of his sword and yanked it from the panel. He turned toward the figure. "Nobody enters my room without my permission!"

"But I have your permission," a deep voice said. "You summoned me. I've come to make your wishes come true—in return for your giving me your soul."

"Who are you?"

"You know who I am," the robed figure said. "I am a part of you."

Savino stepped toward the man. "Don't talk in riddles. Show me your face!" He yanked at the man's hood and let out a piercing scream.

As the hood was pulled back, a huge dark shadow filled the room. Black particles surged from the cloak into Savino's mouth.

Savino made an inhuman sound—like the croak of a raven—and fell to his knees. He clawed at his throat and tried to call for help. All he could manage was a rasping sound. He fell face down on the floor.

Nicholas shuddered. The black cloak remained on the floor next to Savino, but along with the dark shadow the figure that had filled it was gone.

Nicholas thought of entering the armory and helping Savino, as he'd helped his father on that fateful night in San Francisco.

But Savino began to stir. With a moan, he rolled over, pushed himself to a sitting position, and slowly got to his feet.

Nicholas pushed the panel shut. He didn't bother lighting the torch. With his heart pounding, he scooped up the flickering candle and rushed back to his room.

His second encounter with the Dark Shadow was as terrifying as the first. But it added one more piece to the bizarre puzzle that was dominating his life.

CHAPTER 12

A Quiet Visitor

Giovanni Balducci's funeral was attended by throngs of people from both Torre and Chiesta. His rule had been just, and his love for his subjects apparent to all.

Adamo's grief was overwhelming. He looked pale and hollow eyed. Foresta stood arm in arm with him by his father's graveside. To many in attendance, she seemed to be supporting him physically as well as emotionally.

Savino conducted himself with more restraint. He spoke solemnly about his love for his father and his wishes to carry on the good works his father was known for.

Margarita stood next to him, her face covered by a black veil of mourning. Though it concealed her face, it didn't prevent her from observing the frequent looks Savino cast Foresta's way.

That night, Margarita summoned Agnola to her room.

Agnola, as usual, was worried that Margarita would find fault with her for something she'd done. She was pleasantly surprised when Margarita greeted her with a smile.

"I just thought of something, Agnola," Margarita said. "I've never seen you wear a necklace."

"No, my lady," Agnola said, "I never had me one."

Margarita laughed. "What a shame." She held up a chain of pearls with a small crystal set at the center. "Do you like this?"

Agnola nodded. "It's beautiful, my lady."

"Here," Margarita said, "try it on." She stepped toward Agnola and fitted it around her neck. She turned Agnola toward the mirror. "Oh, it looks wonderful on you."

Agnola stared at her reflection, a look of awe on her face. After a moment, she reached back to unfasten it.

"Don't take it off," Margarita said. "You've been a trusted servant. I want you to have it."

"But—"

"You deserve nice things, dear."

Agnola's eyes grew misty. "My lady, I don't know what to say."

"You don't need to say anything," Margarita said. Her brow furrowed. "But I do have a favor to ask of you."

"Anything at all, my lady!"

Margarita raised a finger to her lips. "But it must be a secret just between you and me."

"Of course, my lady."

Margarita smiled. "I want you to have my horse ready for me early tomorrow morning. I have business in town that will be a surprise for my husband. I know you've helped Lacopo prepare the horses before."

"I'll go get him now and bring him to the stable," Agnola said.

Margarita shook her head. "No. Not even he can know about this. Can you do it alone?"

Agnola nodded. "You want one of the brown horses saddled, is that right?"

"Exactly," Margarita said. "Get him ready after midnight and tether him behind the stable."

"I will, my lady."

"Oh," Margarita said, "one more thing. Pack my trunk for a weeklong visit and have someone get a carriage ready for me. I should be finished with my business by midmorning." She patted Agnola's cheek. "You do look lovely in your new necklace."

Agnola blushed. She curtsied and left the room.

The next morning, Nicholas went to the stable earlier than usual to ask a favor from Lacopo. He desperately wanted to tell Ellie about the appearance of the Dark Shadow. Yesterday he hadn't been able to speak to her at Giovanni Balducci's funeral. If Lacopo would let him ride Giotto to Adamo's, he could talk with Ellie and be back to do his stable boy chores before anyone in the Savino household was up.

Nicholas's hopes were high. Lacopo had been so helpful to him, he felt sure he'd grant him the favor. As the minutes passed, he began to worry. The kindly old man usually opened the stable before dawn. The sun was already rising over the mountain, and he still wasn't here.

As he waited, Nicholas heard the sound of approaching hoof beats. Moments later he saw five black warhorses come to a halt at the gate. The riders were all wearing armor. Swords hung at their sides. One of the riders dismounted and opened the gate.

The front door of the main house opened and Savino emerged. He approached one of the riders and spoke to him for several minutes, then returned to the house.

The rider flicked the reins and his warhorse galloped to the stable.

It was Ristro.

"Come on," he said to Nicholas. "You ride with me today." He yanked Nicholas off his feet and set him on the saddle in front of him.

"Where are we going?"

"To Lord Adamo's," Ristro said.

"Why are you all wearing armor?"

"That's not your concern," Ristro said. He spurred his horse. It reared up once and then plunged forward, headed for the road to Chiesta. The four other riders followed close behind him.

Adamo had been drinking heavily since his father's death. Foresta had tried to comfort him, but now she couldn't think of a way to do so. The atmosphere in the household was muted.

Piero had been missing for days, as if the little cat was sharing Adamo's grief. Caterina wandered into the foyer.

"Piero, where are you?" she said in a tiny voice.

"Little girl!" a deep voice said.

She turned and saw Ristro standing in the doorway.

"Hello," she said. "Have you seen my cat?"

Ristro lifted her up and held her in his arms. "Where is Lord Adamo?"

She pointed toward Adamo's office.

Nicholas and four armored men came into the foyer.

Ristro turned to them. "Wait here," he said, and headed for Adamo's office.

"What are you doing in my house?"

Ristro turned and saw Foresta standing in the hallway.

She walked toward him and extended her hands. "Give me my daughter."

Ristro stepped back and nodded to his men.

Two of them stepped from the foyer and gripped Foresta's arms.

Caterina began to cry.

"We're here to collect the three diamonds, on orders from Lord Savino." Ristro said.

"They belong to my husband," Foresta said. "Savino has no right to them."

"Don't tell me about rights!" Ristro said. He hoisted Caterina above his head. "This girl has no right to live here on Lord Savino's property. She came from Venice; we can send her back there today."

Foresta looked stunned.

"But," Ristro said, "If you wish to keep her here with you, Lord Adamo must give up all the possessions of this household. My lord is now possessor of all Lord Giovanni Balducci's assets, including this property."

"Leave us alone! We will leave Savino's land in four days."

Ristro grinned. "You want to make a deal, eh? Well, here's my deal: Give me the diamonds or you will never see your daughter again."

The door to Adamo's office opened and he leaned against the doorway. "Ristro," he said, "what brings you here?" He staggered backwards into his office and banged into his desk.

Ristro stepped into the office and sniffed the air. "Wine before breakfast, Lord Adamo?"

Adamo stared at him, a bewildered look on his face. He looked past Ristro and saw the other men.

"What's going on?"

"I'm here for the three diamonds," Ristro said.

"*My* diamonds?" Adamo said.

"They belong to your brother now. They're part of his inheritance."

Adamo shook his head. "No. That's nonsense. They—"

"I'm not here to argue!" Ristro said.

"Is that my brother's order?" Adamo said.

"It is. Where are they?"

"He can take the diamonds, but he can't take my love away from me," Adamo said. He tottered around the desk and collapsed into his chair.

"Enough talk," Ristro said. "I want them now!"

Ristro snapped his fingers. Two of his men came into the office and began ransacking it.

He gestured to the other two. "Search the second floor!"

They released Foresta's arms and hurried to the stairs.

Adamo pulled the velvet sack from the drawer. He loosened the drawstrings and leaned back in his chair, an odd smile on his face.

Ristro doesn't know there's just the red diamond!

Ristro lowered Caterina to the floor and gripped her hair in one hand. With the other he drew his sword and laid the blade across her throat. "Enough stalling!" he said. "Give me the diamonds now or she dies!"

Foresta screamed.

Adamo raised the velvet sack above his shoulder and stared at it. "You belong to us," he said to the red diamond, as if addressing a person. "Go to Savino now, but return to us!"

He flung the sack at Ristro.

Ristro released his grip on Caterina's hair and snatched at the sack, but not quickly enough. It flew past him and the red diamond slipped free from the sack and bounced across the floor.

Caterina rushed to her mother's arms.

The red diamond bounced into the hallway and a shaft of sunlight through the open foyer door hit it. An array of dazzling lights reflected from the diamond. Multiple lights seemed to rebound from floor to wall to ceiling as it made its way down the hall.

"Get the diamonds!" Ristro yelled to Nicholas.

Nicholas chased the bouncing lights down the hall, but they were moving too fast. They hit the wall at the end of the hallway and ricocheted at a right angle.

He skidded to a stop at the end of the hall and turned to the right. The lights had vanished, but three diamonds lay on the floor: a pink one, a purple one, and a green one. They had stopped just before the open door to the flower garden. He scooped them up. For a moment, he thought of continuing out through the doorway.

Madness!

Ristro and his men would hunt him down like a wounded deer.

As he stood there recovering his breath, an intriguing scent caught his attention: a hint of roses, patchouli, lilies, and musk. He turned to the open door and saw a hooded figure in a green cloak hurrying toward the woods at the far end of the garden. The overhanging branch of a peach tree snagged the hood free and spun the person around, revealing her profile.

Margarita!

She continued to the woods where a brown horse was tied. She mounted it quickly. Without looking back, she rode out of sight.

When Nicholas returned to Adamo's office, Ristro was standing in the doorway. He'd retrieved the velvet sack from the floor. He took the diamonds from Nicholas, tucked them into the sack, and tied the drawstrings. "It's time to go," he said.

"Nicholas!" a girl's voice said.

Nicholas looked past Ristro. Ellie was standing in the office next to Foresta and cradling Caterina in her arms.

Nicholas's heart seemed to leap in his chest. "Ellie!" he said. "I've been looking for you. The Dark Shadow that I saw in my house is—"

"I said let's go!" Ristro said. He grabbed Nicholas's arm and slung him across the hall and into the foyer.

Adamo lurched toward Ristro his fist raised. "You can't do that to a child!"

"Oh, can't I?" Ristro said. He backhanded Adamo and sent him reeling toward the desk. Halfway there Adamo stumbled and fell. His head struck the corner of the desk, and he slumped to the floor.

Ristro barked a short ugly laugh and strode into the foyer. He yanked Nicholas to his feet and dragged him outside to where his warhorse was waiting.

"Adamo!" Foresta took him up in her arms. He was unconscious. She shouted, "Somebody, give me a hand!"

Five of the servants hurried into the room. Their faces had already grown pale.

"One of you, fetch a doctor. Please hurry!" said Foresta. "Help me lay him on the couch!"

Two of them quickly moved the couch closer to him. Then all of them carefully lifted him and laid him down on it.

"Now go check if everybody is safe," said Foresta.

The servants bowed and closed the door behind them.

Foresta sat beside Adamo and held his hand.

"Ellie, please come over here," said Foresta.

Ellie sensed that Foresta wanted to tell her something important. Ellie let Caterina go and went to Foresta. Caterina was still sobbing.

Foresta pulled a handkerchief out from under her garment at the chest.

"This bounced back to me." She opened the handkerchief and showed it to Ellie.

It was the purple diamond!

"The red diamond only exists when the three are in the rightful hand," said Foresta. "I now know that the right owner must always keep a pledge of love, faith, and strength. The magical power wouldn't work even if Savino had gotten all three. We cannot let him take this gem away from us. This is Caterina's inheritance."

Ellie nodded.

Foresta continued, "They might come back here again for this today and tear this place down even worse. I cannot think of a place to hide this. Help me, Ellie."

Suddenly Piero the cat appeared in the room. His golden eyes shone. He started strolling around Foresta and Ellie, brushing his body up against their legs.

"Foresta, do you have anything I can wrap this diamond with?" asked Ellie. "The color should be close to Piero's fur."

Foresta was thinking for a moment. "I think I do." She went to Adamo's desk, opened the bottom drawer, and pulled out something wrapped with a piece of yellowish brown colored leather. It was about the size of a notebook. She untied the wrapping and put the content aside. It was a book summarizing Adamo's agricultural inventions and methods. He had prepared it for a presentation to the Duke and Duchess at his ceremony, which was coming up soon.

Foresta smoothed out the leather and used a dagger on the desk to cut a piece off of the leather.

"How about this?" She handed it to Ellie.

"That will work." Ellie placed the purple diamond on the leather and rolled it up.

"Come here, Piero," Ellie said.

The cat walked to Ellie. She cupped its face with both hands and kissed its head. Piero purred, looking pleased. Ellie tied the leather that contained the diamond around his neck.

Foresta looked relieved. "Thank you, Ellie. What would I do without you? I never would have thought of that."

Ellie grinned and nodded, "You could have done that without me." Then she turned to Piero and said, "Don't let anybody else take this away from you. Now go and hide."

"No! Piero stays here with me at all times!" Caterina cried out with her wet face pouting.

Ellie walked back to her and said, "Caterina, listen to me. You will be a very important person for this village. You'll be okay without him. Please remember that." Then Ellie smiled at her, "Piero will come back to you, I promise."

Caterina was still pouting.

Foresta hurried to her daughter and embraced her with all her heart, "You'll understand later."

Caterina shook head and cried in her mother's arms.

Vigorous sounds of footsteps approached the room and the door swung open. "My lady," said her servant, "the doctor is here!"

The doctor strode in with a worried look on his face. Piero moved through the doorway and vanished into the hallway, leaving crying Caterina behind.

Back in Savino's office, Nicholas stood to the side and watched as Ristro took the velvet sack from his pocket and emptied the three diamonds onto Savino's desktop.

Savino grinned. "Reliable Ristro, you've never let me down." He put them in the palm of his hand and examined them closely. His brow creased. "These look smaller than I thought they'd be. More like cherries than figs."

He shot a glance at Ristro, but said nothing. He set the diamonds back on the table and eyed them from different angles. "Hmm," he said. He picked up the pink one and went over to the window. He gripped the gem between his thumb and forefinger and scraped it across the windowpane. He frowned and scraped the glass again.

"Hellfire!"

He turned to Ristro. "Get over here!"

Ristro strode across the room.

Savino pointed to the windowpane. "What do you see?"

Ristro leaned toward it. He examined it closely and shrugged. "I don't see anything, sir."

"Exactly!" Savino said. "There's nothing to see. Not a mark on the glass. You fool! You brought me ordinary crystals. Diamonds cut glass. These are fake!"

Ristro looked panicked. "Maybe . . . maybe the Venetian lied to Lord Adamo in the first place."

"Not the Venetian; Adamo lied. He fooled you!"

"Perhaps Lord Adamo didn't have the real diamonds in the first place! I remember that he behaved strangely. He grinned when he threw these at me!"

"I don't want to hear any more of your excuses," Savino said. "You disgust me. I'll deal with you later."

He stormed out of his office.

Ristro stood there his eyes downcast, his chin on his chest.

Despite his loathing for Ristro, Nicholas felt a momentary feeling of pity for the humiliated bully.

As soon as Margarita returned from Adamo's she summoned Agnola.

"Is my carriage ready?" she said.

"Yes, my lady," Agnola said. "A driver is waiting for you at the stable."

"Excellent," Margarita said. "Fetch Mariotto for me and then take my horse to the stable. Tell the driver, I'll be there shortly."

Agnola curtsied and headed for the door.

"Agnola?"

Agnola turned back.

Margarita smiled at her. "The necklace looks lovely on you. Perhaps, I'll bring you something that will go with it when I return."

Agnola brought her hands to her chest. "Oh, my lady . . .!" She blushed, curtsied, and hurried from the room.

Margarita had changed into her traveling clothes and was selecting a hat for the journey when Mariotto rushed into the room.

"Mother," he said, "when will I become a king?"

"Hello, my love," she said. She knelt down and hugged him. "Someday you'll be King of the World. But right now, let me show you something magnificent."

She took a knotted handkerchief from her coat pocket and untied it. "These are what will make you a king," she said. She opened the handkerchief and spread it out on the rug, revealing a green diamond and a pink one.

Mariotto pouted. "There are only two. You said we would get three magical diamonds."

"That's all right, dear," she said. She kissed his forehead. "You and I will have the purple one soon. This is just the start for us."

"All right," he said. "Will I be a king then?"

She forced a smile. "Of course, my darling Mariotto. You'll be King of the World."

"Good," he said. "I have to go now. Serafina is waiting to play hide and seek with me. I'm going to hide in my secret place. She never finds me."

She held him back. "One thing, dear," she said. "You mustn't tell your father we have the diamonds. He might try to take them from us so that he can be king instead of you."

Mariotto made a face. "He can't be. I'm supposed to be king."

"That's right. So we have to keep it a secret. I'm going to take these two to your grandfather's house and hide them until we get the purple diamond."

Mariotto grinned. "Can I go play hide and seek now?"

"Of course," she hugged him again. "I'll be away for a little while, but you'll have Nicholas to play with."

"Okay," he said. He pulled away from her and hurried out to the backyard.

Margarita wrapped the diamonds in her handkerchief and put them back in her pocket. She tried on the hat she'd been considering when Mariotto had come in. She checked her appearance in the mirror. As she adjusted the hat, her frustration rushed through her body again.

She didn't realize that Savino would send Ristro to get the gems. When she sneaked into Adamo's house through the back way, she saw the diamonds come bouncing down the hallway and off the walls. She heard the shouts from the other room and knew she didn't have much time. She threw the imitations on the floor, scooped up the real ones and hurried to where her horse was tied.

Not till she got back to her room, she didn't realize she'd only grabbed two of the diamonds. By then it was too late to go back for the purple one.

She tilted the hat to a jaunty angle. It still didn't look right. She sighed. *What does it matter at a time like this? The important thing now is to hide the two diamonds at my father's house.* She'd get the third one from Adamo later.

She headed for the stable where her carriage awaited her.

When Nicholas got to Margarita's room, Agnola was mopping the floor.

"Where's Margarita?" he said.

"Someone hears you call her that, you'll be kicked out of here. Call her *Lady* Margarita."

"All right, Agnola. Where is *Lady* Margarita?"

"What do you want from her?"

"I have to see her right now."

"Well, you can't. She's gone on a trip."

"Where?"

Agnola fondled her necklace, making sure Nicholas would appreciate her new importance. "That's none of your business," she said. "You are nobody at this household."

Nicholas started to speak, but hesitated. Whatever was going on with Agnola, it was clear he'd get nowhere arguing with her. He turned and hurried from the room. Maybe Mariotto knew where his mother had gone.

Mariotto wasn't in his room, the kitchen, or in the backyard. Nicholas finally found him in Savino's armory. He was holding Savino's sword and practicing sword fighting with an imaginary opponent.

"Mariotto," Nicholas said, "do you know where your mother is?"

"I am a king," Mariotto said. "You must bow and fall to your knees before you talk to me." He pointed the sword at Nicholas.

Nicholas thought of taking it away from him, but instead decided to humor him. He bowed and knelt on the floor. "My king," he said, "where did your mother go?"

Mariotto gave Nicholas a fake look. "I don't know," he said.

"You are the king, Mariotto. You should know everything."

"I *do* know everything, but I'm not supposed to tell you where she went." He lowered the sword.

"We're friends, my king," Nicholas said. "I will be your knight and protect you forever if you tell me where she is."

"Are you sure?"

"Of course, my king."

Mariotto thought for a moment. "All right," he said. "But you mustn't tell anyone. My mother and I have two of the magical diamonds. She's gone to hide them at my grandfather's house."

Nicholas had heard Margarita mention that her father was Lord Cosmo Capello. "Where does he live?" he said.

"North of us, in the province of Ferrara."

"Thank you my king," Nicholas said.

"Nicholas," Mariotto said, "I'll be a real king soon and I'll appoint you as my friend forever and the leader of all my knights."

"You are too kind, my king," Nicholas said.

Mariotto held his sword over Nicholas's head. "Nicholas, you are now in charge of the stable."

"No, my king. Lacopo is in charge."

"No. Now it's your turn."

"Why is that, my king?"

"Because the old man died this morning."

Savino stood on the hill behind his manor and looked out at Adamo's land. A flock of chickadees in a nearby stand of trees filled the air with their twittering birdsongs. Savino ignored them. His anger was mounting, his thoughts churning. What was wrong with that blockhead Ristro? How could he have fallen prey to Adamo's trickery? And Adamo? Did he truly believe he could defeat his older brother in a war of wits?

You fooled me this time, Adamo, but you are not a count yet. I will get those diamonds!

He jabbed his sword into the ground, as if sealing a bargain between his soul and the land itself.

The birds went silent.

The Dark Shadow rose up behind Savino. It whispered in his ear: "Savino, my faithful servant, I want you to blow my body over to Adamo's land. It will soon be covered with darkness. Do you understand what I am doing for you?"

"Perfectly—because we are one," Savino said. "There will be no more mornings and daytimes in Chiesta. Only the darkness will remain in Adamo's land and his life. There will be no prosperity, no hope, and no love in that family."

The Dark Shadow flew over to Savino's mouth. He inhaled deeply and then blew out the particles the Dark Shadow had become. They flew toward Adamo's land, spreading through the village, the hills, the forest, the fields, and finally settling over Adamo's house.

"Now I see…" the Dark Shadow said, "the three diamonds transformed into one red diamond when a total eclipse occurred, but they have separated. That red diamond has the magical powers."

"That RED one I saw! It was in my hand!" Savino's body was shaking from enormous anger.

CHAPTER 13

The Invasion

The next day Nicholas got to the stable before first light. As soon as he stepped inside he was overcome with sadness. He'd no longer see Lacopo grooming the horses with loving care. No longer hear the old man talking to them as though they were old friends. He lit a candle and started doing his chores. As he worked, grief came to him in waves. He paused for a while in thought. And then he returned to his tasks and worked even harder. It was a way of honoring Lacopo.

He entered Giotto's stall and patted his muzzle. He wondered if Giotto would miss his old friend. He started to lead him out of the stall, but stopped at the sound of voices. He blew out the candle, pulled the stall gate shut, and peered through the slats.

The main door opened, and Savino and Ristro stepped into the stable.

"When will your men get here?" Savino said.

"Anytime now, sir," Ristro said.

"It had better be soon," Savino said. "When you've saddled our horses, bring them to the house. Then get that brat Nicholas. He'll ride with you."

"Yes, sir."

"I hope you appreciate what I'm doing for you, Ristro. If anyone else had ruined a job like you did, they wouldn't live to tell about it. I want the real diamonds and the little girl. This is your last chance."

"Thank you, sir. I won't fail you this time."

Savino looked at him, but didn't speak. He turned and headed back to the house.

Nicholas's heart was pounding, and he tried to calm himself. He concentrated on taking long slow breaths, and prayed that Ristro wouldn't hear them.

After ten minutes or so, Ristro led two saddled warhorses out of the stable and slammed the door shut.

Nicholas gave Ristro time to take the horses to the house, and then led Giotto out from his stall. In short order, the old horse was saddled and ready to ride. Nicholas opened the side door and led Giotto out to the pasture. When he was out of sight of the house, he mounted him and headed for the rear gate.

When Nicholas got to the gate of Torre, the sun was rising, spreading the light of life over Savino's land. He looked towards his destination, Chiesta. Adamo's land was in the dark shadows under the black clouds as if its life had been taken.

"Let's go, Giotto!" Nicholas snapped the reins.

Foresta woke to the sound of the Chiesta church bells. They tolled seven times. She looked confused; she usually woke up by six or earlier. Then she remembered how late she'd gone to bed. For much of the night, she'd been comforting little Caterina—who'd been terrorized by that beast Ristro. And she'd been caring for poor Adamo. He'd regained consciousness, but hadn't slept tightly. Sometimes he complained of terrible headaches. Other times he drifted into sleep and then woke in a sweat, mumbling disconnected words until he passed out again.

She went to the window and drew back the curtains. The day was gloomy. Could a storm be on the way?

In the dim light, she checked Adamo and Caterina. They were both sleeping soundly now. Somewhat relieved, she put on her robe and went outside.

A dark cloud hung over her house. She walked out toward the cliff and saw that the cloud covered all of Chiesta. But across the valley, Savino's estate and the village of Torre were bathed in sunlight.

Ellie woke up at the usual time and felt something was not right. She threw her blanket around her and strode to the windows. When she opened the curtains, outside in the dark she saw Foresta standing at the cliff. She grabbed a shawl and hurried down there.

Foresta heard footsteps from behind as Ellie approached, but her eyes were still focused on Torre.

"What's happening?" said Ellie.

"Savino must have put a curse on his own brother." Foresta bit her lips.

"Oh, no! We must lift it!" Ellie said.

"I don't know how," Foresta looked at Ellie, "but I'll ask the priest of our church. I might find an answer. Now excuse me, I'd better check on Adamo and Caterina." She turned around and strode back to the manor.

Standing alone, Ellie said herself: *Daniel, hang in there.*

"Papa, my Piero is back!" Caterina said as she came over to Adamo's bed with her cat cuddled in her arms.

Adamo turned the side, kissed Caterina's cheek, and petted Piero. "I am glad Caterina found you," he said to the cat. "We all missed you." He sank back on his pillow.

"He missed you too," Caterina said, her little face serious.

"Oh, there you are," Ellie said to Caterina, "I've been looking for you."

She stepped into the room, followed by Foresta who carried a tray with a cup of soup and a glass of water on it.

"Piero, you are back!" Foresta set the tray on a side table and petted the cat. The gemstone was still at his neck.

Adamo rolled his head to the side. He gave them a weak smile but said nothing.

Foresta pulled up a chair next to Adamo's bed. She sat down and felt his forehead. She frowned and reached for the glass. "Perhaps you should have some water," she said. She brought it to his lips, but he turned away.

"Not now," he said, his voice barely audible.

Foresta looked at Ellie and sighed. "Why don't you and Caterina go out to the back yard and pick some flowers? Later we can make a cheerful bouquet for Papa."

"Good idea," Ellie said. "And Piero can help us." She took Caterina's hand and started out of the room. She paused in the doorway and looked back at Foresta. The two exchanged looks.

Foresta watched as Ellie, Caterina, and Piero headed for the back door. *How fortunate we are to have Ellie,* she thought. *A loving young daughter who is wise beyond her years.*

"Dearest," she said, "I really think you should try a sip of water and then maybe some soup. It will be good for you."

He stared at her for a moment and then got a faraway look in his eyes. "I can't just now," he said in a faltering voice. "More than anything else, I need a good rest . . ."

He closed his eyes . . . and was gone forever.

Nicholas got lost twice while making his way through the woods. Finally he found the path to Adamo's garden and spurred Giotto toward it. When he reached the garden, he saw Ellie and Caterina just heading into the house. Caterina was carrying her little cat, and Ellie had her arms filled with flowers. He tied Giotto's reins to a tree and rushed across the garden.

"Ellie!" he called.

She dropped the flowers and rushed into his arms. "What are you doing here, Nicholas?" she said.

"Ristro's men are on the way!" he said. "You and Caterina have to come with me. My horse is out back."

"They came yesterday," Ellie said.

"I know. But now Savino is with them. I've got to hide you two."

Caterina looked frightened. She clutched at Ellie's leg.

"Are you sure of this?" Ellie said.

"I am! Please there isn't much time."

He turned at the sound of a voice from outside.

It was Savino.

"You three go around back!" Savino said. "We'll take the front!"

"Oh, no," Nicholas said. He picked up Caterina. "Come on," he said to Ellie. He opened the back door and stepped into the hallway.

"The stairs!"

With Ellie right behind him, he dashed to the foyer and ran up the stairs that led to the second floor. They hurried to the room where Adamo and Foresta had first hidden the diamonds in the chest. He climbed onto the chest, reached for a dangling cord, and pulled on it. A hidden door opened and a rope ladder dropped down.

"You first," Nicholas said.

Ellie climbed onto the chest and then up the rope ladder and into to the attic. Nicholas handed Caterina and Piero up to her. He climbed the ladder and pulled it up after him. He tugged on the cord until the door was almost shut. He pulled the cord into the attic and closed the door completely.

When they caught their breath, Nicholas whispered to Ellie, "You look like a princess. I wanted to tell you that sooner."

She was dressed in a silver silk dress with pleated skirt and balloon sleeves, accessorized with a white pearl necklace and earrings. Her bangs were separated at the center and combed to the sides.

Ellie grinned. "I feel like it, too."

By the dim light through the dusty attic window, Nicholas could see Caterina's lower lip trembling. He smiled at her. "We have to be very quiet until the bad men leave. Do you think you can do that?"

She nodded.

He kissed her forehead.

"You're such a brave girl," he said.

Nicholas, Ellie, Caterina, and Piero huddled together. And they waited.

Foresta sat by the bedside where Adamo lay, her head bowed. His hands were crossed over his chest. In accord with the ancient tradition, she had placed coins over his eyes. His face was as pale as white marble, but the expression on his face was peaceful. Finally he seemed at rest.

Her lips moved in steady, silent prayer. All sense of time had escaped her, until she was jolted from her daydreaming by an outcry from her servants.

She got to her feet just as Savino and Ristro charged into the room.

"How dare you invade my house!" she said, her face livid with rage.

Savino looked at Adamo. "Is he dead?" he said, with more curiosity than concern.

Foresta shook her head in disbelief. *Was there no end to Savino's cold-bloodedness?* She said nothing.

Savino went over to the bed. "Too bad," he said. "But he got what he deserved for crossing me."

He turned to Foresta. "I won't take up your time," he said. "I'm here for my three diamonds."

Foresta jabbed her finger toward Ristro and gave him a scornful look. "He already took them!"

Savino sneered. "They were nothing but ordinary crystals."

"That's a lie," Foresta said. "They were the diamonds!"

Savino chuckled. "Did Adamo fool you, too?"

"They were all we had. Now leave us alone!"

"Either your loving faithful husband tricked you, or you tricked him and are now trying to trick me. Which is it?"

"Get off my property now! There is nothing for you here."

"Is that so?" Savino said. "What a shame my brother didn't live long enough to become a count. I now rule this land—and everything in it."

"You can't take anything from the legacy that Adamo earned through his hard work and devotion to his people."

Savino smirked. "Perhaps not. But I can take Caterina. Not that I want her. I really don't care what happens to that child. I can throw her out right now if I feel like. Ristro's companions are searching the house and ground for her even as we talk."

Foresta's face grew pale.

Had Ellie heard Savino's people approaching? Did she have the chance to hide herself and Caterina from those beasts?

"Actually you can't do that," Foresta said, her face now showing confidence. "I suspected you might try something like that and I had her sent back to Venice. Lorenzo's relatives will give her a good home there."

Savino's brow darkened. He gripped Foresta's face with one hand and pushed her against the wall. "Don't try to fool me," he said. "You'll regret it."

Foresta maintained her bluff. With a prayer in her heart that Ellie and Caterina were safe, she said, "Savino, you and your henchmen can look all you want. Caterina is safe in Venice, and I don't have any diamonds."

One of Ristro's men came into the room and shook his head. "No luck," he said. "We checked everywhere. We couldn't find the diamonds or the child."

"Hellfire!" Savino said.

He released his grip on Foresta. "This isn't over," he said. "Your villagers will be mourning Adamo now, and I will allow that—until after the funeral is over. And then I'll return. There are ways to get information from people—some of them very unpleasant. Think about that."

Foresta looked him in the eye but said nothing.

Savino turned to Ristro. "Get your men," he said. "We're leaving."

He looked at Foresta, a malicious grin on his face. "I'll be back."

His shadow expanded behind him, and he left the room.

When it was safe to come down from the attic, Nicholas and Ellie brought Caterina to Foresta, who was absentmindedly sitting beside Adamo.

Caterina burst into tears when she saw her mother.

Foresta put her head up and turned to the cry. "Oh, my love, you were safe!" she ran across the room to her daughter and embraced her tighter than ever.

Ellie and Nicholas left the room and closed the door behind.

It was the first time they'd been alone since they arrived at Savino's. In Ellie's room Nicholas poured out his story of Savino and the Dark Shadow to Ellie.

"I see." Ellie nodded calmly, but her eyebrows were slightly furrowed. That worried Nicholas a little.

"What is it?" Nicholas said.

136

"Nothing, just an image of a painting I've seen in my art book crossed my mind and that image overlapped the scene you've just described to me. Not a big deal. What else did you want to tell me?"

He told her about Margarita's trick with the fake diamonds. "Margarita took them to her father," he said. "But she can't work their magic until she finds the other one. Her father is Lord Cosmo Capello. He lives in the province of Ferrara, north of here. I don't know exactly where, but if we go to Ferrara, we should be able to find him. Do you want to do that?"

"If it's meant to be, then we will go there," said Ellie. "We could leave after Adamo's funeral. We should show our respect for both Adamo and Foresta."

"But our time is running out," Nicholas said. "My father could be the next victim to die like Adamo."

"Remember, Nicholas, time passes differently in this realm. When we return to San Francisco, it will be the same time as it was when we left."

That didn't seem to satisfy Nicholas.

Ellie patted his hand. "Nicholas," she said, "nobody's going to take your father away from you. I promise you we won't let that happen."

That night, Foresta knocked on the door to Ellie's room. Ellie was in bed, about to blow out her bedside candle.

Foresta sat up at the edge of the bed. Ellie sensed Foresta's deepest sorrow from her.

"Ellie, just pray for us and this village. That's the only way we can survive Savino's curse."

"I will find a way to break it!" Ellie said, leaning over towards Foresta.

"I wish we could..." Foresta sighed. "Don't talk about it to anyone, the dark force might hear us and make it worse." She kissed Ellie's cheek and said, "Now go to sleep, my child."

Foresta blew out the candle and left the room.

CHAPTER 14

The Mothers

At the sound of a carriage pulling up in front of his manor, Lord Cosmo Capello went to the window. He broke into a smile and hurried outside. As soon as his daughter stepped down from her carriage, he embraced her.

"Margarita," he said, "what a wonderful surprise!"

She kissed his cheek. "It's always wonderful to see you, Father."

His smile broadened. "What brings you here, my child, business or pleasure?"

"To be truthful, Father, a little of both."

"Well then," he said, "perhaps we should go into my office." He took her arm and escorted her into the house.

Cosmo examined the two diamonds closely and set his magnifying glass on the table. "I'll be delighted to create a necklace for you with these two diamonds," he said. "They're of excellent quality and truly beautiful."

"There's more to them than just beauty," Margarita said.

"Really?"

Margarita gave him a sly smile. "Father, they are magical."

Cosmo raised an eyebrow. "Is that so?"

"Absolutely," she said. "These diamonds are the key to a lifetime of success and happiness for me and Mariotto."

Cosmo stared at her for a moment. Could his daughter be serious? From the intensity of her expression, he decided she was.

"It will take a while to fashion the necklace," he said. "How long can you stay?"

"Not long at all," she said. "I must leave sooner than I would like to. Mariotto is waiting for me at home. But don't worry; I don't need the necklace immediately. In fact, I want you to keep it here in a secure place."

"Why is that?"

Margarita sighed. "The fact is, Savino doesn't know about them. If he did, I'm afraid he'd take them from Mariotto. It pains me to say it, but Savino is jealous of his own son."

"What?"

"Oh, Father," Margarita said, "I feel I'm partly to blame. When I married Savino, I was blind to his faults. I didn't realize how great his vanity was and how jealous he could be. He pretends that he's looking out for your grandson's best interest. In fact, I believe he's afraid that Mariotto will one day become more powerful than he will be."

She brushed at her eyes with her handkerchief and her voice broke. "I fear that he might do something to . . . to prevent that from happening."

"You don't mean—"

"Savino is a revengeful man." She began to sob. "He is capable of anything!"

Cosmo put his arm around his daughter and held her close until she regained her composure.

"You have nothing to worry about, dear child," Cosmo said. "I will set them in a necklace and lock it in my vault until you need it."

"Oh, thank you, Father," she said. "Perhaps things will improve with Savino. But until then, could you keep all this a secret—even from Mother? If Savino ever—"

Cosmo put a finger to her lips. "Hush," he said. "Your secret is safe with me."

Margarita smiled. "Thank you so much, Father. And now after I've had a brief rest, I must return to Torre and my dear Mariotto."

At the house of Adamo Balducci, the servants brought Adamo's coffin to his office. It was there that his passion, his ideas, and his devotion to the people of Chiesta had been cultivated. Foresta sat by it in the soft glow of candlelight as the servants said their farewells to him. She lingered there until the last of them had left. She was about to close the coffin when something brushed against her leg.

It was Piero keeping the purple diamond at his neck.

She lifted him to her lap, surprised at how light he seemed. He mewed softly and pulled himself to the rim of Adamo's coffin. He looked back at Foresta and mewed again. He dropped into the coffin and snuggled next to Adamo. His body went limp, and with a final exhale that sounded like a human sigh, he united with Adamo in death.

A realization came to Foresta. She closed the coffin and strode out to the hallway. She summoned her servants and had them to gather all the torches in the house. They lit them and took them outside.

When they'd arranged them in crosses on all sides of the house, she looked up at the night sky. Neither the moon nor the stars could be seen through clouds that overhung the land. That no longer bothered her. The light from the crosses shone brightly. With a smile on her face, she turned to her people and said: "Never let the fire go out!"

Adamo's funeral was held at the same church in Chiesta where the funerals of Lorenzo de Canal and Giovanni Balducci had been held. The church was packed to overflowing. Late-arriving attendees gathered in the village square to mourn the beloved Adamo.

Romano Bollai, Foresta's father, had paid his respects earlier, but was not in attendance. He and Foresta had agreed that Caterina was in great danger from Savino. Before the actual funeral, he'd taken the child back to his home in Florence. He'd urged Foresta to return with him. She rejected.

"I must finish my duty here," she said. "I have inherited this village and the people from Adamo and Giovanni."

Ellie and Nicholas accompanied Foresta to the church. After Savino's visit, Nicholas had taken Giotto back to the stable, and returned to Adamo's on foot. He felt there was no way he could remain at Savino's house, knowing what he now knew. Since there was no formal agreement regarding his living there, he hoped there was no way Savino could make demands on him.

At Savino's manor Mariotto strutted around in his father's office, the sword in his scabbard almost dragging on the floor. "I'll be a king soon," he said. "The king of everybody."

Savino looked up from his desk. "Mariotto, put your sword away. How many times do I have to tell you to get dressed? We leave for Adamo's funeral in ten minutes."

"Do I have to go?" Mariotto said. "I want stay here and play hide and seek with Bone and Serafina."

"You *do* have to go. Someday that village will be yours, and it's important that the people see you at Adamo's funeral."

"Chiesta is mine now," Mariotto said.

"Don't be silly," Savino said. "As long as I'm alive, it will be mine."

"No, it won't. I'll be a king soon, and a king rules everything!"

Savino smiled. "I admire your ambition. Someday years from now you really may be a king."

Mariotto pulled his sword from its scabbard and pointed it at Savino.

"Put it away," Savino said. "We've got to get going."

Mariotto stepped forward and touched the sword to Savino's belt buckle.

Savino brushed it away, his face reddening. "Stop it!" he said. "What's wrong with you, today?"

"I'll be king soon!" Mariotto said. "Mother said our magical diamonds will make me a king!"

Savino's jaw dropped. "Your mother has them?"

Mariotto remembered it was supposed to be a secret. He covered his mouth with his hand.

Savino struck at Mariotto's sword and sent it flying. "She does have them, doesn't she?" His eyes flashed like those of a madman. "Where is she?"

Mariotto stared at him, frozen with fear.

Savino threw the boy to the floor, knelt down, and straddled him. The Dark Shadow rose up behind Savino like a black flame. It transformed into an angry face and glared at Mariotto.

"Where is she?" a strange fearful voice said—a terrifying mingling of Savino's and the Dark Shadow's voices.

Mariotto's face grew pale. "At Grandfather Cosmo's," he said.

Savino grabbed Mariotto's wrist and stood up. "Let's go!" he said, jerking the boy to his feet. "You'll have to go dressed as you are."

He dragged Mariotto outside, where Ristro was waiting with the carriage. He hauled the boy into the passenger section and pushed him to the floor. "Go!" he yelled to Ristro, and yanked the door shut.

Ristro snapped the reins, and the carriage lurched forward.

Savino looked down at Mariotto, who lay whimpering on the floor. "Today," he said, "we'll say goodbye to my treacherous brother." He laughed, and his face became a mask of hatred. "And when your treacherous mother returns, we'll celebrate my glorious future."

The bells rang out from the belfry of the great tower as the horses' hooves clattered through the paved streets of Torre.

Ristro cracked his whip. "Faster!" he shouted.

His cry went unheard, drowned out by a monstrous roar that rose up from the depths of the earth.

The horses bolted. Wild-eyed, they reared up and tried to break free from their traces.

The reins were ripped from Ristro's hands and the carriage swung wide, pitching him from his perch and sending him sprawling onto the street.

Above him the great tower began to tremble. The belfry cracked open, dislodging one of the two giant bells. It fell to the street, crushing the life from Ristro.

The carriage turned aside in a half circle and slammed into the side of the great tower. The doors were jarred open, and Mariotto's little body flew through the air like a toy. It smashed against a stone wall and fell to the ground, never to rise again.

Savino survived the crash. He got to his feet and surveyed the damage around him. Much of the village square was in shambles, but the earth had stopped shaking. One of his hands was scraped in the fall, but otherwise he seemed unharmed.

Now free of the carriage, the horses ran from the square, their reins trailing behind them.

Savino dusted himself off, and decided to return to his estate. He would walk there if he had to, but perhaps he would find the horses and ride one of them home. Obviously the funeral would be called off. And obviously he had found favor with a higher power.

Could the diamonds already be protecting him? Or could it be the Dark Shadow? Before he could consider the question further, the earth began to shake again.

He heard a shattering sound above him and looked up. The granite cross atop the tower had broken free. It descended on him like an angry child stamping on a snail.

Just after Adamo's coffin was lowered into ground at the cemetery behind the Chiesta church, the earthquake struck. Panicked mourners rushed around the side of the church and streamed toward the village square. Foresta was among those who huddled together there, safe from the fragments of debris that fell from the church. Others were not so lucky.

In the frantic exodus, Ellie and Nicholas were pushed over a railing and went tumbling down a steep slope. They gained momentum until they were speeding toward a jagged stone wall at the bottom of the slope. Nicholas heard Ellie scream, and then felt himself caught up in a whirling blackness that carried him down, down, down into a bottomless pit.

Margarita arrived home two days after the earthquake. The bas-relief profile of Savino above the entrance had lost half its face. Beneath it hung a pair of crossed torches, their burned out heads facing downward.

Agnola, her body trembling, greeted Margarita at the door. "Welcome back, my lady," she said.

Margarita's response was predictable. "The earthquake ruined my trip. It was disastrous to get through the village. Savino must make the villagers repair the damages right away. It's disgusting. I hope none of my things were damaged."

Agnola didn't answer.

Margarita frowned. "Well, were they?"

Agnola shook her head, but couldn't speak.

Margarita grabbed Agnola's shoulders and shook her. "What are you hiding from me?"

"My lady . . . your son . . . the earthquake . . ."

Agnola burst into tears.

Margarita let out an anguished shriek. "No!"

She slapped Agnola's face, knocking her to the floor, and dashed down the hallway toward Mariotto's room.

She paused in the doorway, and her legs went weak.

Her child lay on the bed, his hands crossed over his chest, two coins covering his eyes.

She backed away from the room.

"Savino, you evil man," she said to the empty hallway, "I know it was you! You took my son far away from me forever! What did I do to deserve this?"

She raised her hands toward the ceiling and shrieked out in agony, as if begging God to resurrect the only human being she had ever loved.

CHAPTER 15

We Got Lost

Nicholas was terrified that he might have lost Ellie after the earthquake. He found himself in a foggy, dimly lit area. *Where is Ellie!?* He looked around for her in panic.

"I'm here." Ellie came out of the fog.

Nicholas sighed for relief.

The fog was getting thin, the visibility improved. Ellie spread her arms wide. "Look! We're wearing the clothes we had on back in San Francisco."

"So we are definitely not in Ferrara, Cosmo Capello's property, then." Nicholas was disappointed.

"No, but I don't feel bad about this." Ellie felt a wave of warmth came over her body in where she was not familiar with. *Where is this place?* Somehow she was secretly looking forward to their next encounter.

They were in the middle of a shabby garden of somebody's home property. The flowers were dead and the property was poorly maintained. There was no boundary and objects further around the place. There was only an expansion of space.

A roofed path next to the garden led to a house. A stone staircase at the beginning of the path stretched up to a plateau.

"If we don't have a chance to go to Cosmo Capello's, how can we find the two missing diamonds?"

"It's not clear to me right now," Ellie said. "But I feel that, one way or another, we'll eventually find them. There is a reason why we are here, and we should go back home rather than going to Cosmo Capello's."

"There has to be a way out of here," Nicholas said. "I'll take these stairs. You go through the corridor and check out the house."

He rushed up the stairs to a plateau where another house was located. Dark clouds brooded over it. Was a thunderstorm coming? He looked for an exit, but a high fence enclosed the property. A tall wrought-iron gate in the fence was locked. A dead end.

The house looked new but unlived in. Its windows were closed, the curtains drawn. There was no lawn and no decorative plants in the front yard, just an expanse of gray-pebble ground cover.

Ellie followed the corridor to the house. When she was almost there, the door opened and a fit-looking man in twenty-first-century clothes stepped out. He wore khaki slacks and a blue cotton windbreaker. She guessed he was about her father's age.

He seemed surprised to see her. "Hello," he said. "Can I help you?"

"We got lost."

"We?"

Ellie turned and pointed to Nicholas, who was coming down the stairs.

"What brings you two here?"

"We're trying to go home," Ellie said.

"I see," the man said. "My name is Thomas. And you two are . . .?"

"I'm Ellie and this is Nicholas."

"Nice to meet you both. Would you like to join me for breakfast in the garden? I know it looks shabby, but I make delicious pancakes. I don't often get a chance to have guests in my house. After breakfast I can help you find a way out. What do you say?"

Nicholas cleared his throat, a hint to Ellie they needed to keep going.

"We'd like to," Ellie said, "but we have to get home. Nicholas's father is very ill."

"No problem," Thomas said. He turned to Nicholas. "I'm sorry to hear about your father, and I'm sorry you can't stay awhile. So, kids, where are you heading?"

Ellie and Nicholas looked at each other, unsure what to say.

Thomas seemed puzzled. "You don't know?"

"Well," Ellie said, "we're from San Francisco."

Thomas gave her a questioning look.

"In California," she said.

"Ah, yes," Thomas said. "I think I might have visited there before. I was wondering how you both came to be here. Do your parents allow you to travel so far by yourselves?"

"They really don't know we're here," Ellie said. "You see, we're looking for two special diamonds"

Nicholas looked at Ellie in surprise. *What's happening to her? This is not like her.*

Was it wise to be sharing that information with strangers? Who could you trust? Thomas seemed like a decent person. But he'd thought Savino and Margarita were decent people when he first met them.

"Diamonds?" Thomas said. He seemed to be amused, as if the young people were playing a game. "What will you do with them?"

"They're not for us," Ellie said. "We've got to give back those two and another one to the owner. We already have one of them."

"My wife had a necklace with diamonds," Thomas said. He looked wistful. "She was just so beautiful with that necklace on. I used to imagine she came to our planet on a great comet."

"I've never seen a great comet," Ellie said, "but I've seen pictures of them."

"They're very rare," Thomas said. "Every year hundreds of tiny comets pass through our atmosphere, but only a very few are noticed from the earth. A great comet is one we can see with our naked eyes. It's brighter than the stars and very close to the earth. They show up about every decade or so. Halley's Comet is a great comet, but it only shows up every seventy-five years."

Ellie nodded. "That's why people say that if you see a comet, you should make a wish."

Thomas laughed. "I think you're right, Ellie."

Ellie smiled. "Your wife sounds like a person from a fairy tale."

"Yes, I think so too. She was truly mysterious."

"Was? Where is she now?"

Thomas shrugged. "I don't know."

Ellie was shocked. "You don't—"

"It's strange," Thomas said, looking off into the distance. "One morning when I woke up, my parents were standing beside me and they told me she was gone. Since then I haven't heard from her at all. I miss her, but I can't remember much about her. When I try to think of her, I feel my memories seem to be blocked by black walls. It's frustrating." He lowered his head and stared at the ground.

Thomas's odd conversation was making Nicholas uneasy. He decided to change the subject. "Who lives in the house up there?" he pointed at it.

Thomas shrugged. "I don't know. Over the years, I occasionally see the silhouette of a person in one of its windows. The front gate always seems to be locked."

"But why is it connected to your garden?" Nicholas said.

Thomas shook his head. "I just don't know."

"I see," said Nicholas, "it's a dead end up there. Which way can we go to get out of here?"

"I think that way," Thomas pointed at where his house was. "If you'll excuse me for a minute, I want to get a warmer jacket. It's always chilly here." He turned and went back inside the house.

"Do you trust him? You are acting differently with him from you usually are." Nicholas said.

"I feel like I know him. This kind of thing happens sometimes." Ellie smiled.

"I see," said Nicholas and stared at the direction where they would be heading, "I don't see anything in that direction, but the dim space. I hope Thomas is right about that."

Thomas came out of the house wearing a different jacket.

"Let's go this way." Thomas said.

Nicholas started walking fast ahead. Ellie and Thomas started after him. After a few steps, Ellie stopped and knelt down to tie her shoe. She looked up at Thomas and smiled. "I should use double knots."

Thomas laughed. "Maybe you should try Velcro."

When she was finished, she stood up and stuck out her hand. "It's been nice meeting you," she said. "Thank you so much for your help."

"It was nothing," Thomas said. "I hope you both will come visit me again some time."

When they started walking again, Ellie saw that Nicholas was far ahead them and was waving to her in a hurry-up gesture.

"Nicholas!" Ellie shouted.

Something weird was happening to him. His entire body was distorting, like an image on a TV with bad reception.

She ran toward him as fast as she could.

"Ellie, what's happening to you?" Thomas shouted.

She stopped and looked back. Thomas was running toward her, a panicky look on his face. She looked down and gasped. What was happening to Nicholas was now happening to her. One of her legs had already disappeared. There were patches of empty space in her torso. Could her whole body disappear?

She rushed for Nicholas. He reached out his hand to her. As she grabbed it, Thomas caught up with her and touched on her shoulder.

In the blink of an eye, the figures of Nicholas, Ellie, and Thomas were gone.

CHAPTER 16

The Temptation

"Ouch!"

Nicholas landed on the hardwood floor and looked around in disbelief. "Ellie," he said, "we're back!"

The bedside lamp in Nicholas's room was still on. The white candle had gone out, but a wisp of white smoke rose above its blackened wick. The window was open a crack, and the cold breeze that blew through it made the smoke waver.

Ellie shivered. "*That* explains it!" she said. She went over to the window and closed it all the way. "A strong gust must have blown out the candle and ended our journey."

Nicholas was still in a state of shock. He pinched his cheek hard. "Ouch!" he said again. It was definite: He really *was* back in the Dream House.

"What date is it, Ellie?"

She glanced at the alarm clock on the bedside stand. "It's 9:21, December 7th. We weren't even gone for thirty minutes. We still have almost two weeks left to find the missing diamonds. But we're going to need a lot of help."

"Jerry might help us," Nicholas said, "But…do you think he'll believe what we've just been through?"

Ellie shrugged. "I guess that's a chance we'll have to take."

That night Ellie sat in her bed, opened an art book titled *"Art of the Renaissance"*. She wanted to review the painting that came across her mind when Nicholas told her how the Dark Shadow was created in Savino's office back in time. Her feeling about the painting was stronger this time than it was before. Ellie remembered that painting particularly because it was personalized with calligraphy.

The book was originally given to Renee by one of her friends as a gift when Ellie was born. On Ellie's twelfth birthday, Renee gave it to Ellie as her birthday gift.

There it was. The image of the painting occupied the entire page. It showed a man brandishing a sword with one hand. His other hand was raised behind his head. An elegant woman sat in an armchair near him, holding a book in her hands. Across the bottom of the page—written in elegant calligraphy—were the words: *The Sun to the Moon, Faith to Misery, Light to Darkness.*

She read the words aloud to feel the meaning of it.

I still can't understand it…

She was a little frustrated, closed the book, and turned off the bedside lamp.

At 5:30 AM, December 8.

Allison phoned Renee from the hospital.

Daniel's condition had worsened, and he'd been moved back to the ICU. Renee woke Ellie and Nicholas and told them Allison wanted to see them at the hospital.

When Renee, Nicholas, and Ellie got to the hospital, Jerry and Allison were in the waiting room.

"I'm sorry I brought you all out here at this hour," Allison said. "The charge nurse just told us that we couldn't enter Daniel's room—not even Nicholas. She said it was necessary because the doctors here have never seen a case like Daniel's before. They still don't know what's causing it, or whether it's contagious."

Renee shot a glance at Nicholas and turned back to Allison. "That's all right. At least we know he's getting good care."

Jerry put his arm around Nicholas's shoulders. "They'll fix your Dad," he said. "The doctors here are as good you can find anywhere."

"I hope so," Nicholas said.

"Excuse me," Renee said, "I'm going to get my wake-up coffee from the break room. Does anyone need anything?" The rest shook their head implying "no". "I'll be back." She headed off down the hallway.

Jerry took a seat on the waiting room couch and Nicholas sat down next to him. Allison and Ellie took chairs across from the couch.

Nicholas decided to get right to the point. "Jerry," he said, "I need your help."

"Of course," he said. "Anything I can do for you, just ask."

"It's about the two missing diamonds Mr. Tower wants from Dad," Nicholas said.

Jerry sat up straighter. "What about them?"

"I know where they are."

"You *do*?" Jerry said. He gave Nicholas a skeptical look.

Allison leaned forward, but didn't say anything.

"They're in Italy," Nicholas said. "A place called Ferrara. It's northeast from Chiesta. The diamonds are green and pink. In the sixteenth century they belonged to the Adamo Balducci family, but they were stolen from the family and placed with the Cosmo Capello family."

Jerry looked agitated. "Wait a minute," he said. "Just where did you get this information?"

Nicholas was surprised by his tone of voice. He glanced across at Ellie and saw she was frowning. She moved her head slightly from side to side.

Nicholas decided to change it to a believable story. "Dad told me, after he left the messages for everybody at the museum."

"Well, he said other two diamonds were green and pink. But where did he get that detailed information? I mean, how could that be? Even the Italian team and Father Luciano couldn't trace those diamonds."

"I don't know where he got the information," Nicholas said, "but that's what he told me."

Jerry looked at Allison. "Do you believe any of that?"

"Well, Jerry," Allison said, "it's the first clue we've come up with about the missing diamonds. It might be worth looking into."

"Sure," Jerry said, "like looking for a needle in a haystack. If you want to check it out, go ahead. I'll see what I can find out about Vix Tower and the Oxford Corporation." He stood up and looked at his watch. "I've got to get back to the museum. I'll see you all later."

After Jerry left, Allison asked Nicholas if he had any more information about the Capello family.

"Actually, I do," Nicholas said, "but I don't think Jerry would be interested."

Allison smiled. "I'm interested," she said.

Ellie and Nicholas exchanged looks.

"Go ahead, Nicholas," Ellie said, "I think she'll understand."

Just then Renee returned from the break room and said, "The coffee vending machine is out of order."

"Let's go home and have a breakfast." Ellie said.

"You two go ahead," Allison said, "I'm going back to the museum now and I can drop Nicholas off at school. I'm hungry, too. We can grab breakfast on the way."

Renee looked at Nicholas. "Is that okay with you?"

"Sure," he said.

They all headed for the elevator.

On the way to Nicholas's school, Allison and Nicholas stopped at Mel's Diner. Over breakfast Nicholas added to the information he'd mentioned earlier. Without saying that he and Ellie had time-traveled, he gave Allison a summary of the diamond's history.

When he finished, Allison said, "The Capello family might have shown the diamonds at museums in the past. I think it's certainly worth looking into. I've got vacation time coming and I've got a ton of frequent-flyer miles. I wouldn't mind a quick trip to Italy. I'll talk to the Italian Team. We can first check the museums in Ferrara and maybe some municipal records. I'd also like to dig up the Capello family tree and see if any of the descendants are still around."

"You'd go all the way to Italy?"

"I'd go anywhere if I thought it would help your Dad."

She looked at her watch. "Wow, we'd better get moving. I think we can get you to school on time—just barely."

Nicholas smiled. "Okay," he said. His mood had lightened. Although he'd been hurt by Jerry's indifference, he now felt he had a real ally.

Back at his office in the museum, Jerry ran a computer search for the Oxford Company. Its history read like the Great American Success Story. It began in the early 1940s when William Oxford, a San Francisco entrepreneur, founded an insurance company. Over the years he transformed it from an insurance company to a banking institution with offices throughout the Western United States. When he died in 2006, his only son, Hendry Oxford, inherited the business and ran it in partnership with his college classmate Vix Tower. Since 2009, when Hendry died in a car accident, Tower has been the owner and CEO of the company.

The company was currently thriving. Its stock price had stayed relatively stable during the recent recession and was now booming.

Jerry shook his head. Vix Tower was ridiculously fortunate—and ridiculously wealthy. Why did some people always get the breaks? And why were they always so smug? He thought about Vix's expensive works of art and his elegant furnishings. "I love beautiful things," Vix had told him.

Well who doesn't? It's just that most people can't afford them!

He decided to knock off work early and catch a bus before the rush hour started. He logged off his computer, grabbed his coat, and headed for the exit.

Boy, wouldn't it be nice to have chauffeurs like Vix has.

Jerry stepped from the hallway into his studio apartment and turned on the lights. He closed the door behind him and stood for a moment in the combination living room/bedroom and looked around his apartment. A counter separated the kitchenette from the larger room. A cramped bathroom with a shower completed the rental unit. He shook his head. He could measure the level of his life by his dwelling place. A while back he'd considered upgrading to at least a one-bedroom apartment but had given up on the idea. Rents were outrageous in San Francisco. Even for his current tiny apartment.

He got a beer from the refrigerator and sat down on one of the two stools at the kitchenette counter. He sipped at his beer and stared at the calendar on the door of the mini-fridge at the end of the counter.

A week and a half until payday . . .

He finished the beer and took his wallet and his cell phone from his jacket. He took a business card from the wallet, laid it on the counter, and punched in a number on his cell phone.

"Hello, Jerry," Vix Tower said.

Jerry sucked in his breath. "How did you know it was me?"

"Because I've been expecting your call," Tower said. "Are you ready to accept my offer? I don't have much time. Your window of opportunity will soon close, and my conversation with you will be direct. If you have questions, tell me now—but no negotiations."

"What happed to Hendry Oxford's wife?"

"She disappeared from our sight after Hendry's death. We've never been able to find her."

"One more thing. What was her name?"

"Cypress," Tower said. "Cypress Oxford. Any more questions?"

Jerry paused. "No," he said, "I guess not."

"Fine," Tower said. "Now here's *my* question—and it's the only one I have, Jerry: Are you in or out?"

Jerry didn't hesitate. "I'm in."

"Excellent," Tower said, and hung up.

At the San Francisco Museum of Art History, Allison checked her messages and then went to Philip Rose's office. She wanted to ask him for her time-off with a short notice.

Philip was the executive director of the museum and was responsible for its overall functions. Fundraising for the museum was one of his top priorities. He was also responsible for academic leadership for the museum. Daniel's lecture last month was a result of Philip's good relationship with San Francisco City College. Philip realized that a program of high-quality outreach was essential to making the museum a world-class destination and an acclaimed San Francisco treasure.

When Allison came into his office, Philip took off his reading glasses and gave her a big smile. "Congratulations on your Swords and Daggers Exhibit" he said.

"Thank you. It's going fairly well."

She glanced at some objects hanging on the back wall of Philip's office: two crossed medieval swords with the breastplate of a suit of armor below them. A framed copy of *Tournée du Chat Noir*, a poster that celebrated a famous Paris cabaret of the late nineteenth century, had hung there previously. Philip changed the display from time to time according to what exhibits were being shown at the museum. He found it always impressed visitors to his office, many of whom might be donors to the museum.

"You've got a new look here," Allison said.

"It's here thanks to you," Philip said.

The new display was in honor of the museum's Swords and Daggers Exhibit that Allison had organized with Daniel's support. It was currently the main exhibit at the museum. Daniel'd traveled to Italy in researching it. Through his work with people at the Tuscany Museum of Treasures, he'd arranged for the loan of various medieval swords and daggers to his museum.

"They're beauties, aren't they?" Philip said.

Allison stepped closer and studied one of the swords. She pointed to the decorations on the quillon—the crosspiece between the hilt and the blade that protected the hand of the user.

"This looks like the real thing," she said. "Complete to the sun symbols."

Philip smiled. "The senior blacksmith from Fremont Ironworks duplicated them for us. He's actually an authority on medieval weapons. You did a fine job on the exhibit. I was concerned about how you'd handle your first exhibit, but your passion for the subject made it truly profound."

"I think Jerry Goldman did a terrific job of helping me with the catalog," she said.

"I agree," Philip said. "Another valuable team member. I'm sure he'll put together a wonderful catalog for the Great Diamonds exhibit." He rubbed his hands together. "So how are the preparations going for it? I was wondering if the Italian team has come up with any clues about the whereabouts of the two missing magical diamonds."

"Unfortunately they haven't," Allison said. "But the purple diamond will be a big hit by itself. I think the legend of the three magical diamonds will catch the public's imagination." She paused. "Philip, I need to go to Chiesta and search for something Daniel had been working on before he got hospitalized. This will be my personal time-off."

"Well," Philip clasped his hands together on his desk and leaned toward. "Your passion for your work is admirable. Go ahead. Daniel would be proud of you once again. How soon would you like to go?"

"Possibly today."

Nicholas slogged his way through the day and was relieved when Kayla and Hunter dropped him off at the Dream House.

No one was home. He went straight to his room and lay down for a nap. He needed to catch up on the sleep he'd been losing since that terrifying night and the Allison's call this morning.

Shortly after, Renee dropped off Ellie at the Dream House.

Renee had a part-time job as a teacher's assistant at a kindergarten several blocks from the Dream House. She loved working with young children, and the hours were convenient. She could drop Ellie off at her school before her job started and pick her up when the kindergartener class was over. Usually she came home with Ellie, but sometimes she dropped her off at home and continued on to do domestic chores. Today she was heading for the supermarket to get groceries for the week.

Ellie entered the Dream House and went straight to Nicholas's room. She was concerned about hm. The door was shut. She thought he might be taking a nap. She knew that Nicholas couldn't sleep well at night, so he often took a nap after his school days. She didn't bother knocking on his door. Instead she turned around and went up to her room.

As soon as she'd put her backpack in her room, Ellie came down, hauled the laundry basket to the basement, and put a load in the washing machine. Ellie realized how busy her mother was, and always volunteered to help with the family housework.

She came back upstairs to get a snack. As she was taking a milk carton from the refrigerator, she thought she heard footsteps behind her.

"Hi, Nicholas," she said.

He didn't answer, and she turned from the refrigerator.

No one was there.

Had she imagined hearing the footsteps?

She checked the dining room and the living room. No one was there either.

She went back to the kitchen and felt a strange sensation. It was like hearing a voice—but it was more like *sensing* a voice.

She stood by the kitchen counter for a moment, trying to figure out what was happening. Finally she shrugged and poured herself a glass of milk, took an apple from the fruit bowl, and sat down at the kitchen table to enjoy her snack.

"Ellie, it's me," Thomas said. "Something extraordinary happened to me that day. That's why I'm here with you and Nicholas."

He paused. "I'm right next to you. Can't you see me and hear me?"

Ellie bit into her apple and looked at the dishwasher. That was her next chore. The breakfast dishes were in there, and she'd put them away as soon as she finished her snack.

Thomas shook his head. "I'll try to find a way to get through to you."

After Ellie transferred the laundry from the washer to the dryer, she went back to the kitchen and heard the front door open.

"I'm home!"

"Hi, Mom." Ellie came out to the hallway from the kitchen. "Let me help you put away the groceries."

"Thanks, Ellie. Where is Nicholas?"

"He should be in his room. His door was shut when I came home."

"I'll be back in a minute. I just want to check on Nicholas."

Renee tapped on the door to Nicholas's room, but there was no answer. She opened the door a crack and peeked in.

Nicholas was curled up under the comforter, still sleeping. She watched him for a while. Her heart ached as she thought of the burden the boy had to endure. She eased the door shut and headed back to the kitchen.

"Nicholas is still napping," Renee said. "He sure needs the rest. I called the hospital, and they say Daniel's condition hasn't changed. It's stable, but no sign of improvement."

Ellie frowned. "Do you think we should tell Nicholas?"

"Maybe hold off till we have better news," Renee said. "The poor guy doesn't need to be burdened with depressing information that he can't do anything about."

"I guess not," Ellie said.

"By the way," Renee said, "Your father's company is having a Christmas party on the 20th and I'm going with him. We might be coming home late, so my co-worker will watch you both until we return. You've met her before and you liked her."

"The 20th?" Ellie pause.

"Is that all right for you?" Renee looked worried.

"I just thought that Allison is better for Nicholas," Ellie said.

"You are right. I'll ask Allison."

"Thank you, Mom." Ellie put the last of the groceries away and glanced at the clock. Two hours until dinner. That would give her time to finish her homework. Her mom was making chicken à la king. It was a dish Ellie and her father both loved. Of course her mom would have to put his serving in the refrigerator. He could zap it in the microwave when he finally got home from work. Ellie missed having regular dinners with him. Since they'd moved to the new house, he came home from work after she went to bed and was still asleep when she left for school in the morning.

At least she and her mom could now share their evening meal with Nicholas.

CHAPTER 17

A New Owner of
The Magical Diamonds

December 9, San Francisco, California.

Allison left for Italy today. It was like a miracle that she got a seat for the flight at the last minute. Nicholas had grown close to her. The thought that she was trying to track down the diamonds in Italy was some comfort to him. She seemed more than just an older friend. There was something special about their relationship.

Nicholas went to school as usual. As it had been since the events of that night, it was hard for him to concentrate on his schoolwork—or anything else. Hunter, of course, helped distract him, too. Nicholas considered him a good friend, but he still didn't think he should involve him in his problems—for Hunter's sake as well as his own.

Kayla and Hunter dropped off Nicholas at the Dream House after school.

"We should play new video games sometime soon at my house," Hunter said as Nicholas was getting off the car.

"Yeah," Nicholas said, sounding less enthusiastic than he tried to be, so he felt embarrassed.

"Great. See you tomorrow morning!" Hunter said as cheerful as he could sound.

"Bye, Nicholas. Say hello to Renee and Ellie for me." Kayla waved at him from behind the wheel.

"I will." Nicholas waved at them and saw them off.

He entered the Dream House. "I'm home!" he said aloud, but no response.

He went straight to his room and put his backpack on his desk chair. Then he left a note on Ellie's door which read: "I'm going to Noriega Hill. See you." He had already planned to do it in the car on the way home.

The Noriega Hill was 800-foot high and located several blocks away from his house and the Dream House. That hill held his good memories with his father. For as long as he could remember it had been his favorite retreat. When he was a toddler, his father had carried him there. As he grew older he was able to make the climb himself; hesitantly at first, pausing at the top of each flight of stairs to catch his breath. He counted each step—a total of 328 stairs.

On his ninth birthday—matching his father's progress stride for stride—he made the climb without stopping. That had been a milestone for him. Now he was able to rush up the stairs, mixing speed walking with jogging, panting hard and perspiring heavily. Several small pine and eucalyptus trees surround a huge pine tree at the center of the hilltop. On the last leg of the climb he was careful to avoid the small rocks and roots that could trip up a careless climber.

While recalling his memories, Nicholas had already reached Noriega Street. He walked five more blocks from there.

There it was. He was at the foothill. He looked up the staircases first and then started to climb the 328 stairs. It wouldn't be an easy climb because he hadn't done it for a long time.

He finished climbing the stairs and stepped onto the ground at the top of the staircase. Now he had to climb up to the very top of the hill.

After he carefully avoided tripping over the rocks and roots on the hill, at last he reached the very top. Out of breath, his legs shaking, he got his reward: a panoramic view of the city. To him it seemed like a miniature in a glass case in a museum. To his left lay the Pacific Ocean, the Golden Gate Bridge, and the Marin County Highlands on the other side of the bridge. To the right, he could see the brightly multi-colored Victorian-style houses called "Painted Ladies," some dating from the nineteenth century. Further to the east stretched San Francisco's downtown with its high-rise buildings, including the iconic Pyramid Building. And in the background, the surface of San Francisco Bay's blue water was accented by the white sails of the boats gliding across it.

He could look down on both his own house and the Dream House from there. Compared to the Dream House, his house looked like a matchbox. His parents had moved from a small apartment to that small two-bedroom house when his mother was pregnant with Nicholas so they'd have more space to raise him. But two weeks after giving birth, she died. Daniel had thought about either buying a house or moving from their rented house into a bigger apartment in the city. It hadn't happened. Nicholas sensed that his father was putting off leaving their old house because of the memories it held with his wife.

While Nicholas's mind was wandering, a cold gust of wind swept through the ground and brought him back to the present. Nicholas felt Allison was the only hope he had at that moment.

Chiesta, Italy, December 11.

6103 miles away from San Francisco, Allison sat down in the church with Father Luciano and the head curator of the Tuscany Museum of Treasures.

"It's a pleasure to meet you, Father Luciano. Daniel speaks highly of you." Allison said.

"Thank you. I pray for Mr. Blue's speedy recovery every day," said Father Luciano with sympathy. "We've already started searching for the necklace Cosmo Chapello made. I hope this time we are able to solve the mystery of the diamonds." He clasped his hands together and said with a troubled expression on his face, "I'm concerned about Chiesta's future. Surely the village is decaying. I'm hoping that if the three diamonds come together again, their magic will make Chiesta what it was before. We need Chiesta's lively spirit back."

Allison nodded. "I understand, Father."

"Ms. Kenwood, I'd like to work with you during your visit, but as you know I'm leaving for Rome tomorrow for a holy business for a week. If you need any help from us, just call my church."

"Thank you."

"Miss. Kenwood," the head curator said, "We've found a few exhibits which showed green and pink diamonds. Now, combining his new information, our work got narrowed down." With a serious look on his face, he asked, "How much time do you have here with us?"

"I must return to the U.S. before the 20th," Allison said eagerly.

That night, Father Luciano was too anxious to sleep. It was just a matter of time and then the mystery of the diamonds would be revealed. He slipped out of his bed, dressed properly, and went out of the rectory heading to his church.

He lit two candles in the church. Then he stood at the altar and picked up a sacred box which contained holy words written by a former priest. Five centuries ago, the priest received the holy words from Heaven. Since then the words had been shielded in the sacred box. The box was made of wood. It had some cracks in it, the hinges were rusty and loose, and its color was almost black from being handled frequently. Father Luciano held the sacred box with both hands; one on the bottom of the box and the other on the lid. He exhaled, closed his eyes, and then started to pray for Chiesta's future and for Daniel's speedy recovery.

San Francisco, California, December 18.

Allison returned from her trip to Italy that evening and went straight from the airport to Nicholas's house. She'd called ahead from a stopover in Chicago, and Nicholas and Jerry were waiting for her. By the time she got there she was feeling frazzled. Not just from the jet lag. When she tried to pick up her luggage, she was told it was still back at O'Hare Airport in Chicago.

As soon as she walked in, Nicholas said, "Did you find out where the diamonds are?"

"Not exactly," she said, "but I picked up some very useful information. We're really close to finding them."

"Was the story that Daniel told Nicholas accurate?" Jerry said.

"About the Baldlucci and Capello families?"

"Yeah," Jerry said. "Whatever their names were."

"It was pretty much true. There was an exhibit of historical medieval jewelry at a museum in Bologna in the 1940s. One of the pieces was *The Magical Diamonds*. It appeared again in a jewelry exhibit in Milan in the early 1950s. It was a necklace that has the green and pink diamonds set in a gold plate at the center. A pearl is set in the space where the purple one was intended to be set. The piece had been in the Capello family for centuries.

The cut of the three diamonds was the Point Cut originally. The purple diamond is still in that form. The other two—the pink and the green—were re-cut into a later style—the Rose Cut—and polished to make them brighter, probably in the sixteenth century. They look like little rosebuds."

"Huh," Jerry said. "You think they're the ones we want?"

"It makes sense. As a result of the alterations, the two we're looking for are smaller and brighter than the purple diamond. Here, this is what the necklace looks like." She took out a color photograph and a piece of paper from her purse. "I think you can see the necklace better in this color sketch."

She opened the paper on the coffee table. The pink and green diamonds were set side by side on the gold plate. Below them a tear-shaped pearl was set in the purple diamond's place.

"They meant to set the purple diamond where the tear-shaped pearl is. By the mid-1970s the Capello family had long since dismissed the idea of the diamonds being magical. Their lifestyle and financial status had changed as well. The heirs sold the necklace at an antique auction to a jeweler who operated a boutique in London. His son operates it today."

"How do you know that?" Jerry said.

She cracked a smile. "Because he was at an annual diamond auction in Florence, and I met him."

Jerry seemed stunned. "Does he still have the necklace?"

"No," Allison said. "But he had a record of who purchased the piece in the late 1970s. In fact, he himself closed the deal."

"Who bought it?" Nicholas said.

"A California couple: William and Elizabeth Oxford."

"Interesting," Jerry said. "I think he was the founder of the Oxford Company here in San Francisco—the father of Hendry Oxford."

Allison looked surprised. "That's right," she said. "How did you know that?"

Jerry shrugged. "I learned a bit about the history of the Oxford Company when I was checking out Vix Tower."

"What did you come up with?" Allison said.

"Some useful stuff," Jerry said. "Hendry Oxford inherited the company from his father. He took Vix Tower in as his partner because they'd been good friends in college. He knew Vix was really smart and had a good head for business. After Hendry died in a car accident, Tower became sole owner of the company because of a written mutual agreement they had to that effect. Cypress Oxford—Hendry's widow—vanished after his death."

"Vanished?" Allison said.

Jerry shrugged. "Some people claimed she killed herself out of grief. Maybe went off the Golden Gate Bridge. They didn't have any children or other relatives. After five years, Tower petitioned the state to declare her legally dead and have the rest of Hendry's estate passed on to him."

"Don't you have to wait seven years?" Allison said.

"That's common law in a lot of places," Jerry said, "but it's five years in California."

"Then doesn't Tower have the necklace now?"

"I don't know, but I doubt it," Jerry said. "Otherwise he wouldn't be bugging Daniel for it."

He stood up. "Why don't I see what I can find out about Hendry's assets? Maybe he got rid of the necklace a long time ago. And why don't you see what you can find out about Cypress?"

He took his coat from the rack. "You dug up some great leads, Allison," he said. "I think we're on the right track."

After Jerry left, Allison said, "Nicholas, would you mind if I went into your father's room?"

"Why?" Nicholas said.

"I know it sounds a little strange, but I want to get a sense of what was going on with him when his illness struck."

171

"Sure, go ahead," Nicholas said. After spending so much time with Ellie, it didn't sound strange to him at all.

Allison stepped into Daniel's room and closed the door behind her. She went to the middle of the room and turned in a slow circle, trying to absorb the overall atmosphere. She made an unhurried tour of the room, touching the books on the bookshelves, the objects on his desk, the photographs of him standing at historical sites and ancient villages. She found his journal on the floor. She picked it up and held it against her chest, but didn't open it. She went to his closet and stared into it. The tweed jacket he often wore at work hung there. With her eyes closed, she gripped it with both hands, hoping to somehow communicate with him.

She sat down in his chair and tried to concentrate. Something was missing in this whole puzzle, but what it was eluded her. She closed her eyes. *Tell me what you know, Daniel.*

Nicholas sat down on the edge of his bed and examined his Cup of Mirrors. Could it really tell him what he needed to know? He looked into the mirrors. He sighed. He saw only the same nine reflections of his face that he'd seen that morning.

A tap on his door interrupted him. "Come in," he said.

Allison opened the door. "I'm leaving now," she said. "Do you want me to wait till you're ready and walk you over to Ellie's?"

"That's okay," he said. "I'm going over there now, anyway."

"All right, then, I'll be in touch soon." She paused. "Oh, by the way, I wonder if you'll be free tomorrow afternoon. I plan to visit the old Hendry Oxford mansion. It's up for sale, and the current owners are having an open house. I think Hendry and Cypress might have lived there once. Maybe I could find some clues there. I'd like you to come with me, if you feel like it."

"Sure," Nicholas said. "I'd like that too."

"Great," Allison said. "Let's lock up."

CHAPTER 18

Why Me?

December 19, San Francisco, California.

Allison picked up Nicholas at the Dream House in the late Sunday morning and drove straight to the Oxford Mansion. An open-house lawn sign was posted in the front yard.

The property looked out on the Pacific Ocean on one side and the Golden Gate Bridge on the other. The Victorian mansion was larger than the Dream House. Its exterior was meticulously painted in the popular San Francisco style of vibrantly colored "Painted Ladies."

The front door was open. At the center of the foyer, a woman in a gray pants suit stood by a table arranging flowers in a crystal vase. At the sound of Allison and Nicholas's footsteps, she turned and greeted them.

"Welcome," she said. "I'm Jean Blake, the Realtor." She handed a pamphlet to Allison. "I'm expecting some customers with an appointment soon, but until then I can answer any questions you might have about the property."

"Thank you, Jean." Allison said. She tucked the pamphlet into her purse. "I do have one question for you. Do you know if Hendry and Cypress Oxford ever lived here?"

Jean shook her head. "They may have at one time. I only know the name of the current owner, Mr. Tower. He lived here for thirteen years but now lives in downtown San Francisco." She looked past Allison to where a young couple stood in the doorway. "Oh, dear," she said, "I'm afraid that's my twelve o'clock appointment. If you'll excuse me for a moment, I'll be sure to get back with you. But please feel free to explore."

"Thank you," Allison said.

Jean—another pamphlet in hand—headed toward the newly arrived couple.

Allison took Nicholas's arm and led him to the living room.

The French doors in the living room looked out on a courtyard where a water fountain spouted high in the air and splashed down into a rectangular pool. Two tall holly trees on either side of the pool, their dark green leaves accented by bright red berries, stretched skyward.

"We got a lucky break," Allison said. "She will be showing those people around the main floor while we investigate upstairs. If we're going to find any clues, I think we'll find them in the master bedroom."

A staircase in the living room led up to the second-floor. At the top of the stairs a hallway separated into right and left sections. Allison gestured to the left section. "I'll check the rooms on this side," she said. "You take that one. Look for the biggest room with the best view. That'll likely be the master bedroom. Whoever finds it first should let the other one know."

The first room Nicholas checked was bare of furniture. He opened the single closet in the room and checked for a niche where diamonds could be hidden, but found nothing. A survey of the room itself proved equally disappointing. He noticed a number of large pale rectangles on the walls that revealed where paintings or mirrors once hung. That gave him an idea. He pulled his Cup of Mirrors from his pocket and mirrored the room. It reflected nothing but the bare walls. He pocketed it and headed for the next room.

That room was bare of furniture, but it was much larger than the first room and had two walk-in closets and a full bathroom. Like the first room, its walls showed pale reminders of where works of art had once hung. An empty gilded picture frame leaned against the wall in one of the closets. A large bay window looked out across the Golden Gate channel and offered a spectacular view of the Marin Highlands.

Nicholas's heart began to beat faster. This had to be the master bedroom!

He started toward the hallway to tell Allison what he'd found but paused. He pulled the Cup of Mirrors from his pocket again. Just as in the other room, the mirrors reflected nothing but bare walls—until it faced the empty picture frame in the closet.

Nicholas gasped, and a chill shot up his spine.

The frame was still empty, but the octagonal mirror in the center of the Cup of Mirrors reflected the portrait of a woman. She stood on a huge rock next to a tree, her hair flying in the wind. Behind her, ocean waves crashed against the shore. And around her neck she wore the necklace with the pink and the green diamonds in it.

"Are you all right, Nicholas?" Allison said. She stood in the doorway, a concerned look on her face.

Nicholas turned to her. "Allison," he said, "Cypress has the necklace!"

"What?"

"Look!" he said, holding the Cup of Mirrors up to her.

She stared into it for a moment, and then shook her head. "I just see an empty picture frame."

"You don't see her?" Nicholas said. He turned the Cup of Mirrors toward himself. "But Allison, she's there as clear as can be! She's . . . oh, wait!"

He lowered the Cup of Mirrors and looked at Allison. "Now I understand. This mirror was intended just for me—to show me the truth. That's what you told me, right?"

Allison looked confused for a moment, and then she nodded her head. "That's absolutely right, Nicholas," she said. "And I think our work is done here. It's time for you and me to have a long talk."

The Italian restaurant was in North Beach, a few blocks from the Fisherman's Wharf area. "It's not all that fancy," Allison said, "but the food is terrific. I know I should experiment, but I always order the same thing here—spaghetti and meatballs."

"I'll have that too," Nicholas said.

After the waiter took their order, Nicholas took a roll from the basket. "Allison," he said, "you never told me where you bought the Cup of Mirrors. I wonder if there are magic stores or some kind of places where you can get things like that."

Allison smiled. "There might be, Nicholas, but I've never seen one. I actually *didn't* buy the Cup of Mirrors. I found it on a beach during a family picnic when I was eight years old. I saw a star-like beam coming from the sand and ran over to it. The beam was sunlight reflecting from the mirrors. I was excited because I felt it had sent a signal especially to me to find it—my own special treasure.

When I was little, I didn't have a good relationship with my mother. She seemed to criticize everything I did, said, or wanted to do. She favored my younger sister. My father either wasn't aware of how she treated me, or didn't want to challenge her about it. I didn't do anything wrong, but in her eye I was wrong all the times. Why was she against me? I sometimes prayed to the mirrors for an answer.

When I was fourteen, I stood by the window in my bedroom at night and used the Cup of Mirrors to reflect beams from the streetlights onto the walls. I hoped that they'd create a path through the walls to another world where I could leave my life behind forever."

She smiled. "Needless to say, that never happened."

"One day when I came home from school, my mother was in my room looking through my stuff. One of our neighbors told her that he saw a flashlight shining from my window every night. He thought I was sending some kind of signals to someone out on the street and he thought my mother should know about it.

I showed her the Cup of Mirrors and explained what I'd been doing with it and told her the reason that I did it.

She snatched it from me and peered into it. After a while, she turned to me, a look of despair on her face. 'I look like my mother.' she said. 'And I realize that I talk and act like her too. Her life was hard, and she was filled with disappointment and bitterness. I've tried not to become like her. But the harder I try, the more like her I become. Please try to forgive me.'

She began to sob, and for the first time in years we embraced. Finally her tears seemed to wash away her shame and regrets."

"What happened then?" Nicholas said.

Allison smiled. "After that day, our relationship changed for the better."

"What about the story behind the mirrors you told me at the hospital? Did you make that up?"

"No. That day when I found it at the beach, my parents and their friends were all busy talking with each other—grown up stuff. I wandered down to the shore to wash sand off from the mirrors. A very old lady—or she seemed very old to me; remember I was only eight then—came up to me and said, 'You're a lucky girl. Those mirrors can show you the truth: not what you *want* to know but what you *need* to know.' And then she told me the story that I told you that day at the hospital."

"Wow!" Nicholas said. "Thank you for sharing that with me." He hesitated. "Allison, you've always been honest with me. But the thing is, I can't say I've always been honest with you."

"Oh?"

"It's about the story of the diamonds. The whole story. You see, we— Ellie and I—were afraid nobody would believe us."

Allison reached across the table and put her hand on his. "I'm sure you had your reasons. I trust you both, and if there's something you want to keep to yourselves, that's your business."

Nicholas shook his head. "No. I don't want to keep it to myself. I want to tell you, and it's important that I do."

"Okay," Allison said, "I'm all ears."

Nicholas took a deep breath. "First of all," he said, "Ellie and I were *there*."

Allison cocked her head. "Where?"

Nicholas stared her in the eye. "In Tuscany—in the sixteenth century."

Allison nodded slowly. She didn't seem surprised. "Ah," she said. "You time-traveled, is that right?"

Nicholas looked both relieved and embarrassed. "Uh-huh."

Allison smiled. "Are you both gifted?"

"Ellie is, but I'm not," he said. "She took me with her and we went back there and . . ." He paused. "It's a long story, Allison."

"We've got plenty of time," she said.

"Okay," Nicholas said, and for the next half hour he recounted the story of his and Ellie's adventures in Tuscany and of Daniel's encounter with Vix Tower and the Dark Shadow.

When Nicholas was finished, Allison came around to the other side of the table and hugged him tightly. "Thank you, Nicholas," she said. "That explains so much." She smiled. "I know a place where we can get a great dessert and start our search for Cypress."

The uniformed security guard at the Oxford Company recognized Jerry from his previous visit. He led him to the bank of elevators and gestured to a different elevator than the one he'd taken before. The door was open.

"This one goes directly to Mr. Tower's office," the security guard said.

Moments later Jerry stepped out of the elevator and into a large room packed with cubicles. The people in some cubicles had their eyes glued to computers, doing whatever to increase Vix's fortune on a Sunday.

A woman in a business suit was waiting to meet Jerry. "This way please, Mr. Goldman," she said, "Mr. Tower is expecting you." She guided him through the maze of cubicles to a mirrored wall at the back of the room. As they approached it, a door in the wall that he hadn't noticed slid open.

Vix Tower was seated behind a modernistic glass and metal desk, his back to a view of the San Francisco cityscape, a stack of paperwork in front of him.

Vix looked up and smiled. "Come in, Jerry," he said. "And welcome aboard."

When they were both seated on a luxurious leather couch, Vix's expression grew serious. "What have you got for me?" he said.

"Good news," Jerry said. "We found out where the two missing diamonds ended up."

"And...?"

"They're in an antique necklace that belonged to Hendry Oxford's wife."

Vix frowned. "Cypress. I might have known she'd be the key to the mystery."

Jerry didn't know how to respond. Vix hadn't welcomed his news as he'd hoped he would.

"Well," Vix said, "at least it might point us in the right direction. Her parents live somewhere in Big Sur. They're a pair of leftover hippies. They weren't any help when we had declared legally Cypress was dead, but maybe you can get a line on the necklace. If there really is such a thing."

Vix leaned forward. "She pulled a vanishing act. Nobody's seen her in years. She's legally dead, but nobody knows if she's *factually* dead. Or in hiding."

Jerry gave him a questioning look.

"Cypress was very eccentric," Vix said. "But she was also a strong woman, in a way."

"You were Hendry's best friend and business partner and he left all his assets to you," Jerry said. "I guess you must have known *her* well, too."

"You've done your due diligence on me, Jerry, but it's none of your business."

On the way to the meeting, Jerry had tried to figure out how to avoid Vix's dominance of him. It came to him now. He looked Vix in the eye. "You had something to do with Hendry's death, didn't you?"

Vix kept his composure. "It's not your place to ask questions of me."

Jerry wasn't backing down. "You killed Hendry Oxford and his wife to take over their fortune."

Vix thought for a moment, and then shrugged. "Well, Jerry," he said. "I guess you're one of us now. I won't keep secrets from you. Hendry was easy to handle, but not Cypress. She fought against us. She was our obstacle. Because of her it's taken such a long time to accomplish our plan. She's still fighting us. I can feel it."

"What do you mean?"

"She is very powerful. Her force could destroy our plan, even in another dimension of our lives, if we let her."

"I don't understand what you mean. And who else is working with you on this plan, whatever *that* is?"

Vix smiled. "More will be revealed in time, Jerry. And you'll meet my partner eventually—I guarantee it. What you should do now is check out Cypress's parents and—one way or another—bring the three diamonds to me by midnight of December twentieth at the latest. You'll get what you want then and you'll know what you want to know."

"Why does it have to be by the twentieth?"

"Remember what I said about questioning me?"

"Vix, you underestimate me," Jerry said, his voice rising. "You take me too lightly—and your offer is shabby compared with what you want me to do for you."

"So, Jerry," Vix said, the hint of a smile coming to his face, "what are you trying to tell me?"

Jerry spitted out the words. "I need twice as much money as you offered me!"

Vix grinned broadly, and a demonic gleam came to his eyes. "Jerry," he said, "you are just the man we needed!"

After Nicholas and Allison left the restaurant, she drove to a coffee shop. She opened her laptop at an empty table in the corner and handed Nicholas a twenty-dollar bill. "They've got great desserts here," she said. "Get me an espresso and whatever you want for yourself. Meanwhile I'll start checking published notices of the deceased."

The café was crowded. It took ten minutes to get their desserts.

Nicholas came back to the table with Allison's espresso and a cherry-ginger scone and a cup of cocoa for himself. He slid the change to her. "Any luck?" he said.

She shook her head. "Uh-uh. I'm going to see if there are any missing-person websites. There were a bunch of them."

But after ten minutes or so, none of them appeared results for a "Cypress Oxford."

"Nicholas," she said, "what can you think of that a wealthy woman—who's not a celebrity of some kind—might do to get herself listed on the Internet?"

They both wracked their brains until Nicholas said, "Rich people donate money."

"Brilliant!" Allison said.

After a dozen searches Cypress Oxford's name turned up as a past donor to the Community Hospital of the Monterey Peninsula.

"Bravo!" Allison said as she closed her laptop. "I'll take you home now, so you can get a good night's sleep. Tomorrow we're hitting the road."

"Tomorrow everything will be over and my dad will get better, right?" Nicholas said.

Allison looked into his eye, "We'll do our best. If we cannot find the diamonds, there is another way to resolve it." She made a tough smile.

While Nicholas was spending time with Allison, Ellie and Renee went downtown for Christmas shopping. Renee wanted to make this year's holidays something special by lifting up holiday spirit for her family and Nicholas'. She had been looking forward to a Christmas shopping spree with her daughter.

The parking lots near Union Square were all full when they got there, so they parked the car in the financial district and walked four blocks back to Union Square. The streets were filled with holiday shoppers, Christmas carols, Salvation Army representatives, tourists, and creative street performers. Renee and Ellie took each other's hands and moved forward in the crowd.

They shopped at two boutiques and two department stores there. When they came out of the second department store, the sun was starting to set.

"We better go home now," said Renee. "I don't want Nicholas to wait for us. Tomorrow we're going to Fillmore Street to finish off the rest of our gift list."

"Okay, Mom. Let's go home before he gets home." Ellie said.

They threaded through a crowd of people admiring the fancy holiday window displays of the department store and headed to their parking lot.

A block away from the parking lot, Ellie saw a familiar face across the street.

That's Jerry. Ellie stopped walking. With shopping bags in both hands, Renee kept walking without realizing her daughter was not with her.

Jerry had just come out of a high rise building and was standing by the curb in front of it.

Ellie waved at him, but he didn't seem to notice her. He seemed to be waiting for someone. Soon a black limousine slowly pulled over next to him. The driver got out and opened the door for him. One of the shaded windows in the back seats rolled down. Ellie saw a profile of a man in a black suit. His black hair was sleekly combed back. He seemed like an important person by his mannerisms.

Vix Tower, Ellie thought.

Jerry got into the car and then the limousine took off.

"Ellie, I was almost loosing you!" Renee strode to Ellie with a worried look on her face.

"Can we go across the street, Mom? I just want to know what that building is."

Just then the traffic light changed to green and lots of the pedestrians started to move. Ellie pulled Renee's hand. They crossed the street and walked over to the marble steps of the building. Renee read the gilt lettering on the building: *The Oxford Company.* She looked up at the beautiful skyscraper and seemed impressed by it. Ellie, on the other hand, was sensing a heavily unpleasant feeling.

When Allison dropped off Nicholas at the Dream House, she told Renee she was going to Monterey the next day on business related to Daniel's upcoming Great Diamonds exhibit.

"Would it be all right if Nicholas came along with me?"

"Of course," Renee said. "It would be a nice treat for his Christmas vacation. And I think it would take his mind of Daniel's situation."

"Anything new on that?" Allison said.

"Not really," Renee said. "Still pretty much the same."

Allison sighed. "As long as it's not worse, there's always hope."

Renee nodded. "Oh, by the way," she said, "Kevin and I are going to his company's Christmas party tomorrow night. We might be coming home late, and I wonder if you could watch the kids. My co-worker will be available tomorrow, but Ellie and I thought Nicholas would be more comfortable with you."

"The twentieth," Allison said. Her heart was pounding. "Of course," she said and checked her watch. "I've got a few things to wrap up this evening, but I'll come by in the morning around eight, if that's okay."

"Perfect," Renee said. "Ellie and I still have some Christmas shopping to do." She gave a little smile. "And it's best that Nicholas doesn't go with us."

That night, Renee made beef steak tacos, guacamole, and chips for dinner. Nicholas was feeling better emotionally and his appetite was good after what happened with Allison today.

"You two go ahead and eat dinner. I'll put the laundry into the dryer now." Renee said and left the dining room for the basement.

"I saw Jerry downtown today," Ellie said. "I think he was in Vix's building and I don't like it."

"He must have been checking out Vix and the company," said Nicholas as he bit into his taco. "This is delicious!"

"Jerry got into Vix's limousine," said Ellie. "You should not trust him."

Nicholas' mood was lifted up a moment ago, but now it was down again. "Jerry is a long time friend of my father's and mine. He won't betray us. He doesn't believe anything sounds supernatural. That's all there is to it." Nicholas got up from his chair, "I don't know who or what to believe anymore. My father is the only family I have and I'm losing him. Why is this happening to *me!?*"

"Because *we* know you can get through this. That's why." Ellie said.

"Who are *we?*"

"The people who protect you. You might not understand it now."

"No, I don't." Nicholas looked away from her and went out of the dining room.

"Nicholas!"

He didn't stop.

Ellie sighed softly. At that point, all she could do was watch him leave.

Renee came back from the basement, "Where is Nicholas?"

"He's in his room. He is worried about his father."

"Poor boy, let's not pressure him with anything. I'll put his dinner in the refrigerator. He might be hungry later." Renee looked at Ellie's plate, "You haven't touched your dinner yet. Let's eat."

Ellie nodded, picked up one of her tacos. "Mom, do you remember you gave me an art book on my last birthday?"

"Yes, I do."

"You told me that it was a gift for you from one of your friends. Have I met that person before?"

"No, you haven't. She moved to another state after you were born. I knew her only a short period of time; I'd say less than a month. I don't know how she is doing now."

"What was she like?"

Renee looked hesitant. "Why are you suddenly asking these questions?"

"You know the words written in calligraphy on one of the pages? They are beautiful. I just want to know the meaning of the words. I think she's the one who wrote them…That's okay. I'll figure it out myself then." Ellie took the first bite of her taco.

"Check out this guacamole, Ellie." Renee scooped it up with a chip and brought it into her mouth. "Woo, delicious! And I made it!" she said and then laughed.

"Of course, you are a great chef, Mom!" Ellie also laughed but she tried to keep the tone of her voice low. She felt guilty about Nicholas while she was having fun with her mother at dinner.

Sometime after one o'clock that night, Nicholas woke up feeling hungry because he hadn't eaten much at dinner.

He turned on his bedside lamp, put on his slippers, and headed for the kitchen. On his way there, he noticed a flickering light and odd sounds coming from the entertainment room.

Had someone forgotten to turn off the TV?

He stepped into the room and was taken aback at the sight of a man sleeping on the couch. The TV was muted; it was the man's snoring he'd heard.

A liquor bottle and an empty glass were on the side table next to the couch.

He guessed it was Ellie's father. He left the TV on and continued to the kitchen. Nicholas opened the refrigerator and saw his dinner in there, ready to zap in the microwave. He put it into the microwave and pushed the start button. The machine sounded loud in the middle of a quiet night. He poured himself a glass of water. As he rinsed out the glass, a voice said, "Hi. You must be Nicholas."

Startled, Nicholas spun around and saw the man standing in the doorway.

"I'm Kevin," the man said. "Ellie's father."

"Hello," Nicholas said. "I'm sorry if I woke you."

"That's okay," Kevin said, his words a little slurred. "Going upstairs to bed, anyway. I need some water too."

On his way to the sink, he brushed past Nicholas. He reeked of alcohol. He poured himself a glass of water, downed it in one swallow, and set the glass on the sink board. "Well, Nicholas," he said, "welcome to my castle." He attempted a smile. "Although it's not even mine."

He headed for the hallway, and Nicholas heard him stumble a few times as he made his way up the stairs.

The Dream House had problems Nicholas hadn't been aware of.

CHAPTER 19

The Portrait of a Woman

December 20, San Francisco, California.

The schools were off for the winter break starting from today. Ellie was still in her bathrobe and pajamas when Allison came by for Nicholas. She followed them out to the sidewalk.

Nicholas was quiet the whole time. The conversation at the dinner table from last night had been affecting him. Ellie thought it's understandable and hoped that Nicholas could accept the truth.

"Have a good trip!" Ellie waved goodbye as the car pulled away. She turned back to the Dream House, her teeth chattering from the cold. She hugged herself to keep warm and hurried up the steps. There was something she'd planned the night before for Nicholas.

Renee met her at the door. "Breakfast is on the table," she said. "Then you better get ready for shopping."

"Okay, Mom, but can we be done by three? I forgot to tell you, I signed up for an educational tour for kids for this afternoon at Daniel's museum."

"Sure, but now finish your breakfast and get dressed. We've got the last shopping to do."

Allison and Nicholas drove for a little more than two hours and hit Monterey about 10:15 AM. The hospital turnoff was a mile or so past the turnoff to downtown Monterey. The hospital itself was just a few hundred yards from the highway. Tall Monterey pines lined the entranceway. She pulled into it and continued on to the underground parking lot. "We made pretty good time, Nicholas," she said. "You can play the radio, if you want. It shouldn't be long." She got out of the car and went into the hospital alone.

She took the elevator to the main lobby. She checked the hospital directory and followed the arrows to the Hospital Foundation Development office.

According to her nametag, the gray-haired woman at the counter was Lorene. She greeted Allison with a smile. "Can I help you?"

"I hope so, Lorene," Allison said. "I'd like to make a contribution to the hospital."

"Well, thank you. We truly appreciate the help we get from our donors." Loren took two forms from a desk drawer and passed them to Allison. "The top one is for information about you. The other is to indicate individuals or organizations you might wish to honor or memorialize."

"Oh," Allison said, "I *did* have that in mind. My friend Cypress Oxford has always praised the work you do here."

Lorene's face lit up. "Her generous endowment funded our pediatric wing."

"She mentioned that," Allison said. "You know her, I take it."

"By name only. I've only been volunteering here for a few years."

Allison tried to cover up her disappointment.

"But," Lorene added, "Whenever Dylan and Gabrielle come up from Big Sur, they always drop by this office to say hello."

Allison gave her a questioning look.

Lorene's brow furrowed. "The Harts," she said. "Cypress's parents."

"Of course." Allison said. "Dylan and Gabrielle." She smiled. "I always call them Mr. and Mrs. Hart."

"Lovely people," Lorene said.

"They certainly are," Allison said. She looked at her watch. "Oh my goodness! I'm already late for a dental appointment in Carmel." She folded the forms, stuck them in her purse, and headed for the door. "I'll fill these out later and send them in with my check. Thanks for your time, Lorene. Have to run."

Allison looked for the phone number and address of a D. Hart in Big Sur as soon as she came out of the office.

"I think we're in business," she said to Nicholas in the car, and set up the navigator for the address.

"Did you find her?" Nicholas said.

"No, but I've got her parents' number." She made a call.

On the third ring, a man picked up.

"Gabby?" he said.

"No, I'm Allison Kenwood, and I'm calling for Mr. Hart."

"That's me," the man said. "Sorry. My wife was supposed to be back from shopping by now. I figured the car broke down or something. What can I do for you?"

"I'm from the San Francisco Museum of Art History. I'm doing research for an upcoming exhibit and I'd like to talk with you about a necklace your daughter once had."

"Oh, that," he said. "Where are you?"

"I'm near the Community Hospital in Monterey. I'm on my way to Big Sur."

"You're not far from here. I'm busy out back right now, but if you want to chat, you should be here in forty, fifty minutes. An hour maybe, depending on the traffic."

"That would be great," Allison said.

"If I'm still out back, just yell," he said. "I may be old, but I'm not deaf—at least not yet. Here's how to get here."

Allison gave Nicholas a thumbs-up and jotted down the information on the back of the road map.

They followed the scenic highway for a half hour or so. On their right, the Pacific Ocean waves surged against the rocky shoreline; the Santa Lucia Mountains rose up on their left.

Nicholas glanced at the dashboard clock. "We're almost there," he said.

"I was worried that we'd hit heavy traffic," Allison said, "So far, it's been—"

"Allison, STOP!" Nicholas shouted.

She slammed on the brake, and skidded to a stop.

"What is it?" she said.

"Back up," Nicholas said. "I just saw the place where the woman in the painting at the Oxford Mansion was standing."

Allison looked over her shoulder, put the car in reverse, and backed up about a hundred yards.

"That's it," Nicholas said.

She parked on the side of the road and they both stepped out.

On the edge of a cliff that overlooks the ocean, a tree grew next to a large rock. Distorted by the prevailing winds off the Pacific, its trunk protruded seaward, but its branches stretched toward the mountains.

Nicholas pointed. "The woman was on that huge rock and that big tree was behind her. That's what the Cup of Mirrors showed me in the empty picture frame."

"Do you know what kind of tree that is?" Allison said.

"Yes," he said. They both smiled and said together: "A cypress tree!"

The Harts lived in an old, but well-maintained, two-story wooden house. It was located about a quarter of a mile up a road that branched off Highway 1. A hand-painted sign on the front gate read: "Home Is Where the Harts Are!"

Allison parked on the side of the road and she and Nicholas got out. They followed a flagstone path up to the porch and rang the bell.

They waited a minute or so, but there was no answer.

"Should I yell?" Nicholas said.

There was no need to. The door swung open and a tall and thin man—his white hair tied back in a ponytail—stepped onto the porch. He seemed surprised to see Nicholas. "You must be Allison Kenwood," he said to her. He looked down at Nicholas and smiled. "But who is this young whippersnapper?"

Nicholas returned the smile. "I'm Nicholas Blue, sir," he said.

"I'm Dylan Hart. Call me Dylan." He stepped to the side. "Come on in."

A short hallway led to the living room. Nicholas stopped there to examine a framed poster that hung on the wall.

It showed a man brandishing a sword with one hand. His other hand was raised behind his head. An elegant woman sat in an armchair near him, holding a book in her hands. The clothes they wore and the interior of the background were familiar to Nicholas. He was sure that the time frame was the same as in Adamo and Savino's time. The word "Renaissance" was printed across the top of the poster.

"Do you like it?" Dylan said. "It's my favorite poster."

"I do," Nicholas said. He pointed to the top of the poster and said, "Renaissance."

Dylan nodded. "A French word meaning 'rebirth.' It refers to the cultural movement that occurred between the fourteenth and seventeenth centuries. It began in Florence, Italy, and affected intellectual life all over Europe."

"Remember the swords and daggers exhibit at the museum?" Allison said. "They were made in that period."

"It's beautiful," Nicholas said.

"Cypress gave it to us," Dylan said. "She saw the painting in one of her art books and had a poster made of it. She did the calligraphy."

"Superb work," Allison said.

They all moved into the living room and an elderly woman came through the doorway at the other end. Her salt and pepper hair draped on the back. She grinned at them.

"This is my wife, Gabrielle," Dylan said. "Seems her car didn't break down after all." He gestured toward a half circle of chairs in front of a stone fireplace and said, "Grab a seat, and let's see what we can do for you."

"First of all," Allison said, "I want to thank you for taking the time to see us."

"Our pleasure," Dylan said.

"As you may have read, the San Francisco Museum of Art History is having an exhibit of historical diamonds. We've been told that your daughter owns a historical piece—a necklace—with a unique story behind it. I've been trying to locate her to ask her some questions about it because we have a limited amount of time to put all the information together before the exhibit opens."

"Well, we don't know where she is now," Dylan said. "Last time we saw her was about fourteen years ago."

"We haven't seen her not hair of her since then," Gabrielle said.

Allison looked dumfounded. "Have you tried to locate her?"

"Not necessary," Dylan said. "When she wants to, she'll let us know where she is."

"Why are you so sure of that?" Allison said.

He grinned. "Because that was what she told us."

"Could I see a photograph of Cypress?"

"We don't have any photographs of her," he said.

"But she's your child."

"She told us not to keep any pictures of her last time we saw her. And we threw the last several pictures of her. She didn't like picture taken since she was young." Gabrielle said. Her eyes looked straight into Allison's.

"Miss," Dylan said, "we keep her image in our minds and hearts. She's special. She's different from most people, because she's been gifted in so many ways. She can feel and sense your concealed feelings, see invisible events or objects, and hear voices of the spirits. All of those ordinary human beings are not able to do." He paused and then said, "Do you two believe in miracles?"

Nicholas and Allison exchanged looks. "I think so," Allison said.

"But you're not sure," Dylan said. "You think one might happen, but you don't have faith in it. You have seen a miracle, yet you still think it was just a coincidence. Is that it?"

Gabrielle took Dylan's hand in hers. "We think something magnificent will happen soon. Cypress is leading us to open the door to it."

Both Allison and Nicholas seemed at a loss for words.

"Signs and wonders," Dylan said. "Cypress always has said, 'there is a reason for everything that happens.' Anyways, the last time we saw our daughter she predicted someone from a museum might come for her necklace someday. When they did, she told us, we should give it to them." He spread his hands wide. "Well, today three people *did* come by."

Allison and Nicholas looked thunderstruck.

"*Three* people?" Allison said.

"Uh-huh," Dylan said. "You two and your colleague from the museum, Jerry something."

"*Jerry Goldman?*"

"That's the name. He came by early this morning and picked it up."

Dylan noticed the look on Allison's face.

"You didn't know?" He chuckled. "I think you museum people just might have a communication problem."

Half a mile from the Hart's house, Allison pulled to the side of the road, and called Jerry. The phone rang a half-dozen time and went to voicemail. Allison frowned. At the beep, she left a message. "Jerry, I've just come out of the Hart's place in Big Sur. I wish you'd told me you were going there. As soon as you get the two diamonds appraised, please give me a call and let me know the results. As you know, today is the 20th. It's really important." She turned to Nicholas and smiled. "If those two diamonds are real, we're in business."

Nicholas nodded but didn't say anything.

On the way back to San Francisco, Allison said, "You seem awfully quiet, Nicholas. Are you worried about what Jerry did?"

"What?" he said. "Oh, I just thought…it's not like him." He had been thinking about what Ellie said about Jerry last night at the dinner.

"I think so, too. There must be a reason for it," said Allison.

Nicholas wanted not to think about Jerry anymore, "I was also thinking about Mr. and Mrs. Hart. They seemed really nice and everything, but a little bit . . . I don't know—"

"Crazy?" Allison said.

Nicholas looked embarrassed. "No, not that so much. But the way they talked about Cypress . . . and they didn't have any photographs of her. It was just so strange."

"I know what you mean. They were odd, but nice. I think maybe they talked about Cypress that way to keep her memory alive. She's still alive in their hearts, and they want to believe she's still alive in reality."

"Do you think she *is* still alive?" Nicholas said.

"I don't know what to believe about that, but I'm glad that Dylan and Gabrielle do."

Jerry came back to San Francisco from Big Sur and parked his rental car in his museum parking lot. He got out of the car with his brief case and headed to the office of the director of the museum.

Philip Rose intently examined the documents Jerry had given. Philip set them down on the desk and smiled. "Terrific job, Jerry," he said. "What a great start to my week!" He patted the jewelry box on his desk. "It's clear that the necklace belongs to Mr. Tower. I'll have our lawyers draw up a waiver of rights for the purple diamond today and we can fax it to him today or tomorrow. In the meantime, you can deliver the necklace to Mr. Tower in person. You've earned it." Philip said.

"Mr. Tower said he'd return the necklace as soon as he had a gemologist examine it."

"Understandable, Jerry. He'll need a certification that they're genuine before he officially delivers them to us. We'll also have them certified before the exhibit and again when we return them to him after it closes. Along with the purple diamond, of course."

Jerry nodded.

"Mr. Tower's loan is exceptionally generous, and his offer to permanently donate artwork to the museum in the future is beyond belief," Philip stood up and shook Jerry's hand, "your finding Mr. Tower won't be forgotten by our board of directors."

Jerry smiled modestly.

"Now you'd better be on your way," Philip said. "I imagine Mr. Tower is as eager to see his treasure as we are to feature it in our exhibit."

"Yes, sir," Jerry said. He put the jewelry case in his briefcase and headed for the door.

Vix Tower examined the diamonds in the necklace with his naked eyes. He shrugged and carried the necklace over to the plate glass window in his office. He pressed the necklace against the glass at head level and pulled it down. Two scratches—like a set of ski tracks—appeared in the glass.

"They're the real deal," Jerry said, beaming.

Vix laid the necklace on his desk and shrugged again. "Maybe."

A voice on the intercom said, "Mr. Malibu is here."

"Send him in," Vix said.

A moment later the door slid open, and a man with salt-and-pepper hair stepped through it. He was pulling a wheeled aluminum case behind him.

"Good afternoon, Mr. Malibu," Vix said. He pointed to the necklace. "Here it is."

Malibu ignored Jerry and nodded to Vix. "Good afternoon," he said. He picked up the necklace and took it over to the window. He noticed the scratch marks on the pane and chuckled. He held the necklace up to the sunlight and turned it this way and that. "Looks like a genuine sixteenth-century piece," he said. "And the diamonds are eye flawless."

Vix said nothing.

Jerry cleared his throat.

Malibu took some equipment from his case and laid it out on Vix's desk. He sat down at the desk and began to examine the diamonds. Silence remained. After fifteen minutes or so, he turned to Vix and held up the necklace. "Natural diamonds usually have minor imperfections," he said. "But with synthetic diamonds, you don't find obvious flaws—such as inclusions of foreign material. These diamonds are close to flawless—except for an orange fluorescence, which is absent in real diamonds. That's a sure indication that they're synthetic diamonds, which, by the way, will scratch glass."

He laid the necklace on the table and began returning the tools of his trade to the aluminum case.

"Thank you, Mr. Malibu," Vix said. "Your check is ready at the front desk."

When the door slid closed behind Malibu, Vix glared at Jerry. "Idiot! Cypress made a total fool of you! Get the diamonds back from her, and don't make the same mistake again!"

Jerry's face was pale and damp with sweat.

"This isn't a game, Jerry. There are real consequences for failure in this matter. And Jerry, those consequences are horrific beyond your darkest nightmares."

The light in the room grew dim, and a dark shadow began to grow behind Vix's back. Jerry couldn't tell if what he saw was real or just a hideous illusion.

The Dark Shadow began to speak, and Jerry began to tremble. Jerry realized that the grotesque figure was all too real.

"Her force is coming closer," the Dark Shadow said. "She is no longer alone. She has found a woman to be her agent in this earthly world. Through her, Cypress could destroy us. It must not happen!"

The shadow subsided, and Vix hit the button on the intercom.

"Yes, sir," a voice said.

"Have a car ready for me. I'm on the way down."

Vix looked at Jerry. "I imagine you want to make things right—is that the case?"

"Yes sir," Jerry said.

"I thought so," Vix said. "On our way to the museum you can call your boss and tell him you and Mr. Tower would like to view the purple diamond today. Got it?"

Jerry nodded.

Vix smiled. "Let's go."

Renee pulled up in front of the San Francisco Museum of Art History. Ellie had told her mother she was going to take part in an educational museum tour for children. Although she felt bad about lying to her mother, she didn't want Renee to worry her. The truth was she wanted to check up on Jerry.

"Remember, I'm going to a Christmas party at your Dad's company tonight," Renee said.

"So I won't be home when you get back. I won't be later than ten o'clock. Allison and Nicholas will be there."

"I know, Mom. But we'll all be at Nicholas's house."

That was true. Ellie was going to help Nicholas save Daniel.

Renee kissed Ellie's cheek. "Okay, dear, enjoy the tour."

"Danger, Ellie! Don't go in there!"
Thomas realized she didn't hear him. He still couldn't break through.
With his heart unbearably heavy, he faded away.

CHAPTER 20

The Real Agent of Our Doom

llie blended into the crowd that was entering the museum. Once inside, she separated from the other visitors and ducked into an alcove. Gilt lettering on the door across from her indicated it was the conference room. Nicholas had given her a tour of the museum, including the administration offices. She remembered the offices were in the same corridor as the conference room, but she couldn't remember which one was Jerry's.

That problem was solved when Jerry and a man she recognized stepped from the office right next to the conference room. Jerry escorted the man from his office into the conference room.

The corridor was empty. As soon as Jerry closed the conference room door behind him, Ellie scooted across the corridor and tried his office door. It was unlocked. Ellie looked up at the gilt lettering on the door. It said: Daniel Blue. The office was no longer Daniel's but Jerry's now. She glanced up and down the corridor. Still no one in sight. She stepped into his office and closed the door.

The conference room was delightfully warm and full of light. All the blinds were open and sunlight poured into the room.

Vix sat facing the windows and his shadow grew on the wall behind him.

Philip Rose extended his hand. "It's an honor to finally meet you, Mr. Tower."

"The pleasure's all mine. And please call me Vix."

"Certainly . . . Vix," Philip said, "I'm pleased to say the purple diamond is ready for viewing." He opened a small jewelry box and slid it across the conference table to Vix. "When it's set in the necklace with the other two diamonds, the effect should truly be stunning."

"Yes," Vix said. "It should be indeed." His shadow grew bigger and pounded like a beating heart.

Philip took off his glasses and rubbed his eyes. "By the way," he said, "when do you think the inspection of the necklace will be completed?"

Vix stared into Philip's eyes and smiled. "Oh, I think by tomorrow."

As he said those words, the Dark Shadow rose up behind him and covered the entire room like a cocoon.

Philip became frozen in space, as immobile as a marble statue. Time itself seemed to be frozen.

"Hey, what's going on?" Jerry said.

Vix gave him a condescending look. He reached into his pocket and pulled out a gem. It was a synthetic duplicate of the purple diamond. He took the original from the jewelry box and replaced it with the replica. He stuck the original into his pocket and grinned at Jerry. "One down," he said. "And I don't think I need to remind you that I'll need the other two by midnight."

After Vix said it, the Dark Shadow faded away.

Philip looked a little confused. He shook his head and put his glasses back on.

"Tomorrow, really?" he said. "That's wonderful. You certainly don't like to waste time, do you?"

Vix stood up. "I don't," he said. "And I'm sorry to say, I've got to get back to my office."

"Well, I hope you can wrap it up in time to watch the eclipse tonight," Philip said. "It's going to be spectacular."

"I forgot all about that," Vix said. "If I have time, I'll give it a look."

Ellie had pressed her head to the wall between Daniel's office and the conference room, hoping to hear what was going on in there. But the wall was too thick. Well, she could give the room a quick search and see if that would turn anything up. It was worth a try.

Jerry walked Vix out to his limousine. When they got to it, he said, "Vix, I've got a question for you."

Vix looked amused. "Questions, questions, Jerry. You're a very curious young man." He slid into the back seat of the limousine and started to close the door.

Jerry grabbed the handle and held the door open. "What went on back in the conference room was really strange. I mean, how come Philip didn't know the Dark Shadow was there, but you and I did?"

Vix grinned. "That's a fair question, Jerry. The answer is: You're now a part of the Dark Shadow—and he's now a part of you."

Vix yanked the door shut, and the limousine pulled into traffic.

Ellie checked the drawers in Jerry's desk without finding anything useful. She thought of trying the file cabinets but decide to make a quick check of his closet instead. Half a dozen empty metal coat hangers were suspended over a metal rod that ran from one side of the closet to the other. A beat up raincoat was crumpled on the floor. There was a shelf with several boxes on it at the back of the closet. She was about to check them out when she heard footsteps outside the office door. She pulled the closet door shut and waited, her heart pounding.

The office door opened and closed with a bang. She heard a click, and a line of light showed under the door. She prayed that Jerry wouldn't want his raincoat. As she concentrated on controlling her breathing, the light under the closet began to darken. When it was almost solid black she heard a deep, hollow voice.

"Jerry," it said, "forget the woman!"

"What are you doing here?" Jerry said. "What do you want with me?"

"No questions!" the voice said. "Listen and obey! The woman is no longer Cypress's earthly agent. The real agent of our doom is now a young girl. Find her! Deal with her!"

The line under the door grew light again.

Ellie felt totally bewildered. What had all that been about? As she tried to collect her thoughts, she heard a jangling sound. It was faint at first, but grew louder by the second. For some reason the coat hangers were moving. She reached back to hold them steady as a loud rumbling sound began to fill the air. The floor moved under her feet in a rolling motion and the closet began to rock from side to side.

She grabbed the metal rod for support, but it pulled away from the closet wall and she felt herself falling to the floor.

"No!" Thomas shouted.

He reached out to catch her, but his hands slipped though her body.

Ellie screamed as she landed face down on the floor.

That was an earth quake. Jerry was a Californian, and he'd experienced a number of earthquakes. He'd even been in Oakland during the devastating Loma Prieta Earthquake of 1989. This one was no way near that strong, but it got his attention.

Jerry crawled out from under his desk and looked toward the closet. Had he heard a woman's cry from there or was it just his imagination?

"Who's in there?" he shouted.

There was no response.

He looked around for anything he could use as a weapon. He picked up a folding chair that had been knocked over during the quake and moved toward the closet.

With one hand, he held the chair in front of him like a lion tamer. With the other he yanked the closet door open.

The body on the floor wasn't a woman.

Jerry thought of the Dark Shadow's warning. He smiled at the sight of Ellie—a young girl.

Allison and Nicholas were on Highway 101 about fifteen minutes south of San Francisco when her phone rang. "Maybe this is Jerry," she said. She took the call on the car speakerphone.

It wasn't Jerry, but a representative from the San Francisco Airport. They'd finally located her luggage. It was only one suitcase, but it held all her notes and documents from her trip to Italy.

A few minutes later she turned off the highway and headed into the airport.

By 4:25 PM they were out of the airport parking lot and about to hit the highway.

At 4:30 PM the earthquake struck, and the traffic to San Francisco became a nightmare.

At 7:00 PM Allison finally dropped Nicholas off at the Dream House. The porch and the foyer lights were on. "I'm heading museum now," she said. "Maybe Jerry left a message for me on my desk. I'll be in touch soon."

Nicholas entered the Dream House. "Ellie!" he called. There was no response.

He knew Renee would be at Kevin's company helping him set up the Christmas party, but Ellie was supposed to be home.

He turned on the lights in the living room and the kitchen. No sign of her. He checked the entire house. No one was home. In his own room there was a large envelope on his bed. A Post-It note on it said: "Nicholas—this might be useful. See you soon—Ellie."

Could she have gone to the party with her parents? No, she wouldn't do that.

He left a note for Ellie on the door to her room, turned off all the lights except for the porch and foyer lights, and headed for his own house with the envelope.

The last night of autumn—the moon was full, the air crisp and clear.

When Nicholas got to his house, he went to the kitchen and made himself a cup of hot cocoa. He brought it to the living room, sat down on the couch, and opened Ellie's envelope. In it was a book titled *Art in the Renaissance.*

He moved aside several magazines on the coffee table and set the book down on the cleared space. He opened it to a bookmarked page. The image from the poster at the Hart's house occupied the entire page. On the bottom of the page, there were words written in calligraphy: The Sun to the Moon, Faith to Misery, Light to Darkness.

Did Ellie leave the book for me because it referred to Vix Tower and the Dark Shadow? Was this once Cypress's book? And was the handwritten message on the bottom hers? If so, how did Ellie get this book?

He tried to figure how it all fit together.

"The Sun to the Moon, Faith to Misery, Light to Darkness."

Did the Darkness refer to the Dark Shadow? Back in Torre—500 years ago—Savino had summoned the Dark Shadow when he cursed and threw his sword at the armory wall. In the twenty-first century, had Vix Tower also summoned the Dark Shadow to help him get the diamonds? What would happen if Allison, Ellie, and I found the diamonds and gave them to Tower? Would it save my father? Would Tower and the Dark Shadow go away? Or could it mean that Tower and the Dark Shadow would prevail forever? The questions tossed and turned in his mind. Fatigue finally hit him, and he stretched out on the couch and closed his eyes. He took a deep breath, felt as if his body were sinking into the couch...

No, no time for napping! He sat up on the couch and opened his eyes. He blinked and looked around in confusion. He was no longer in his house but back in Thomas's garden.

Have I time-traveled again?

Everything looked the same as before. A figure appeared in the distance and moved toward him.

"Allison! How did you get here? Did you find the diamonds?"

She didn't answer, but reached out her hand to him, offering him something. He opened his hand and she dropped a gold key into his palm. It looked like the key on Ellie's pendant.

She pointed to the house on the plateau next to Thomas's house. The dark clouds still hovered above it.

Key in hand, Nicholas climbed the stairs and went to the gate. It was still locked. He stuck the key in the rusty keyhole and turned it. The gate swung open, and he stepped into the yard. A thin beam of sunlight broke through the clouds. To his amazement, plants sprouted up from the soil, some bursting into flowers. Others became bushes and trees that bore green leaves, nuts, and fruit.

He walked up the path to the house and tried the lock with his gold key. The door opened, and he entered the foyer. A larger beam of sunlight shone through the sunroof. He looked up and saw the dark clouds gradually breaking away.

He followed a long hallway to a room at the rear of the house. The glass door to the room was engraved with flowers and vines. A silhouette moved inside the room.

He tried the door, but it was locked. As he put the key in the keyhole, the ringing of a telephone startled him. He pulled back from the door and dropped the key. He scooped it up, but lost his concentration by the ringing, he had trouble fitting it into the keyhole.

It was growing hotter, and he was perspiring so much that the key almost slipped from his fingers. He finally forced it into the keyhole and tried to turn it. The lock resisted his efforts, but finally gave way. He pushed the door open as the ringing grew so loud...

CHAPTER 21

Complete the Puzzle

Nicholas sat bolt upright and realized he was back in his own house and the kitchen phone was ringing.

He rushed to the phone, picked up the handset, and shouted, "Hello!"

A woman's voice said, "Nicholas?"

"Yeah, it's me, Allison," he said groggily.

"Are you okay?"

He looked up at the kitchen clock. He'd slept for almost three hours!

"I'm fine," he said to Allison. "I suddenly fell asleep on the couch, and the phone woke me."

"Is Ellie there?" Allison said. "I tried to call her, but could only get the answering machine."

"No, she isn't with me."

"Renee and Kevin are at his company's Christmas party. Renee asked me to look after Ellie and you tonight until they come back. Could you look and see if she's home now?"

"Just a second," he went to the front window and opened the curtains. The only lights on at the Dream House were the porch light and the foyer light. He went back to the kitchen. "Nobody's there," he said. "And I don't think Ellie went to the party with them. I know she wants to help me tonight."

"This is strange," Allison said. "Someone put her key pendant in my inbox at work."

"Why?"

"I don't know, Nicholas. It doesn't make sense at all,"

"How can we ever get the diamonds now?" Nicholas said, his voice cracking.

"We'll try to come up with something," Allison said. "Maybe we can negotiate with Vix to give us more time to find the diamonds. I'll try to find Jerry and talk to him. I don't know what he's up to, but it's the only tactic we have left. Stay where you are. I'm coming right over."

Within twenty minutes, Alison arrived at Nicholas's house and showed him the key pendant. "It looks like the one Ellie always wears," she said, "And I found this." She turned it over and showed him the etching on the back: "Pierce with a light of faith."

"That's incredible." Nicholas said. "Here, look at this." He opened *Art in the Renaissance* to the book-marked page.

Allison looked at the bottom of the page and read the handwritten words aloud: "The Sun to the Moon, Faith to Misery, Light to Darkness."

"Ellie left this book for me today," Nicholas said. "I think it's the book Mr. Hart mentioned. And I think the handwriting is like Cypress's calligraphy. It's all got to tie together somehow."

Allison thought for a moment. "There *could* be a connection."

Nicholas nodded. "Remember the message Dad left for you, Mr. Rose, and Jerry the day he got hospitalized. He said he suspected that something might happen to the three diamonds on December twentieth. At the time, I thought he was out of his mind."

"Uh-huh," Allison said.

"So did Vix. He said December twentieth would be 'a night of miracles.' That's what Lorenzo told Adamo and Foresta. The three diamonds became one red diamond."

"My God!" Allison said. "There actually *will* be a miracle tonight—a total lunar eclipse!"

"You're right," Nicholas said. "The sun, the earth, and the moon will align and become as one. And if Vix and the Dark Shadow have the three diamonds, they will become one. The magical power will be theirs!"

"But they don't have them," Allison said. "They still want us to get the other two for them."

Nicholas nodded and said, "Something is telling me that what we actually have to do is not so much finding the diamonds as finding a way to destroy the Dark Shadow. Otherwise, my father will never be free from it. I told you I saw the Dark Shadow swallow Dad. That's why he's in the hospital now. I don't think he'll ever get better as long as the Dark Shadow exists."

"But *how* do we destroy it?" Allison said.

"I'm not sure yet." Nicholas said. He gazed at the words on Ellie's pendant: *Pierce with a light of faith*. Did that hold the answer?

The kitchen phone rang, and Nicholas rushed to answer it.

"Hi, Nicholas," Renee said. "I came back from the Christmas party earlier than I planned to check any damages in the house. Kevin had to stay at party because he's in charge. I see that you kids didn't touch the meals I cooked for you. Come on over; I smuggled some cookies from the party for you." Her voice brightened.

"Where's Ellie?" Nicholas said.

There was a pause. "I thought she was with you," Renee said. "Ellie was on a kid's tour at Daniel's museum this afternoon. After the earthquake I called the museum and spoke with Jerry. He said everything was all right at the museum, he'd give her a ride home." She paused. Her tone changed. "Isn't she there?"

"Stay right where you are," Nicholas said. "Allison and I are on our way over."

He hung up the phone. "This looks bad, Allison," he said. "Jerry told Renee he'd give Ellie a ride home from the museum."

Allison's face grew pale. She took her cell phone from her purse and speed-dialed a number.

"Hello," Jerry said, "I figured you'd call."

"What's going on, Jerry?" Allison said, unable to mask the tension she was feeling.

"Frankly I thought you'd call sooner when you found Ellie's pendant."

"Where is she?"

"Hey, no need to take that tone. She's here with me."

"Where are you? And just what's going on with—"

"That's enough, Allison! Listen carefully, because I don't intend to repeat myself. The diamonds in the necklace were fakes. Bring the two real ones to the peak of Noriega Hill before midnight. Don't worry about Daniel's purple diamond. Philip traded that to us for a lovely synthetic duplicate. But we do need the others before midnight tonight. Don't be late."

"What makes you think I have them?"

Jerry laughed. "A big bird told me you'll have them soon—a big black bird. He tells me a lot of things now."

"You're working for Tower, Jerry, aren't you? Have you got no shame? Have you forgotten all Daniel has done for you?"

"You need to calm down, Allison. Oh, and by the way, you were terminated as of today."

"What? Philip won't allow you to do that."

"Actually, he's been so pleased with my work lately that he gave me all the executive powers Daniel used to have. Terminating an individual is one of them." He paused. "Noriega Hill before midnight. And don't even *think* of substituting fake diamonds like Cypress did!"

"Who do you—?"

Jerry had already hung up.

Allison stuck her cell phone back in her purse and made a silent vow to herself.

I will bring Daniel back to life.

Renee lost her self-control in her state of grief and Allison and Nicholas did what they could do to calm her.

The three sat at the Dream House kitchen table, cups of cocoa in front of them that Nicholas had prepared.

Renee hadn't touched hers. Her eyes were red, and her hands were trembling. She lowered her head when she spoke. "Jerry said Ellie was safe and she was in the museum cafeteria at the moment. When I told him I'd come get her, he said not to bother. He'd drive her home because Allison hadn't come back from Monterey yet."

She raised her head. "Allison, what's going on with Jerry? Is there something the matter with him that I don't know about? Do you think Jerry has . . . *taken* Ellie from us?"

Allison put her hands on Renee's. "Renee," she said, "He is not capable of doing such a thing. I guarantee that she's fine. Jerry's upset about something at work. Sometimes he acts kind of childish, and this is just his inappropriate way of getting attention. I guarantee that she's fine. I'm meeting him soon, and I'll resolve the problem. I'll bring her back in a couple of hours."

"I don't understand any of it, Allison. You *have to* explain it to me."

"Please, Renee, you've got to trust me on this. Ellie is all right. The whole thing really has nothing to do with Ellie. It's about something at the museum that Jerry misunderstood. It'll be simple to clear up once I meet with him. Basically it's a minor personnel matter. That's all I can say right now."

Renee fixed her eyes on the wall. "I want to trust you," she said. "And I guess I do. But it's just . . ."

She looked at Allison. "I don't know. I feel it's my fault. I thought I made a right decision for us to move to San Francisco and start our new life. I was wrong. We should have stayed in that small apartment."

Allison was more concerned with what she and Nicholas would be doing within two hours than hearing about what had brought the Spark family to the city. Still, she realized that Renee needed to distract herself from her worries about Ellie's situation.

"What made you decide to move here?" Allison said.

"My husband—Kevin, you haven't met him—owned a company in Seattle. It was a small business, but he took pride in the fact that it was his own. When the economy got sluggish and a huge contract with a customer fell through, his company took a dive. Kevin lost the company. He had to take whatever job he could find to survive and start our lives all over again.

I took odds jobs to help support us. I worked as a nanny for my friend, a next-door neighbor, which helped a little. But not enough. We had to give up our house. We put most of our belongings in storage and moved to a one-bedroom apartment. Ellie slept on a foldout couch in the living room. Then four months ago, the friend who'd hired me as a nanny told me about another friend whose husband was a San Francisco executive. He'd just been offered a lucrative promotion. He'd be setting up and managing a branch office in Singapore. The problem was, he'd have to live there for at least four years, and he'd just purchased this house."

Allison and Nicholas both looked surprised. "Here?" Allison said.

"That's right," Renee said. "They needed a caretaker, and my friend recommended me. The arrangement was that we could live here free of charge; we just had to keep the house in good shape, pay our own utility bills, and be willing to move out on a month's notice when the man's Singapore job was completed.

Kevin thought it was a big risk, but I persuaded him to make the move. Our savings didn't amount to much, but Kevin found a job here as a manager of a small start-up that we both think has potential. He's still haunted by the failure of his own company, but he's really working hard to make this company succeed."

She choked up for a moment. "It's my fault we moved here. And if something happens to Ellie, I could never forgive myself. How could I apologize to Kevin and to Ellie's mother?"

She burst into tears.

Allison and Nicholas did double takes. "What do you mean Ellie's mother?" Allison said.

Renee sighed. "I'm not Ellie's biological mother," she said. "We adopted Ellie when she was born because her mother was ill. Her mother was afraid she was going to die, and she begged us to take care of her daughter."

"Does Ellie know about this?" Nicholas said.

Renee shook her head. "We haven't told her. We promised her mother we'd wait until Ellie's thirteenth birthday. Her mother asked us to give her a pendant and an art book on her twelfth birthday and to tell her how we came to adopt her on her thirteenth."

"Ellie loaned the book to me," Nicholas said. "It's beautiful."

"I remember Ellie's pendant. It's very unique," Allison said.

Renee paused. "Excuse me," she said. "I'll be right back." She went upstairs and came back a moment later with a small safe in her hands. She opened the combination lock, took out an envelope from it, and handed to Allison. "This is an invitation to Ellie's thirteenth birthday party that we're sending to her grandparents."

Allison glanced at the envelope and passed it to Nicholas. The address was written in ornate handwriting. The intended recipients were Dylan and Gabrielle Hart in Big Sur.

"Who *is* Ellie's birth mother?" Allison said.

"Her married name was Cypress Oxford."

Allison nodded. "Renee," she said, "You may have the key to helping us all. Please tell me everything you know about Cypress."

"I'll do *anything* that will help me get Ellie back," Renee said. "Thirteen years ago, Cypress and I were patients in a Seattle hospital, and we met in the cafeteria one day. She wanted to buy some juice, but had forgotten to bring her wallet. I paid for her juice and told her not to worry about it. But that afternoon she came to my room to pay me back and brought me a bouquet of flowers. We began to talk, and we quickly developed a friendship. Cypress was due to give birth in two weeks, but her contractions had started early, and she was there for observation. I was going to have a baby, but I lost it again for the second time. And the doctors had told me I'd never be able to have a child.

I was depressed, of course, and she was very supportive of me. As we got to know each other, she told me that her husband had died in a car accident eight months earlier and that she had medical problems that the doctors hadn't been able to diagnose. She asked if anything should happen to her, would Kevin and I adopt her baby. It seemed bizarre to me, but she said she wouldn't want her child to fall into the wrong hands if she were put up for an adoption by an agency.

Of course I was desperate to have a child, but I wondered if she wasn't imagining a worst-case scenario. I even wondered if she just didn't want to raise a child by herself. Nevertheless, I talked with Kevin and we agreed. The very next day her attorney brought papers for all of us to sign. Here are the papers." Renee took them out of the safe and handed to Allison. After that, nothing was left inside the safe.

"What happened to her?" Allison said.

Renee paused, struggling to control her emotions. "Cypress died shortly after she gave birth to Ellie. Kevin and I took care of her funeral. She'd made us promise not to let anyone know about this, not even her own parents. She loved them very much, but for reasons of her own, she didn't want them to know about their granddaughter until her thirteenth birthday. We've kept our promise—until now."

"I'm sorry," Allison said.

Nicholas said nothing, but in his mind, images of his mother and Cypress overlapped. "Did Cypress leave anything else for Ellie besides the pendant and the art book?" Allison asked.

"No. Except for some glass beads that she'd collected in her own childhood. She thought her child would enjoy them the same as she did."

"Does she have them still?"

"No," Renee said. She turned to Nicholas. "Remember when you had your bike accident with Ellie? They got broken or scratched up, and she threw them away."

"Not all of them," Nicholas said.

Renee looked puzzled. "Are you sure?"

"Uh-huh," Nicholas said. "I think she keeps them in a little sack. Could we check in her room?"

"I guess so," Renee said. "Let's take a look."

In Ellie's room, Renee found the beads in a small leather sack in the top draw of Ellie's dresser.

"You were right, Nicholas," Renee said. She emptied them into her hand. There were four of them. Two of the beads were round and the size of cherries. One was orange, the other blue. Both were shiny, but chipped here and there. The two others were smaller and shaped like rosebuds. One was pink and the other green. They looked duller than the other two, but appeared to be in good condition.

Allison put the pink and green beads back in the sack. "We need to borrow these, Renee," she said. "If that okay with you. I promise we'll bring them back along with Ellie."

Renee nodded. She looked more resigned than enthusiastic.

Allison handed Nicholas the sack and said, "We'll be back soon." They headed to the front door.

Renee went back to the kitchen and sat down at the table. She picked up her cup of cocoa, which by now was cold. She set it back down and stared at a colorful drawing of a galaxy on the refrigerator door that Ellie had done in art class. It was truly beautiful. The tears came to her eyes, and she felt as lonely and unhappy as she'd ever felt in her life.

When Allison and Nicholas got to the sidewalk, Nicholas seemed energized. "I've got an idea," he said, "and I think it's a good one. We've got to go to my house first."

He dashed toward his house, with Allison not far behind him.

Once inside, Nicholas set the sack on the coffee table in front of the couch. "Sit down, Allison," he said. He handed her Cypress's book. Open the page with Cypress's handwriting. "I'll be back in a minute." He turned and hurried to his bedroom.

Nicholas opened his closet. Many boxes of collected objects were stored. Daniel had brought Nicholas souvenirs from his travels since Nicholas was little.

Nicholas looked for a wooden shell. It was about the same size as his hand and was given to him from Daniel for his last birthday. Daniel found that in an antique shop near City Collage when he gave a lecture there a few months ago.

"There!" He grabbed it and rushed back to the living room.

Allison had the book open to the page.

Nicholas showed Allison the wooden shell.

"I remember this…" said Allison.

Nicholas gave her a little smile. "I hope this works."

"Dad said, 'Maybe someday if you're confused and desperately need help, that shell will provide you with an answer—if you put your faith in it. Just blow your breath into the shell and then put it up to your ear.' Cross your fingers and say a prayer for me."

He took a deep breath, closed his eyes, and brought the wooden shell to his lips. His lips moved, but he made no sound. And then Nicholas blew into the shell and brought it to his ear.

He stood there in silence for almost a minute, listening to what only he could hear.

"Nicholas . . .?" Allison said.

He turned to her. "It worked, Allison—it really did!"

"What happened?" she said.

"I know what we need to do. Cypress's spirit wants us to destroy the Dark Shadow!" He pointed to the open page. "What she wrote on this page: *The Sun to the Moon, Faith to Misery, and Light to Darkness.* I now know what she wanted to tell us. This is how to destroy the Dark Shadow and end the curse once and for all."

"Why do you think that?"

"Because Cypress led us to the Harts, to her book and the words in it, and to her pendant. Most of all, because she led us to the missing diamonds."

He pointed to the page again. "She says here: *The Sun to the Moon, Faith to Misery, and Light to Darkness.* On the pendant she had made for Ellie, it says: *Pierce with a light of faith.* That implicated the image of the poster we saw at the Harts and the way Savino created the Dark Shadow. She wrote a word on that poster, "Renaissance", which means 'rebirth.' It sounds like 'reverse.' Don't you see? Cypress is telling us to *reverse* Savino's spell, the spell that created the Dark Shadow. Savino created the Dark Shadow through his jealousy, anger, and resentment—the *misery* that haunted him. Savino summoned him when he threw his sword and pierced his own shadow on the armory wall. I remember that the cross guard between the hilt and blade of his sword had a crescent design on it—the *moon*. And when he pulled the sword from the fireplace, the blade was covered with ashes—the *darkness*."

"So the *light* means a fire," Allison said.

Nicholas nodded. "And the *sun* means a sword that represents the sun. With a sword like that, with fire, and with our *faith* we can break his spell!"

Allison stared at him with wonder and awe in her eyes. "You figured it all out with the help of the wooden shell that your Dad gave you."

"Yes," he said. "And by following what my heart tells me."

"Nicholas, I'm very proud of you."

Nicholas blushed.

Allison leaned toward him and kissed his cheek. "Okay, Nicholas," she said, "what do we do now?"

"First of all, we need a sword that represents the sun."

"There were two in the Swords and Daggers exhibit that we did," Allison said. "They had suns on their crosspieces–Oh, no! But they've already been shipped back to Italy."

"I wonder if any antique stores would still be open." Nicholas said.

She shook her head. "I doubt it. Even if there were some, they probably wouldn't have any swords like that on hand." She thought for a moment, and then her face lit up. "I've got it!" she said. "Philip had replicas made of those two swords and hung them in his office!"

She stood up and grabbed her coat. "We need to go ahead with the meeting with Tower and Jerry. If I don't show up by midnight, do you think you can handle them? I know it's a lot to ask."

He got on his feet. "I can do it," he said. "Whatever it takes, I'll give it my best." He picked up the little sack and tucked it into his pocket.

When they got out to the street, Allison glanced at her watch. It was 11:05 PM. The eclipse would start in just over half an hour. Nicholas headed for the Dream House. She headed for the next block, where she'd parked her car.

CHAPTER 22

The Magical Night

The museum parking lot was closed. Allison parked on the street and rushed to the employee entrance. She looked up at the sky. The white full moon seemed to float in a field of sparkling stars.

At the employee entrance she pushed the emergency button and presented her face and badge to the security camera. It scanned her irises and her badge and buzzed her in. *Jerry, my employment is not over yet,* she thought.

Philip's office was unlocked, and she went in and flicked on the light. She gasped.

A framed poster that showed the Hope Diamond hung on the wall where the two swords had been hanging.

What had Philip done with them?

She searched frantically through his closet, but they weren't there. She rushed to the conference room and switched on the lights. Not there either.

She checked Daniel's office, remembering as she did that it was now Jerry's. The swords weren't there.

Out in the hallway, she glanced at her watch. It was just eleven-thirty. The total eclipse would start soon in a few minutes. Should she call Philip at his home and find out where the swords were? What if Jerry hadn't been bluffing and she really *was* terminated?

She took a deep breath and then a thought struck her. Philip had praised her for her efforts in putting the Sword and Daggers Exhibit together. Would he have rewarded her with a gift of the swords?

She rushed into her laboratory and turned on the lights.

Success! The swords were hanging on the wall behind her desk. She pulled one from its mount and hurried for the exit.

Allison threw open the employee entrance door, ran toward where she parked...

"Stop!" She shouted.

Too late.

The truck was already pulling into the street with her car in tow. She rushed to the curb, just in time to see the tow truck and her car disappear around a corner. She looked down at the curb. It was painted red. In her rush to get into the museum, she'd parked in a tow-away zone.

When Nicholas got to the Dream House, Renee looked exhausted.

"Renee," he said, "I need to borrow a couple of your torches."

She didn't ask why. She nodded and led him down to the front yard where eight four-foot-long bamboo torches were fixed in the ground. They had metal fuel containers at the top with wicks running through them. "I forgot to light them this evening" Renee said. "I've been so . . ." Her words trailed off.

"I understand," Nicholas said. "It's okay. I don't need them lit right now. Is there fuel in them?"

"We filled them this morning," Renee said.

"Great," Nicholas said, and pulled one from the ground. Renee pulled up another one and handed it to him. They were heavier than he'd thought.

Renee took one of the torches from him. "Nicholas," she said, "I'm going with you. Wherever that is."

"We're going to climb Noriega Hill."

He looked up at the sky. The total eclipse had begun. The shadow of the Earth was slowly casting downward over the white moon. Now the moon was looking like a crescent facing upward.

Nicholas and Renee walked in silence. After they'd gone four blocks, Nicholas noticed Renee was breathing hard. He stopped walking and turned to her. "Are you okay?" he said.

She coughed. "No, not really, Nicholas. I'm sorry; I guess I overestimated my condition. Actually I'm exhausted. The stress…it hasn't been easy for me today."

"Of course not," Nicholas said. "It's probably better that you go home now in case Ellie calls."

Renee sighed. "I suppose so." She hugged him. "All right dear. God bless you." She handed him her torch and headed back to the Dream House.

When Nicholas got to the first flight of stairs, he took a deep breath. Even though he'd have to lug both heavy torches all the way to the top, he was glad Renee had gone home. Maybe Jerry was just bluffing and Ellie was safely home. Even if that wasn't so, he didn't think Renee would be up to dealing with what he and Allison would be facing.

He set the torches down and checked his jacket pocket to make sure his lighter was there. It was. He took another deep breath, picked up the two torches, and prepared to deal with the stairs—all 328 of them.

Two-thirds of the way up the hill, Nicholas set the torches down again. Hot and sweating in his jacket, he took off the jacket and wrapped it around his waist. He looked up at the night sky. The moon was starting to turn a yellowish brown, moving deeper into its total eclipse phase. Before long it would appear to be red—a "Blood Moon."

He lit the two torches and resumed his climb.

Nicholas stepped on the soil of the hill top. His eyes were watery from the cold air and his vision was blurry. He brushed his eyes with his hands. On the very top of the hill he could see the huge pine tree silhouetted against the sky. He headed for it. When he drew near, he could make out three indistinct figures in front of the tree. Nicholas wanted to see the fourth figure; his target—The Dark Shadow.

"You're fifteen minutes late," the familiar voice said.

Nicholas's heart seemed to freeze in his chest.

Vix!

He stuck one of the torches into the ground. He held the other in one hand and moved forward. In the light from the torches he could make out Vix Tower, and just behind him, the Dark Shadow. A few feet away Jerry and Ellie stood. A strip of duct tape covered Ellie's mouth. She stepped toward Nicholas, and Jerry grabbed her arm and yanked her back. Her body twisted, and Nicholas could see that her hands were tied behind her.

The red moon was nearing the maximum eclipse phase, and it glowed high above the pine tree.

"Have you got the diamonds?" Vix said.

Nicholas held up one hand. "They're right here," he said.

"Good. Bring them to me. Do it fast, or say goodbye to your father."

"Do it, Nicholas. Now!" Jerry joined in.

Nicholas shook his head. "Free Ellie first."

"No," Vix said. "Give me the diamonds first. If they're real we'll release her."

Nicholas moved several steps toward Vix and set the green diamond on a rock. He moved back to where he stood before.

Vix walked over to the rock, and picked up the diamond. He transferred it to his other hand, which also held the purple diamond. The two diamonds began to glow. They rose a foot or so above Vix's hand. They hovered there for a moment and then began to swirl in separate, glowing circles—one purple, one green. Finally the circles merged into one orbit.

Vix smiled. "Excellent, young man," he said, his tone more pleasant now. "The diamond is real. Now if you'd please bring me the other one."

"No," Nicholas said. "Set Ellie free first."

"That's not going to happen," Vix said, his voice sinister again. "Don't think that I won't hurt you just because you're a child."

The Dark Shadow began to expand.

Nicholas stood still. He faced Vix and the Dark Shadow, but his eyes glanced around the area, searching . . . searching . . .

Where are you, Allison? Please get here before it's too late!

"Nicholas, just do it." Jerry said. "Your time is running out."

Ellie struggled to break free from Jerry again, but he held her tight. As she slackened her efforts, she sensed a curious presence near her. She didn't recognize it. Although she couldn't free herself from Jerry, she experienced a feeling of hope. Perhaps the time to escape wasn't right now, but it might be soon.

"Ellie," Thomas said, "I'm trying to free you from him, but I'm slipping away from everything! Keep your faith. There is hope. Stay strong."

Nicholas gave Jerry a scornful look. "You don't get the diamond until you free Ellie," he said. "It's *your* time that's running out!"

The moon had changed its color to blood red with an outer rim of bright turquoise color. It was seventeen minutes past midnight—the maximum eclipse was taking place.

Nicholas glanced around the area again.

Where are you, Allison? We need you!

"Do what I say!" another voice said. It was deep, threatening, unearthly—a tone no human being could duplicate.

224

The Dark Shadow rose up behind Vix higher than the pine tree and formed into a man in a military suit. He was bald and obese, with a black patch over one eye like a pirate. The other eye gazed down at Nichola, menacing under the thick eyelid. Then one of his huge hands grabbed Nicholas by the neck. And then it changed its form into that of a whirlwind. It lifted him into the air and spun him around in dizzying circles until finally it spewed him out onto the ground.

Nicholas's torch flew from his hand and his shin slammed against a rock. Excruciating pain shot through his body.

The whirlwind took the form of the one-eyed giant again. It reared up once more and fixed its eye on Nicholas.

"Get up, Nicholas!" Thomas said. "You must resist the dark forces!"
He slipped away as he'd done before.

Nicholas forced himself up to his knees. As he tried to rise to his feet, the pink diamond slipped from his hand and bounced toward Vix.

The giant's eye gleamed. He picked up the pink diamond and dropped it into Vix's palm, where it joined the other two diamonds.

All three began to swirl in separate circles above his palm.

The one-eyed giant became the Dark Shadow again.

Jerry, his face ashen, stared at Vix and the Dark Shadow. He shook his head slowly from side to side. "No," he said softly, "this can't be." He released Ellie's arm and took a few cautious steps backward. "God forgive me. This is . . ."

His voice cracked and he couldn't finish. Cold sweat streaming down his face, he turned away from the terrifying spectacle. His half bottom couldn't move. He crawled on the rocky hill just to get away from the scene. Then he finally got on his feet, dashed for the pathway to the stairs, and vanished into the night.

Ellie stood frozen in place, too stunned to move. A moment later her mind cleared, and she hurried to Nicholas's side. She turned her back to him, squatted down, and with her hands still bound, helped him to his feet.

Now the separate circles of the swirling diamonds were merging into one orbit. Vix stared at them, his eyes wide. The swirling stopped when they had merged. The three diamonds dropped into his palm, and then began to integrate. He looked to the sky and laughed maniacally.

"This power is now with us forever!"

Nicholas stripped the tape from Ellie's mouth and began to untie her hands.

"We've got to *reverse* the spell to destroy the Dark Shadow! We need to pierce the Dark Shadow with a sword that represents the sun now and run the touch fire on the blade of the sword to the Dark Shadow and burn The Darkness for once and for all!" Ellie said.

"I know," Nicholas said. "But we need Allison."

"I'm here!" a voice said.

Nicholas and Ellie turned and saw Allison rush toward the Dark Shadow, a sword in her hand. She thrust it forward with all her might, piercing the Dark Shadow. As she hammered the sword into the pine tree with a rock, its form became the frowning face of a nineteenth century Japanese warrior in full armor. His face distorted in agony under his war helmet and he let out a bone-chilling moan.

The warrior looked toward Vix. "Pull this out of me! Hurry, you fool!"

"Wait, it's almost done," said Vix. He was focused on the three diamonds integrating into one.

Nicholas pulled the burning torch from the ground and handed it to Allison. "Run this on the blade of the sword to the place where it entered his chest."

She gripped the torch with both hands, pressed the flame against the length of the sword's blade, and jammed it against the Dark Shadow's chest.

The warrior's body began to burn with little smoke, and then burst into flame.

As the fire spread, he screamed again. "Get it off me!"

Vix turned his head toward the warrior form of the Dark Shadow. "Wait! The diamonds aren't done yet!"

Still in human form, the Dark Shadow roared over the sound of the flames at Allison.

"I'll get you!"

She stepped backward and stumbled over a root. The torch fell from her hand and landed on a rock, dislodging the fuel container. The fuel spilled out and soaked into the ground.

"Hellfire! Vix, pull this sword out of me!"

Vix started toward him and stopped. "I can't move!" He said. "Something's holding me back!"

The warrior form of the Dark Shadow sucked in a deep breath and exhaled with such force that the flames were extinguished. "Hah!" he cried out. He raised his hands to the hilt of the sword and began to pull it out, trying to free it from the tree and from his body. His face was a mask of violent anger and hatred. "I will destroy you all!"

"The fire isn't strong enough to defeat him!" Nicholas was devastated.

Nicholas and Allison stared at the monstrous figure as he pulled out the sword inch by inch.

Ellie inhaled and exhaled deeply to try to calm herself as much as she could first. She closed her eyes, her brow furrowed in concentration…She opened her eyes, "Nicholas, the Light is the great light of the Universe! The sun, the moon, and the stars."

Nicholas reached into his jacket pocket, "I've got it!" He pulled out the Cup of Mirrors and held it up toward the sky. He adjusted its angle so that he could collect the lights of the stars, the light from the red moon, and the turquoise light that rimmed it.

As the beams of light were drawn into the Cup of Mirrors, Nicholas tilted it toward the monstrous figure the Dark Shadow had assumed.

The beams struck the blade of the sword. They coursed through its entire length, sparking and flashing and igniting the Dark Shadow's body again.

"It's working!" Ellie said.

"Ah!" Nicholas pointed at the burning Dark Shadow.

The Dark Shadow was changing its form into many different kinds of men and some of women, from different time periods. They all struggled in the flames with agony.

In the form of a malicious man in the flames, the Dark Shadow grazed at Nicholas, Ellie, and Allison. "You think you can destroy me?" He took another deep breath and exhaled, quelling the flames once again. He let out a furious roar of laughter.

That voice sounded familiar to Nicholas. When the flames decreased, he could see the man's face clearly.

"It's Savino!" Nicholas cried out.

"Watch this!" The Dark Shadow in Savino's form began pulling out the sword again.

"No!" Nicholas looked up at the night sky, searching for he knew not what.

"Look!" Vix turned towards the Dark Shadow. "The three diamonds have just become one!" He opened his hand and revealed the glowing red diamond. Then he turned to Nicholas, Ellie, and Allison. "You thought you could defeat us," he said. "Now you'll learn how powerful we are!"

Ellie grabbed Nicholas's arm. "There!" she pointed to the sky. "A great comet!"

High above them a brilliant comet streaked across the heavens.

Nicholas lifted his hands toward it and was jolted backwards as the light from the comet surged into the Cup of Mirrors. Ellie held his hand and the Cup of Mirrors tight, he regained his balance, and together they spun around.

"Hold on a little longer!" Thomas said. He placed his hand over theirs.

"I'll have you!" The Dark Shadow in Savino's form dislodged the point of the sword from the tree and was pulling it out from his chest.

No longer held in place, Vix took steps towards Nicholas and Ellie.

Ellie and Nicholas tilted the Cup of Mirrors toward the Dark Shadow and a burst of energy from the comet's light surged forth. It struck the sword's blade with a thunderous roar that muffled the Dark Shadow's cry of agony.

He vanished in a dazzling flash of light. Black ashes swirled in the air, fell to the ground, and were transformed into a heap of dust. A sudden gust of wind scattered the heap into the night air until nothing remained.

By the enormous impact of the energy of light thrusting into the Cup of Mirrors, the mirrors got shattered with an explosion like a firework. It lit up the entire hill in the night.

Vix Tower echoed the Dark Shadow's scream as nine red-hot shards of glass streaked from the Cup of Mirrors and tore through his body. He fell to the ground, his body smoking, all life drained from him.

The red diamond rolled from Vix's lifeless hand and was transformed into three separate diamonds: one green, one pink, and one purple.

Allison walked over to the diamonds and picked them up. A smile spread across her face. "Come here Ellie," she said.

Ellie went over to her.

"Stick out your hand," Allison said.

Ellie did, and Allison dropped the three diamonds into her palm.

The diamonds began to glow. Soon the three merged and became one. A beautiful red diamond the size of a fig.

"This is the red diamond that Lorenzo told Adamo about," Ellie said. An image of Caterina's spouting face came to Ellie's mind.

"This is incredible!" Allison held her breath.

Ellie said, "Each of the three diamonds represents the elements that require the three to become one red diamond. To keep the red diamond with its magical powers, the owner must have the quality of the three elements."

"What are the three elements, Ellie?" Nicholas said.

"Love, Faith, and Strength." Ellie said.

Nicholas nodded. "Now it's truly in the hand of its rightful owner." He said.

Ellie stared up at the sky. "It was a great comet, Nicholas, wasn't it?"

"It sure was, Ellie. One of the greatest!"

"The Dark Shadow and Vix Tower are gone for good. After five centuries, the curse is finally lifted," said Allison.

"We won the battle," Nicholas said. "I have my father back!"

"Yes," Allison said. "We do have him back." She pulled Nicholas and Ellie to her and hugged them both.

"Ouch!" Nicholas cried out. Looking at his right palm.

"What's wrong?" Allison glanced at it. Its skin was all red and began to blister, burned by the sizzling mirrors.

"I'll take you to Daniel's hospital right now." Allison put her arm around Nicholas's shoulders and looked up at the sky. Tears of joy streamed down her face.

CHAPTER 23

The Truth and Freedom

A police officer on patrol dispatched a message: "What was that fiery explosion on Noriega Hill!?" He made an emergency u-turn and hurried to the hill. He drove up the steep street and was almost at the foothill. Only a few cars passed by on the way.

SCREECH!!!

The officer slammed on the brake and his body lurched forward in his seat by the sudden stop. A man ran into the car as he was running down the stairs from the hilltop. He rolled up onto the car in front of the windshield.

Their eyes met.

The police officer pulled out his gun, jumped out of the car behind the door, and aimed at the man.

"Don't move! Put your hands up!" He shouted.

The man held up his hands and leaned back from the car slowly.

The officer approached him, still aiming the gun at him.

"What were you doing up there?"

"I was…" The man was shaking.

"What's your name?"

"Jerry…Jerry Goldman."

As the police officer padded him down to search him, Alison, Ellie, and Nicholas came down from the hilltop. And Allison approached the officer.

"This man is guilty of kidnapping this girl. Please take him in," said Allison.

Jerry burst into tears and said, "I'm sorry. I don't understand why I did such a thing." Two backup patrol cars arrived. The officer handcuffed Jerry and put him in the back of his cruiser.

In the hospital at the sound of the alarm, the night shift nurse dropped the report she was working on and looked up at the monitor. "Code blue!" she shouted. Something was going wrong in Room 213.

She dashed down the hallway and threw open the door to 213.

"What in the world . . .!" The nurse was in a panic.

Daniel was standing by his bed. The tubes and wires that had been monitoring his condition were all disconnected from him.

"What happened to me? What are these all about?" Daniel said in confusion.

"You've been hospitalized in a coma for two weeks," she said as calmly as possible.

Daniel was speechless.

Two other nurses and a doctor hurried into the room. They stood there, stunned.

The doctor shook his head. "It's a miracle," he said.

Daniel shrugged. "If you say so. But whatever it is, I've never felt better in my life."

After the police officers released Allison, Ellie, and Nicholas at the foothill, Allison headed to the Dream House first. On the way in the back seat, Nicholas said to Ellie, "I'm sorry I was rude to you when you told me about Jerry. I knew you were right, but I guess I couldn't accept the truth. I apologize."

"That's okay, I understand. I know you trust me." Ellie smiled.

"Thanks, Ellie." Nicholas wondered how much more she knew about him; perhaps things that he himself didn't realize.

"Nicholas," Ellie said, "But the other two diamonds. . . where did you find them?"

"They were in your beads box, Ellie. They were among the one's that survived in my famous bike accident."

Ellie looked stunned. "I don't understand."

"Ellie," Allison said, "I think I'd better tell you something before you get in your home. It might be a lot to handle, but I think you'll be able to deal with it."

Allison parked the car in front of the Dream House.

"Go ahead," Ellie said. "After what just happened on Noriega Hill, I think I can deal with anything."

"I don't doubt it." Allison recounted the story of how Renee and Kevin came to adopt Ellie. When Allison finished the account, Ellie looked drained.

Would the information add to the trauma Ellie had just been through?

By telling her such a personal story, had Allison overstepped her boundaries?

She hadn't.

"For a long time, I've suspected something like that," Ellie said. "It's nice to know I was close to the truth."

Allison and Nicholas were relieved.

"I've got a question, Allison," Nicholas said.

"Okay."

"How did Jerry know we'd find the real diamonds?"

"I wondered that myself," Allison said. "Then I remembered that when I called him this evening, he said something strange about a big black bird telling him things. I couldn't understand what he meant then. Now I think he was talking about the Dark Shadow."

"Maybe so," Nicholas said. "Nothing will ever surprise me again."

Back at the Dream House, Renee held Ellie in a tight embrace. "Thank God you're all right!" she said. "I couldn't bear to ever lose you again."

"You'll never have to, Mom. Not ever."

Renee suppressed a sob. "I know that, my love," she said, and rocked her from side to side. Kevin's eyes were red, but not from drinking. He'd wept like a baby when Ellie returned safely.

He knelt down beside her. "I'm sorry for how I've acted lately," he said. "I wasn't like that before my business problems in Seattle, and I don't want to ever be like that again. I'll try to make it up to you and your mother. I want you to know that I've always loved you as much as your real parents could."

"Dad, you've both always been my real parents, too," Ellie said. "And you always will be."

Kevin began to cry again, but this time he was smiling through his tears.

"Goodbye, dear child," Thomas said. "I must go now. She's waiting for me."
He kissed Ellie's forehead and was gone.
He had finally broken through to the other world.

Ellie raised her hand to her forehead.

"What is it, Ellie?" Renee said.

"It felt like something just touched me."

Renee kissed Ellie's forehead. "Who knows?" she said. "Maybe it was your guardian angel."

Chiesta, Italy, December 21.

Nine hours ahead of San Francisco at the time Nicholas and Ellie defeated the Dark Shadow. Father Luciano had just finished with his morning mass. Alone in his church, he put his hands on the pulpit and dropped his head. *We've got to save this village!* The church's attendance was noticeably getting less and less every year.

Two days ago his heart was as light as a feather. Upon his return from his business trip, he was pleased to hear that the museum teams had proved that the legendary diamonds actually exist, and they found the missing diamonds. But a piece of bad news came through; those diamonds were synthetic.

Father Luciano walked to the altar and picked up the sacred box. He held the box with both hands, exhaled and closed his eyes, and then started to pray for Chiesta. That's what he always did every day for years. But today his prayer was distracted by an urgent desire: *I want to read the holy words!*

At that moment he lost his concentration.

"No!" He cried out.

The sacred box slipped away from his hands, fell on the floor, and shattered into pieces. The inside was exposed, revealing a small book wrapped with leather. It looked in a delicate condition. He picked up the book and carefully removed the wrapping. He opened the book. His heart was pounding hard. Standing still, he skimmed through the pages.

"Good God!"

He strode out of the church with the book and went to his office to make an urgent call to the local museum.

The blue sky was appearing above the village of Chiessa.

CHAPTER 24

You Rise

San Francisco, December 25.

On the Christmas Day Allison cooked her spaghetti with meatballs for dinner at the Blue's house. Nicholas had requested that in advance. She made it from scratch with her own recipe. The tomato sauce shimmered on the stove. The house was filled with the warm air and Nicholas's favorite Christmas carol "*O Come All Ye Faithful*" was playing.

While Daniel was getting an extra chair for Allison from the garage, Nicholas sneaked into his father's room.

Nicholas put back the picture of his mother into the bedside table drawer with his left hand. His right palm hurt every day, and it reminded him of how wonderful it was to stay in his own power.

"The dinner is served!" Allison called.

They all gathered at the kitchen table. As soon as Nicholas sat down, he took a big bite of Allison's steamy dish.

"This is better than the one we had at the restaurant, Allison!" said Nicholas.

"That's the best complement I've had for a long time." Allison gave him a bright smile.

"You know, Nicholas." Daniel said. "I think it's about time for us to move to a bigger house."

Nicholas nodded, "Good idea. We'll need it once you and Allison are married."

Daniel rocked back in his chair. He turned to Allison. "Did *you* tell him?"

Nicholas and Allison look at each other and grinned.

"Of course she didn't, Dad," Nicholas said. "The wooden shell told me."

"You have your faith in it." Daniel's face grew serious.

Nicholas nodded, "What is the story behind it?"

"Well, the story was my dream I had almost two months ago. Remember, I went to the City Collage to give my lecture. That morning." Daniel said. "It's about love between a man and a woman…

He was a talented young wood carver living in a mountain village. Although he loved the mountains, he felt a strong urge to see the ocean. He decided to leave his village and see for himself what he'd dreamed about for so long.

After traveling for many days, at last he reached the sea.

One morning, he met a young woman on the beach. She was a mute. Her dress was as blue as the sky, her hair as dark as midnight, her eyes as deep green as the kelp in the sea, and her skin as beige as the sand.

He fell in love with her and asked her to marry him. She looked into his eye and shook her head. He felt as if his whole world had fallen apart. 'Why not?' he said.

Just then a huge wave pounded against the shore. It withdrew and another even larger wave rolled in. It crashed harder than the first and formed into a giant hand.

Time seemed frozen.

She was the only thing that moved in the stillness. She picked up a shell from the sea, inhaled deeply, and blew her breath into it. She handed it him and walked toward the giant hand, and climbed into it. She smiled at him, and the watery fingers of the hand closed over her.

And just like that, the wave retreated into the sea, leaving on the shoreline a lacey pattern of foamy white bubbles that gradually burst and faded away.

Marriage was prohibited by the god of the sea because she was a fairy of the sea. She must stay at sea.

Brokenhearted, he returned to his mountain village. One day an idea struck him, and he began carving beautiful wooden copies of the seashell she'd given him. The people of the village admired them and soon they were in great demand in both his village and in the neighboring villages.

Eventually he fell in love with a young maiden in his village, and she was in love with him. He wanted to marry her, but he was worried that he might not be ready for marriage. One night he held the shell and said, 'I'm so confused. I don't know what I should do,' and then blew his breath into it.

From the shell a strange sound came; not of the sea, but of a woman's voice. Although he'd never heard the mute speak, he knew the voice was hers.

'I'll send you the power, the strength, and the energy to move forward in your life.' She said.

'But you must decide for yourself. You've already known the answer in the bottom of your heart.'

He knew in his heart.

The next day he asked the young maiden from his village if she would marry him.

Her answer was simple: 'Yes.'

And so the two were wed, and they both lived happily ever after…."

"That's beautiful." Allison said.

"Hours later, I saw the wooden shell in the antique shop nearby the collage. I thought it meant something to me." Daniel smiled. "I was right."

"That young man in your dream is *you* then." Allison said.

"So who do you think that mute is, Dad?"

"Hmm," Daniel was looking at the far walls and then put his silver down on the table.

"What's the matter?" Allison put her hand on his softly.

"Nicholas, she is your mom," Daniel said. "Olivia was guiding both of us to the right path. She helped me to make an important decision and move on with my life—I wanted the answer to *my* question to be 'Yes'..."

Nicholas was stunned and felt an incredible joy. He looked up in the air to an unknown place and said, "Thanks, Mom."

In late January, the burn in Nicholas' palm from the sizzling mirrors was healed.

One afternoon as Nicholas was checking the mail box, a black shinny Cadillac passed in front of his house and it took his attention. It parked elegantly in front of the Dream House. Two well-dressed men with black attaché cases got out of the car and went straight up to Spark's. *They must have come for Ellie*, Nicholas thought. Ellie's parents answered the door promptly and the men entered the house.

In the Dream House, the two men sat in the sofa across from Renee, Ellie, and Kevin. A man with grey hair was from the Oxford Company and the other was the attorney for the company.

"Well, after DNA testing it proved that Ellie Spark is the daughter of Hendry Thomas and Cypress Oxford—the former owner of the Oxford Company and of his widow. Mr. Tower died late last year, apparently from a freak lightning strike on Noriega Hill. He left no heirs, but the Oxford Company and its assets. Therefore, Ellie is officially the heiress of the Oxford Company and its assets—including the Red Diamond." The attorney said.

"Hendry wanted to be called 'Thomas' by close friends outside work," the grey haired man said. "If Thomas had known he had a daughter, he must have been delighted. Life is often unfair." He shook his head regretfully.

The Great Diamonds Exhibit at the San Francisco Museum of Art History was a huge success. Nicholas and Ellie were invited to the grand opening as the special guests, and Aunt Joyce accompanied with them. During the opening ceremony, Philip announced he was retiring in early June and that Daniel was chosen to replace him. Allison was selected to fill Daniel's current position.

The crowd of the worldly famous diamonds was expectedly big. Nicholas, Ellie, and Joyce passed through that section and moved straight to the true star of the exhibit; *Caterina Balducci/Light of Faith Diamond*. The red diamond was named after Caterina and her life.

A bigger crowd appeared ahead of them. Nicholas held Ellie's hand tight so that they wouldn't be separated when they walk through it. Joyce followed behind them.

"That is like the crowd for Mona Lisa at Louver Museum in Paris!" said Joyce.

They threaded their way through the massive audience and finally stood in front of the red diamond.

"The red diamond is incredibly big," Joyce said. Her eyes stared at it as she spoke.

Caterina Balducci/Light of Faith Diamond sent out glowing colors of the rainbow in the spot light. It took everybody's breath away.

"When a total eclipse occurred last month, the three diamonds integrated into one red diamond... Isn't it incredible, Nicholas?" Joy said.

"Do you believe in it, Aunt Joyce?" Nicholas was curious about her answer.

"Yes, I do! Your father clarifies the wonders of the world for all of us. I'm proud of him... Do you think you were born under a lucky star, Nicholas?" Joyce winked at him.

"Yes, I think so, too," said Nicholas. It was genuine.

"Good for you," Joyce wiped her tears away with her fingers and moved on.

"Wow, this is the necklace that the pink and green diamonds were once set in. What a gorgeous pearl necklace that is!" Joyce was allured by the necklace that Margarita Balducci had her father designed. It was set with synthetic replicas of the purple, green, and pink diamonds for the display.

Jerry's face popped up in Nicholas's mind, but he quickly erased the memory.

"I miss Jerry..." Joyce made a sore face, but soon she moved on. "On this last panel, it's about you, Ellie," said Joyce. "The current private owner has decided to donate the gem as a gift to Chiesta village in Italy. The owner chose the church of Chiesta as a guardian for it and it will be housed at the Tuscany Museum of Treasures. The museum will present the diamond and its legacy to people from all over the world. It's your parent's keepsake for you. Is your decision still the same?"

"Yes. I want to give this diamond back to her village where Caterina Balducci family rests. This is my wish and I'm sure that Light of Faith wishes to be there, too."

"Well done, Ellie, well done." Joyce padded Ellie's shoulders.

"Nicholas," Ellie said, "Can I ask you something?"

"Sure, you can ask me anything," Nicholas said.

"Would you be my co-owner of Light of Faith?"

"Me?" He was so stunned that he almost choked.

Ellie nodded with a serious look on her face. "Yes, I want you to be."

Still in shock, Nicholas said, "Yes, it's an honor!" He stuck his hand and they shook their hands together.

"This is just wonderful! We have to celebrate. I'll make a feast this weekend." Joyce was already planning what she would cook for the party. "I have to tell Daniel about it. I'll be back." Joyce hurried through her way back to Daniel's office.

Ellie and Nicholas looked at each other and giggled as they moved forward.

In the last case, Foresta's original journal was displayed along with copies of it translated into English.

"Dad said that Father Luciano accidentally found the journal in the sacred box in his church on the same day that we defeated the Dark Shadow." Nicholas said.

Ellie said with a look of satisfaction across on her face, "I think Foresta and Caterina wanted to expose their lives to let us learn something from it."

Nicholas nodded. "Let's see what happened in their lives after the earthquake."

Together they read through a summary of the journal provided on a panel at the forefront of the case:

Margarita left Torre for her home after Mariotto died from the earthquake. She didn't want to deal with the chaos in the village where her son's life was taken. Now I rule both Chiesta and Torre, living in Chiesta.

Today Caterina finally came back from Florence at last after two weeks of separation. I'm blessed. Now we live one day at a time. I keep only one torch. The supply of the oil for torches is limited.

At the age of 14, Caterina works hard for the lands. She practices Adamo's agriculture methods in Torre and Chiesta. The results in Torre are a tremendous success but not in Chiesta. Even though the amount of food is not enough to satisfy our stomachs, her efforts saved all of us.

Caterina loses her hope in the restorations from time to time. I could have left this cursed land for her, with the fortune we would have made from the purple diamond. Nevertheless, I still keep the secret of the purple diamond from Caterina. I'm worried that the darkness would worsen our lives if I spoke about the diamonds.

At age of 18, Caterina is married to a young man from Florence, who shares his dreams with her and vice versa. She is now a free light of faith. They live in Giovanni's estate and rule both Chiesta and Torra. I still stay in Chiesta where my heart is.

Fifteen years has passed since the earth quake, yet the restorations aren't completed yet. The dark clouds have been fading slowly. Today Caterina gave us the light once again; she gave birth to twins, a boy and a girl. My consciousness of the diamonds is faded, but my fears of the dark force remain deep in my mind.

Caterina is the Sun, Adamo is the Earth, and I am the Moon

Foresta Balducci

Eighteen years passed after the earth quake. My mother, Foresta Balducci, died of pneumonia. Today I found this journal and learned about the story of the three magical diamonds. I let the torch go out naturally.

Now I must live as a bright light of faith. Not as a woman, nor as a man, but as an eternal light of faith that floats in time. My obstacles only drive me further and improve my determination to accomplish my mission. My struggles lead me to gain wisdom and grow my soul.

Two decades passed after the earth quake. The restoration was finally done. I wish my mother could have seen this with her own eyes. My husband and I are appointed to a count and countess by the Duke because of the work we've done for the church, monastery, and villagers.

Some of black clouds have faded. Now our land is shrouded by dark gray clouds. We never see blue sky again and the spirit of Chiesta is still not the same as before. Our duties must continue.

At this last stage of my life before God takes me from this world, I will bring this journal to my trusted priest and monks at the church of Chiesta. I'll ask them to pray to God to break Savino's curse once and for all.

Caterina Balducci

"What remarkable women Foresta and Caterina were!" Ellie said.

"Yes, they were," Nicholas said. "You know, Ellie, I'm bothered about the future of the red diamond. What if a massive earthquake hits Tuscany again, do you think the diamond would be absorbed into the earth?"

"Perhaps."

"And what if our entire planet is destroyed someday?"

Ellie shrugged. "Another like it will be created," she said. "And we'll all go to the place where Foresta and Caterina's light of faith and my mother's wishes traveled–That is the spiritual world."

"Where *is* the spiritual world?"

Ellie said, "We can't see it, but it exists in a close distance—and we belong to that world, where our spirit comes and goes. Foresta and Caterina's light of faith—their spirit—found you because your father discovered the purple diamond. Their spirit knew you would find the other diamonds. When my mother was alive, she tried to destroy Vix and the Dark Shadow with her power, but their negativity ruined her health. While she lived, she did everything she could to protect me from them. When she became a spirit, she knew it would take a while for me to develop the gifts she passed onto me. She was right. I needed time to strengthen my power, so that you and I could defeat Vix and the Dark Shadow."

"I still wonder how we were able to do that," Nicholas said.

"The energy from my mother and Caterina and Foresta made it happen," Ellie said. "Spiritual energy exists forever."

"My mother watched me from the spiritual world," Nicholas said, "and so did your father Thomas. But why didn't Thomas know you were his daughter?"

"He was not able to see things clearly because of Vix and the Dark Shadow's negative energy. That place where my father was in between the earth and the spiritual world," Ellie said. "He couldn't go to the spiritual world, because he didn't know he was dead. Vix and the Shadow caused the car accident that killed him. But he thought he was still alive in this world because he missed my mother so much."

"That house with dark clouds above Thomas's property was in my dream on the day of the eclipse," Nicholas said. "In the dream, I opened that house with your pendant key and I saw the silhouette of someone through the glass door at the end of the hallway. Who was that?"

"Cypress—my mother," Ellie said. "Vix and the Dark Shadow's negative energy trapped her spirit there with their curse. But now and forever, my mother and father are together in the spiritual world where they belong. What you saw in your dream was a metaphor for your unlocking the curse. The Universe showed you your future in that dream."

"The Universe?"

"Yes. You can call it God too, whichever word you feel a connection to something greater. It's the place where the truth is. Even if the truth is beaten down at times, it rises eventually. That's why we could defeat the Dark Shadow and Vix Tower."

Nicholas nodded. "I want to express my passion from the bottom of my heart and create something great in this world. If I can do that, I'll be a very, very happy person."

"Yes, Nicholas, you will," Ellie said. "That is your liberation. Look around you. See what gifts you've received and treasure them. That helps you start to make your wishes come true."

Gifts? The word jolted Nicholas. He recalled his dream he had in the morning at Savino's. In the dream, someone promised him a gift.

A realization came to him: *Ellie was the gift!*

"Do you think we were meant to meet each other?" Nicholas said.

"I think so."

He paused for a second and said, "Who are *you*?"

Ellie smiled. "I'm a messenger sent to guide you to the right path," she said, "Nicholas, let your Light of Faith guide you into the right direction like a torch to accomplish your mission in the time given to you."

Nicholas nodded and said, "Have you accomplished *your* mission, Ellie?"

She shook her head. "No, Nicholas. Even as we speak, somebody in somewhere is looking for my help."

She smiled. "I can feel it."

THE END

Author Biography

Hanna Ireland first showed interest in art and creating stories and images in her early childhood. She often daydreamed that some day she would be an author of her own books.

Diamond Quest was written for age 13–18, but the novel can also apply to adults who still have their inner child and anyone who may need an entertainment boost of healing and transformation.

Visit **www.hannaireland.com**